THE STORY OF A BAD BOY

We crept with fear and anguish under our flimsy shelter

THE STORY OF A BAD BOY

BY

THOMAS BAILEY ALDRICH

ILLUSTRATED BY

EDWIN JOHN PRITTIE

THE JOHN C. WINSTON COMPANY

CHICAGO   PHILADELPHIA   TORONTO

PRINTED IN THE U. S. A.
AT THE INTERNATIONAL PRESS
THE JOHN C. WINSTON COMPANY, PROPS.
PHILADELPHIA

Story of a Bad Boy

CONTENTS

LIST OF ILLUSTRATIONS

CHAPTER I

IN WHICH I INTRODUCE MYSELF

THIS is the story of a bad boy. Well, not such a very bad, but a pretty bad boy; and I ought to know, for I am, or rather I was, that boy myself. Lest the title should mislead the reader, I hasten to assure him here that I have no dark confessions to make. I call my story the story of a bad boy, partly to distinguish myself from those faultless young gentlemen who generally figure in narratives of this kind, and partly because I really was not a cherub. I may truthfully say I was an amiable, impulsive lad, blessed with fine digestive powers, and no hypocrite. I didn't want to be an angel and with the angels stand; I didn't think the missionary tracts presented to me by the Rev. Wibird Hawkins were half so nice as Robinson Crusoe; and I didn't send my little pocket money to the natives of the Fiji Islands, but spent it royally in peppermint drops and taffy candy. In short, I was a real, human boy, such as you may meet anywhere in New England, and no more like the impossible boy in a story book than a sound orange is like one that has been sucked dry. But let us begin at the beginning.

Whenever a new scholar came to our school, I used to confront him at recess with the following

1

words: "My name's Tom Bailey; what's your name?" If the name struck me favorably, I shook hands with the new pupil cordially; but if it didn't, I would turn on my heel, for I was particular on this point. Such names as Higgins, Wiggins, and Spriggins were deadly affronts to my ear; while Langdon, Wallace, Blake, and the like, were passwords to my confidence and esteem.

Ah me! some of those dear fellows are rather elderly boys by this time—lawyers, merchants, sea captains, soldiers, authors, what not? Phil Adams (a special good name that Adams) is consul at Shanghai, where I picture him to myself with his head closely shaved—he never had too much hair— and a long pigtail hanging down behind. He is married, I hear; and I hope he and she that was Miss Wang Wang are very happy together, sitting cross-legged over their diminutive cups of tea in a sky-blue tower hung with bells. It is so I think of him; to me he is, henceforth, a jeweled mandarin, talking nothing but broken Chinese.

Whitcomb is a judge, sedate and wise, with spectacles balanced on the bridge of that remarkable nose which, in former days, was so plentifully sprinkled with freckles that the boys christened him Pepper Whitcomb. Just to think of little Pepper Whitcomb being a judge! What would he do to me now, I wonder, if I were to sing out "Pepper!" some day in court? Fred Langdon is in California, in the native-wine business—he used to make the best licorice water I ever tasted! Binny Wallace sleeps in the Old South Burying Ground; and Jack Harris, too, is dead—Harris, who commanded us boys, of old, in the famous snowball battles of Slatter's Hill. Was it yesterday I saw him at the head of his regiment on its way to join the shattered Army of the Potomac? Not yesterday, but six years ago. It was at the battle of the Seven Pines, that Gallant Jack Harris never drew rein until he had dashed into the Southern battery! So they found him—lying across the enemy's guns.

How we have parted, and wandered, and married, and died! I wonder what has become of all the boys who went to the Temple Grammar School at Rivermouth when I was a youngster?

"All, all are gone, the old familiar faces!"

It is with no ungentle hand I summon them back, for a moment, from that Past which has closed upon them and upon me. How pleasantly they live again in my memory! Happy, magical Past, in whose fairy atmosphere even Conway, mine ancient foe, stands forth transfigured, with a sort of dreamy glory encircling his bright, red hair!

With the old school formula I commence these sketches of my boyhood. My name is Tom Bailey; what is yours, gentle reader? I take it for granted it is neither Wiggins, nor Spriggins, and that we shall get on famously together, and be capital friends forever.

Chapter II

IN WHICH I ENTERTAIN PECULIAR VIEWS

I WAS born at Rivermouth, but, before I had a chance to become very well acquainted with that pretty New England town, my parents removed to New Orleans, where my father invested his money so securely in the banking business that he was never able to get any of it out again. But of this hereafter.

I was only eighteen months old at the time of the removal, and it didn't make much difference to me where I was, because I was so small; but several years later, when my father proposed to take me North to be educated, I had my own peculiar views on the subject. I instantly kicked over the little negro boy who happened to be standing by me at the moment, and, stamping my foot violently on the floor of the piazza, declared that I would not be taken away to live among a lot of Yankees!

You see I was what is called a "Northern man with Southern principles." I had no recollection of New England: my earliest memories were connected with the South, with Aunt Chloe, my old negro nurse, and with the great, ill-kept garden in the center of which stood our house—a whitewashed stone house it was, with wide verandas—shut out from the street by

4

lines of orange, fig, and magnolia trees. I knew I was born in the North, but hoped nobody would find it out. I looked upon the misfortune as something so shrouded by time and distance that maybe nobody remembered it. I never told my schoolmates I was a Yankee, because they talked about the Yankees in such a scornful way it made me feel that it was quite a disgrace not to be born in Louisiana, or at least in one of the Border States. And this impression was strengthened by Aunt Chloe, who said, "Dar wasn't no gentl'mcn in the Norf no way," and on one occasion terrified me beyond measure by declaring that, "if any of dem mean whites tried to git her away from marster, she was jes' gwine to knock 'em on de head wid a gourd!"

The way this poor creature's eyes flashed, and the tragic air with which she struck at an imaginary "mean white," ، re among the most vivid things in my memory of th٠ ٩e days.

To be frank, my idea of the North was about as accurate as that entertained by the well-educated Englishmen of the present day concerning America. I supposed the inhabitants were divided into two classes—Indians and white people; that the Indians occasionally dashed down on New York, and scalped any woman or child (giving the preference to children) whom they caught lingering in the outskirts after nightfall; that the white men were either hunters or schoolmasters, and that it was winter pretty much all the year round. The prevailing style of architecture I took to be log cabins.

With this delightful picture of Northern civilization in my eye, the reader will easily understand my terror at the bare thought of being transported to Rivermouth to school, and possibly will forgive me for kicking over little black Sam, and otherwise misconducting myself, when my father announced his determination to me. As for kicking little Sam—I always did that, more or less gently, when anything went wrong with me.

My father was greatly perplexed and troubled by this unusually violent outbreak, and especially by the real consternation which he saw written in every line of my countenance. As little black Sam picked himself up, my father took my hand in his and led me thoughtfully to the library.

I can see him now as he leaned back in the bamboo chair and questioned me. He appeared strangely agitated on learning the nature of my objections to going North, and proceeded at once to knock down all my pine-log houses, and scatter all the Indian tribes with which I had populated the greater portion of the Eastern and Middle States.

"Who on earth, Tom, has filled your brain with such silly stories?" asked my father, wiping the tears from his eyes.

"Aunt Chloe, sir; she told me."

"And you really thought your grandfather wore

a blanket embroidered with beads, and ornamented his leggings with the scalps of his enemies?"

"Well, sir, I didn't think that exactly."

"Didn't think that exactly? Tom, you will be the death of me."

He hid his face in his handkerchief, and, when he looked up, he seemed to have been suffering acutely. I was deeply moved myself, though I did not clearly understand what I had said or done to cause him to feel so badly. Perhaps I had hurt his feelings by thinking it even possible that Grandfather Nutter was an Indian warrior.

My father devoted that evening and several subsequent evenings to giving me a clear and succinct account of New England; its early struggles, its progress, and its present condition—faint and confused glimmerings of all which I had obtained at school, where history had never been a favorite pursuit of mine.

I was no longer unwilling to go North; on the contrary, the proposed journey to a new world full of wonders kept me awake nights. I promised myself all sorts of fun and adventures, though I was not entirely at rest in my mind touching the savages, and secretly resolved to go on board the ship—the journey was to be made by sea—with a certain little brass pistol in my trousers pocket, in case of any difficulty with the tribes when we landed at Boston.

I couldn't get the Indian out of my head. Only

a short time previously the Cherokees—or was it the Comanches?—had been removed from their hunting grounds in Arkansas; and in the wilds of the Southwest the red men were still a source of terror to the border settlers. "Trouble with the Indians" was the staple news from Florida published in the New Orleans papers. We were constantly hearing of travelers being attacked and murdered in the interior of that state. If these things were done in Florida, why not in Massachusetts?

Yet long before the sailing day arrived I was eager to be off. My impatience was increased by the fact that my father had purchased for me a fine little mustang pony, and shipped it to Rivermouth a fortnight previous to the date set for our own departure—for both my parents were to accompany me. The pony (which nearly kicked me out of bed one night in a dream), and my father's promise that he and my mother would come to Rivermouth every other summer, completely resigned me to the situation. The pony's name was *Gitana*, which is the Spanish for gypsy; so I always called her—she was a lady pony—Gypsy.

At length the time came to leave the vine-covered mansion among the orange trees, to say good-by to little black Sam (I am convinced he was heartily glad to get rid of me), and to part with simple Aunt Chloe, who, in the confusion of her grief, kissed an eyelash into my eye, and then buried her face in the bright bandana turban which she had mounted that morning in honor of our departure.

I fancy them standing by the open garden gate; the tears are rolling down Aunt Chloe's cheeks; Sam's six front teeth are glistening like pearls; I wave my hand to him manfully, then I call out "good-by" in a muffled voice to Aunt Chloe; they and the old home fade away. I am never to see them again!

CHAPTER III

ON BOARD THE "TYPHOON"

I DO not remember much about the voyage to Boston, for after the first few hours at sea I was dreadfully unwell.

The name of our ship was the "A No. 1, fast-sailing packet 'Typhoon.'" I learned afterwards that she sailed fast only in the newspaper advertisements. My father owned one quarter of the "Typhoon," and that is why we happened to go in her. I tried to guess which quarter of the ship he owned, and finally concluded it must be the hind quarter—the cabin, in which we had the cosiest of staterooms, with one round window in the roof, and two shelves or boxes nailed up against the wall to sleep in.

There was a good deal of confusion on deck while we were getting under way. The captain shouted orders (to which nobody seemed to pay any attention) through a battered tin trumpet, and grew so red in the face that he reminded me of a scooped-out pumpkin with a lighted candle inside. He swore right and left at the sailors without the slightest regard for their feelings. They didn't mind it a bit, however, but went on singing—

"Heave ho!
With the rum below,
And hurrah for the Spanish Main O!"

I will not be positive about the "Spanish Main," but it was hurrah for something O. I considered them very jolly fellows, and so indeed they were. One weather-beaten tar in particular struck my fancy —a thick-set, jovial man, about fifty years of age, with twinkling blue eyes and a fringe of gray hair circling his head like a crown. As he took off his tarpaulin I observed that the top of his head was quite smooth and flat, as if somebody had sat down on him when he was very young.

There was something noticeably hearty in this man's bronzed face, a heartiness that seemed to extend to his loosely knotted neckerchief. But what completely won my good will was a picture of enviable loveliness painted on his left arm. It was the head of a woman with a body of a fish. Her flowing hair was a livid green, and she held a pink comb in one hand. I never saw anything so beautiful. I determined to know that man. I think I would have given my brass pistol to have had such a picture painted on my arm.

While I stood admiring this work of art, a fat, wheezy steam tug, with the word AJAX in staring black letters on the paddle box, came puffing up alongside the "Typhoon." It was ridiculously small and conceited, compared with our stately ship. I speculated as to what it was going to do. In a few minutes we were lashed to the little monster, which gave a snort and a shriek, and commenced backing

us out from the levee (wharf) with the greatest
ease.

I once saw an ant running away with a piece of
cheese eight or ten times larger than itself. I could
not help thinking of it, when I found the chubby,
smoky-nosed tug boat towing the "Typhoon" out
into the Mississippi River.

In the middle of the stream we swung round, the
current caught us, and away we flew like a great
winged bird. Only it didn't seem as if we were moving. The shore, with the countless steamboats, the
tangled rigging of the ships, and the long lines of
warehouses appeared to be gliding away from us.

It was grand sport to stand on the quarterdeck
and watch all this. Before long there was nothing to
be seen on either side but stretches of low, swampy
land, covered with stunted cypress trees, from which
drooped delicate streamers of Spanish moss—a fine
place for alligators and Congo snakes. Here and
there we passed a yellow sandbar, and here and there
a snag lifted its nose out of the water like a shark.

"This is your last chance to see the city, Tom,"
my father said, as we swept round a bend of the
river.

I turned and looked. New Orleans was just a
colorless mass of something in the distance, and the
dome of the St. Charles Hotel, upon which the sun
shimmered for a moment, was no bigger than the
top of old Aunt Chloe's thimble.

What do I remember next? the gray sky and the fretful blue waters of the Gulf. The steam tug had long since let slip her hawsers and gone panting away with a derisive scream, as much as to say, "I've done my duty, now look out for yourself, old 'Typhoon'!"

The ship seemed quite proud of being left to take care of itself, and, with its huge white sails bulged out, strutted off like a vain turkey. I had been standing by my father near the wheelhouse all this while, observing things with that nicety of perception which belongs only to children; but now the dew began falling, and we went below to have supper.

The fresh fruit and milk, and the slices of cold chicken looked very nice; yet, somehow, I had no appetite. There was a general smell of tar about everything. Then the ship gave sudden lurches that made it a matter of uncertainty whether one was going to put his fork to his mouth or into his eye. The tumblers and wineglasses, stuck in a rack over the table, kept clinking and clinking; and the cabin lamp, suspended by four gilt chains from the ceiling, swayed to and fro crazily. Now the floor seemed to rise, and now it seemed to sink under one's feet like a feather-bed.

There were not more than a dozen passengers on board, including ourselves; and all of these, excepting a bald-headed old gentleman—a retired sea captain —disappeared into their staterooms at an early hour of the evening.

After supper was cleared away, my father and the elderly gentleman, whose name was Captain Truck, played at checkers; and I amused myself for a while by watching the trouble they had in keeping the men in the proper places. Just at the most exciting point of the game, the ship would career, and down would go the white checkers pell-mell among the black. Then my father laughed; but Captain Truck would grow very angry, and vow that he would have won the game in a move or two more, if the confounded old chicken coop—that's what he called the ship— hadn't lurched.

"I—I think I shall go to bed now, please," I said, laying my hand on my father's knee, and feeling exceedingly queer.

It was high time, for the "Typhoon" was plunging about in the most alarming fashion. I was speedily tucked away in the upper berth, where I felt a trifle more easy at first. My clothes were placed on a narrow shelf at my feet, and it was a great comfort to me to know that my pistol was so handy, for I had no doubt we should fall in with pirates before many hours. This is the last thing I remember with any distinctness. At midnight, as I was afterwards told, we were struck by a gale which never left us until we came in sight of the Massachusetts coast.

For days and days I had no sensible idea of what was going on around me. That we were being hurled somewhere upside down, and that I didn't like it, was about all I knew. I have, indeed, a vague impression that my father used to climb up to the berth and call me his "Ancient Mariner," bidding me cheer up. But the Ancient Mariner was far from cheering up, if I recollect rightly; and I don't believe that venerable navigator would have cared much if it had been announced to him, through a speaking trumpet, that "a low, black, suspicious craft, with raking masts, was rapidly bearing down upon us!"

In fact, one morning, I thought that such was the case, for bang! went the big cannon I had noticed in the bow of the ship when we came on board, and which had suggested to me the idea of pirates. Bang! went the gun again in a few seconds. I made a feeble effort to get at my trousers pocket! But the "Typhoon" was only saluting Cape Cod—the first land sighted by vessels approaching the coast from a southerly direction.

The vessel had ceased to roll, and my seasickness passed away as rapidly as it came. I was all right now, "only a little shaky in my timbers and a little blue about the gills," as Captain Truck remarked to my mother, who, like myself, had been confined to the stateroom during the passage.

At Cape Cod the wind parted company with us without saying as much as "Excuse me"; so we were nearly two days in making the run which in favorable weather is usually accomplished in seven hours. That's what the pilot said.

I was able to go about the ship now, and I lost no time in cultivating the acquaintance of the sailor with the green-haired lady on his arm. I found him in the forecastle—a sort of cellar in the front part of the vessel. He was an agreeable sailor, as I had expected, and we became the best of friends in five minutes.

He had been all over the world two or three times, and knew no end of stories. According to his own account, he must have been shipwrecked at least twice a year ever since his birth. He had served under Decatur when that gallant officer peppered the Algerines and made them promise not to sell their prisoners of war into slavery; he had worked a gun at the bombardment of Vera Cruz in the Mexican War, and he had been on Alexander Selkirk's Island more than once. There were very few things he hadn't done in a seafaring way.

"I suppose, sir," I remarked, "that your name isn't 'Typhoon'?"

"Why, Lord love ye, lad, my name's Benjamin Watson, of Nantucket. But I'm a true blue Typhooner," he added, which increased my respect for him; I don't know why, and I didn't know then whether Typhoon was the name of a vegetable or a profession.

Not wishing to be outdone in frankness, I disclosed to him that my name was Tom Bailey, upon which he said he was very glad to hear it.

I lost no time in cultivating the acquaintance of Sailor Ben

When we got more intimate, I discovered that Sailor Ben, as he wished me to call him, was a perfect walking picture book. He had two anchors, a star, and a frigate in full sail on his right arm; a pair of lovely blue hands clasped on his breast, and I've no doubt that other parts of his body were illustrated in the same agreeable manner. I imagine he was fond of drawings, and took this means of gratifying his artistic taste. It was certainly very ingenious and convenient. A portfolio might be misplaced, or dropped overboard; but Sailor Ben had his pictures wherever he went, just as that eminent person in the poem—

"With rings on her fingers and bells on her toes"
—was accompanied by music on all occasions.

The two hands on his breast, he informed me, were a tribute to the memory of a dead messmate from whom he had parted years ago—and surely a more touching tribute was never engraved on a tombstone. This caused me to think of my parting with old Aunt Chloe, and I told him I should take it as a great favor indeed if he would paint a pink hand and a black hand on my chest. He said the colors were pricked into the skin with needles, and that the operation was somewhat painful. I assured him, in an offhand manner, that I didn't mind pain, and begged him to set to work at once.

The simple-hearted fellow, who was probably not a little vain of his skill, took me into the forecastle and was on the point of complying with my request, when my father happened to look down the gangway —a circumstance that rather interfered with the decorative art.

I didn't have another opportunity of conferring alone with Sailor Ben, for the next morning, bright and early, we came in sight of the cupola of the Boston State House.

CHAPTER IV

RIVERMOUTH

IT was a beautiful May morning when the "Typhoon" hauled up at Long Wharf. Whether the Indians were not early risers, or whether they were away just then on a warpath, I couldn't determine; but they did not appear in any great force—in fact, did not appear at all.

In the remarkable geography which I never hurt myself with studying at New Orleans, was a picture representing the landing of the Pilgrim Fathers at Plymouth. The Pilgrim Fathers, in rather odd hats and coats, are seen approaching the savages; the savages, in no coats or hats to speak of, are evidently undecided whether to shake hands with the Pilgrim Fathers or to make one grand rush and scalp the entire party. Now this scene had so stamped itself on my mind, that, in spite of all my father had said, I was prepared for some such greeting from the aborigines. Nevertheless, I was not sorry to have my expectations unfulfilled. By the way, speaking of the Pilgrim Fathers, I often used to wonder why there was no mention made of the Pilgrim Mothers.

While our trunks were being hoisted from the hold of the ship, I mounted on the roof of the cabin, and took a critical view of Boston. As we came up the harbor, I had noticed that the houses were huddled together on an immense hill, at the top of which was a large building, the State House, towering proudly above the rest, like an amiable mother hen surrounded by her brood of many-colored chickens. A closer inspection did not impress me very favorably. The city was not nearly so imposing as New Orleans, which stretches out for miles and miles in the shape of a crescent along the banks of the majestic river.

I soon grew tired of looking at the masses of houses, rising above one another in irregular tiers, and was glad my father did not propose to remain long in Boston. As I leaned over the rail in this mood, a measly-looking little boy with no shoes said that if I would come down on the wharf he'd lick me for two cents—not an exorbitant price. But I didn't go down. I climbed into the rigging, and stared at him. This, as I was rejoiced to observe, so exasperated him that he stood on his head on a pile of boards in order to pacify himself.

The first train for Rivermouth left at noon. After a late breakfast on board the "Typhoon," our trunks were piled upon a baggage wagon, and ourselves stowed away in a coach, which must have turned at least one hundred corners before it set us down at the railway station.

In less time than it takes to tell it, we were shooting across the country at a fearful rate—now clattering over a bridge, now screaming through a tunnel; here we cut a flourishing village in two, like a knife, and here we dived into the shadow of a pine forest. Sometimes we glided along the edge of the ocean, and could see the sails of ships twinkling like bits of silver against the horizon; sometimes we dashed across rocky pasture lands where stupid-eyed cattle were loafing. It was fun to scare the lazy-looking cows that lay round in groups under the newly budded trees near the railroad track.

We did not pause at any of the little brown stations on the route (they looked just like overgrown black-walnut clocks), though at every one of them a man popped out as if he were worked by machinery, and waved a red flag, and appeared as though he would like to have us stop. But we were an express train and made no stoppages, excepting once or twice to give the engine a drink.

It is strange how the memory clings to some things. It is over twenty years since I took that first ride to Rivermouth, and yet, oddly enough, I remember as if it were yesterday, that, as we passed slowly through the village of Hampton, we saw two boys fighting behind a red barn. There was also a shaggy, yellow dog, who looked as if he had commenced to unravel, barking himself all up into a knot with excitement. We had only a hurried glimpse of the battle—long enough, however, to see that the combatants were equally matched and very much in earnest. I am ashamed to say how many times I have speculated as to which boy got licked. Maybe both the small rascals are dead now (not in consequence of the set-to, let us hope), or maybe they are married, and have pugnacious urchins of their own; yet, to this day, I sometimes find myself wondering how that fight turned out.

We had been riding perhaps two hours and a half, when we shot by a tall factory with a chimney resembling a church steeple; then the locomotive gave a scream, the engineer rang his bell, and we plunged into the twilight of a long, wooden building, open at both ends. Here we stopped, and the conductor, thrusting his head in at the car door, cried out, "Passengers for Rivermouth!"

At last we had reached our journey's end. On the platform my father shook hands with a straight, brisk old gentleman whose face was very serene and rosy. He had on a white hat and a long, swallow-tailed coat, the collar of which came clear up above his ears. He didn't look unlike a Pilgrim Father. This, of course, was Grandfather Nutter, at whose house I was born. My mother kissed him a great many times; and I was glad to see him myself, though I naturally did not feel very intimate with a person whom I had not seen since I was eighteen months old.

While we were getting into the double-seated wagon which Grandfather Nutter had provided, I took the opportunity of asking after the health of the pony. The pony had arrived all right ten days before, and was in the stable at home, quite anxious to see me.

As we drove through the quiet old town, I thought Rivermouth the prettiest place in the world; and I think so still. The streets are long and wide, shaded by gigantic American elms, whose drooping branches, interlacing here and there, span the avenues with arches graceful enough to be the handiwork of fairies. Many of the houses have small flower-gardens in front, gay in the season with china asters, and are substantially built, with massive chimney-stacks and protruding eaves. A beautiful river goes rippling by the town, and, after turning and twisting among a lot of tiny islands, empties itself into the sea.

The harbor is so fine that the largest ships can sail directly up to the wharves and drop anchor. Only they don't. Years ago it was a famous seaport. Princely fortunes were made in the West India trade; and in 1812, when we were at war with Great Britain, any number of privateers were fitted out at Rivermouth to prey upon the merchant vessels of the enemy. Certain people grew suddenly and mysteriously rich. A great many of "the first families" of today do not care to trace their pedigree back to the time when their grandsires owned shares in the "Matilda Jane," twenty-four guns. Well, well!

Few ships come to Rivermouth now. Commerce

drifted into other ports. The phantom fleet sailed off one day, and never came back again. The crazy old warehouses are empty; and barnacles and eel-grass cling to the piles of the crumbling wharves, where the sunshine lies lovingly, bringing out the faint, spicy odor that haunts the place—the ghost of the old West India trade!

During our ride from the station, I was struck, of course, only by the general neatness of the houses and the beauty of the elm trees lining the streets. I describe Rivermouth now as I came to know it afterwards.

Rivermouth is a very ancient town. In my day there existed a tradition among the boys that it was here Christopher Columbus made his first landing on this continent. I remember having the exact spot pointed out to me by Pepper Whitcomb! One thing is certain, Captain John Smith, who afterwards, according to the legend, married Pocahontas —whereby he got Powhatan for a father-in-law— explored the river in 1614, and was much charmed by the beauty of Rivermouth, which at that time was covered with wild strawberry vines.

Rivermouth figures prominently in all the colonial histories. Every other house in the place has its tradition, more or less grim and entertaining. If ghosts could flourish anywhere, there are certain streets in Rivermouth that would be full of them. I don't know of a town with so many old houses.

3

Let us linger, for a moment, in front of the one which the Oldest Inhabitant is always sure to point out to the curious stranger.

It is a square, wooden edifice, with gambrel roof and deep-set window frames. Over the windows and doors there used to be heavy carvings—oak leaves and acorns, and angels' heads with wings spreading from the ears, oddly jumbled together; but these ornaments and other outward signs of grandeur have long since disappeared. A peculiar interest attaches itself to this house, not because of its age, for it has not been standing quite a century; nor on account of its architecture, which is not striking—but because of the illustrious men who at various periods have occupied its spacious chambers.

In 1770 it was an aristocratic hotel. At the left side of the entrance stood a high post, from which swung the sign of the Earl of Halifax. The landlord was a stanch loyalist—that is to say, he believed in the king, and when the overtaxed colonies determined to throw off the British yoke, the adherents to the Crown held private meetings in one of the back rooms of the tavern. This irritated the rebels, as they were called; and one night they made an attack on the Earl of Halifax, tore down the signboard, broke in the window sashes, and gave the landlord hardly time to make himself invisible over a fence in the rear.

For several months the shattered tavern remained deserted. At last the exiled innkeeper, on promising to do better, was allowed to return; a new sign, bearing the name of William Pitt, the friend of America, swung proudly from the door post, and the patriots were appeased. Here it was that the mail coach from Boston twice a week, for many a year, set down its load of travelers and gossip. For some of the details in this sketch, I am indebted to a recently published chronicle of those times.

It is 1782. The French fleet is lying in the harbor of Rivermouth, and eight of the principal officers, in white uniforms trimmed with gold lace, have taken up their quarters at the sign of the William Pitt. Who is this young and handsome officer now entering the door of the tavern? It is no less a personage than the Marquis Lafayette, who has come all the way from Providence to visit the French gentlemen boarding there. What a gallant-looking cavalier he is, with his quick eyes and coal-black hair! Forty years later he visited the spot again; his locks were gray and his step was feeble, but his heart held its young love for Liberty.

Who is this finely dressed traveler alighting from his coach and four, attended by servants in livery? Do you know that sounding name, written in big valorous letters on the Declaration of Independence— written as if by the hand of a giant? Can you not see it now?—JOHN HANCOCK. This is he.

Three young men, with their valet, are standing

on the doorstep of the William Pitt, bowing politely, and inquiring in the most courteous terms in the world if they can be accommodated. It is the time of the French Revolution, and these are three sons of the Duke of Orleans—Louis Philippe and his two brothers. Louis Philippe never forgot his visit to Rivermouth. Years afterwards, when he was seated on the throne of France, he asked an American lady, who chanced to be at his court, if the pleasant old mansion were still standing.

But a greater and better man than the king of the French has honored this roof. Here, in 1789, came George Washington, the President of the United States, to pay his final complimentary visit to the State dignitaries. The wainscoted chamber where he slept, and the dining hall where he entertained his guests, have a certain dignity and sanctity which even the present Irish tenants cannot wholly destroy.

During the period of my reign at Rivermouth, an ancient lady, Dame Jocelyn by name, lived in one of the upper rooms of this notable building. She was a dashing young belle at the time of Washington's first visit to the town, and must have been exceedingly coquettish and pretty, judging from a certain portrait on ivory still in the possession of the family. According to Dame Jocelyn, George Washington flirted with her just a little bit—in what a stately and highly finished manner can be imagined.

There was a mirror with a deep filigreed frame

hanging over the mantelpiece in this room. The glass was cracked, and the quicksilver rubbed off or discolored in many places. When it reflected your face you had the singular pleasure of not recognizing yourself. It gave your features the appearance of having been run through a mincemeat machine. But what rendered the looking-glass a thing of enchantment to me was a faded green feather, tipped with scarlet, which drooped from the top of the tarnished gilt moldings. This feather Washington took from the plume of his three-cornered hat, and presented with his own hand to the worshipful Mistress Jocelyn the day he left Rivermouth forever. I wish I could describe the mincing genteel air, and the ill-concealed self-complacency, with which the dear old lady related the incident.

Many a Saturday afternoon have I climbed up the rickety staircase to that dingy room, which always had a flavor of snuff about it, to sit on a stiff-backed chair and listen for hours together to Dame Jocelyn's stories of the olden time. How she would prattle! She was bedridden—poor creature!—and had not been out of the chamber for fourteen years. Meanwhile the world had shot ahead of Dame Jocelyn. The changes that had taken place under her very nose were unknown to this faded, crooning, old gentlewoman, whom the eighteenth century had neglected to take away with the rest of its odd traps. She had no patience with new-fangled notions. The old ways

and the old times were good enough for her. She had
never seen a steam engine, though she had heard
"the dratted thing" screech in the distance. In her
day, when gentlefolk traveled, they went in their own
coaches. She didn't see how respectable people could
bring themselves down to "riding in a car with rag-
tag and bobtail and Lord-knows-who." Poor old
aristocrat! the landlord charged her no rent for the
room, and the neighbors took turns in supplying
her with meals. Toward the close of her life—she
lived to be ninety-nine—she grew very fretful and
capricious about her food. If she didn't chance to
fancy what was sent her, she had no hesitation in
sending it back to the giver with "Miss Jocelyn's re-
spectful compliments."

But I have been gossiping too long—and yet not
too long if I have impressed upon the reader an idea
of what a rusty, delightful old town it was to which
I had come to spend the next three or four years of
my boyhood.

A drive of twenty minutes from the station
brought us to the doorstep of Grandfather Nutter's
house. What kind of house it was, and what sort of
people lived in it, shall be told in another chapter.

CHAPTER V

THE NUTTER HOUSE AND THE NUTTER FAMILY

THE Nutter House—all the more prominent dwellings in Rivermouth are named after somebody; for instance, there is the Walford House, the Venner House, the Trefethen House, etc., though it by no means follows that they are inhabited by the people whose names they bear—the Nutter House, to resume, has been in our family nearly a hundred years, and is an honor to the builder (an ancestor of ours, I believe), supposing durability to be a merit. If our ancestor was a carpenter, he knew his trade. I wish I knew mine as well. Such timber and such workmanship don't often come together in houses built nowadays.

Imagine a low-studded structure, with a wide hall running through the middle. At your right hand, as you enter, stands a tall, black mahogany clock, looking like an Egyptian mummy set up on end. On each side of the hall are doors (whose knobs, it must be confessed, do not turn very easily), opening into large rooms wainscoted and rich in wood carvings about the mantelpieces and cornices. The walls are covered with pictured paper, representing landscapes

31

and sea views. In the parlor, for example, this enlivening figure is repeated all over the room: A group of English peasants, wearing Italian hats, are dancing on a lawn that abruptly resolves itself into a sea beach, upon which stands a flabby fisherman (nationality unknown), quietly hauling in what appears to be a small whale, and totally regardless of the dreadful naval combat going on just beyond the end of his fishing rod. On the other side of the ships is the mainland, again with the same peasants dancing. Our ancestors were very worthy people, but their wall papers were abominable.

There are neither grates nor stoves in these quaint chambers, but splendid open chimney places, with room enough for the corpulent backlog to turn over comfortably on the polished andirons. A wide staircase leads from the hall to the second story, which is arranged much like the first. Over this is the garret. I needn't tell a New England boy what a museum of curiosities is the garret of a well-regulated New England house of fifty or sixty years' standing. Here meet together, as if by some preconcerted arrangement, all the broken-down chairs of the household, all the spavined tables, all the seedy hats, all the intoxicated-looking boots, all the split walking sticks that have retired from business, "weary with the march of life." The pots, the pans, the trunks, the bottles—who may hope to make an inventory of the numberless odds and ends collected in this be-

wildering lumber room? But what a place it is to sit
of an afternoon with the rain pattering on the roof!
What a place in which to read *Gulliver's Travels*, or
the famous adventures of Rinaldo Rinaldini!

My grandfather's house stood a little back from
the main street, in the shadow of two handsome elms,
whose overgrown boughs would dash themselves
against the gables whenever the wind blew hard. In
the rear was a pleasant garden, covering perhaps a
quarter of an acre, full of plum trees and gooseberry
bushes. These trees were old settlers, and are all
dead now, excepting one, which bears a purple plum as
big as an egg. This tree, as I remark, is still standing,
and a more beautiful tree to tumble out of never
grew anywhere. In the northwestern corner of the
garden were the stables and carriage house, opening
upon a narrow lane. You may imagine that I made
an early visit to that locality to inspect Gypsy.
Indeed, I paid her a visit every half hour during the
first day of my arrival. At the twenty-fourth visit
she trod on my foot rather heavily, as a reminder,
probably, that I was wearing out my welcome. She
was a knowing little pony, that Gypsy, and I shall
have much to say of her in the course of these pages.

Gypsy's quarters were all that could be wished,
but nothing among my new surroundings gave me
more satisfaction than the cosy sleeping apartment
that had been prepared for myself. It was the hall
room over the front door.

I had never had a chamber all to myself before, and this one, about twice the size of our stateroom on board the "Typhoon," was a marvel of neatness and comfort. Pretty chintz curtains hung at the window, and a patch quilt of more colors than were in Joseph's coat covered the little truckle-bed. The pattern of the wall paper left nothing to be desired in that line. On a gray background were small bunches of leaves, unlike any that ever grew in this world; and on every other bunch perched a yellow bird, pitted with crimson spots, as if it had just recovered from a severe attack of the smallpox. That no such bird ever existed did not detract from my admiration of each one. There were two hundred sixty-eight of these birds in all, not counting those split in two where the paper was badly joined. I counted them once when I was laid up with a fine black eye, and falling asleep immediately dreamed that the whole flock suddenly took wing and flew out of the window. From that time I was never able to regard them as merely inanimate objects.

A washstand in the corner, a chest of carved mahogany drawers, a looking-glass in a filigreed frame, and a high-backed chair studded with brass nails like a coffin constituted the furniture. Over the head of the bed were two oak shelves, holding perhaps a dozen books—among which were Theodore, or The Peruvians; Robinson Crusoe; an odd volume of Tristram Shandy; Baxter's Saints' Rest,

In a lidless trunk in the garret I unearthed another collection of novels
and romances

and a fine English edition of the Arabian Nights, with six hundred woodcuts by Harvey.

Shall I ever forget the hour when I first over-hauled these books? I do not allude especially to Baxter's Saints' Rest, which is far from being a lively work for the young, but to the Arabian Nights, and particularly Robinson Crusoe. The thrill that ran into my fingers' ends then has not run out yet. Many a time did I steal up to this nest of a room, and, taking the dog's-eared volume from its shelf, glide off into an enchanted realm, where there were no lessons to get and no boys to smash my kite. In a lidless trunk in the garret I subsequently un-earthed another motley collection of novels and ro-mances, embracing the adventures of Baron Trenck, Jack Sheppard, Don Quixote, Gil Blas, and Char-lotte Temple—all of which I fed upon like a book-worm.

I never come across a copy of any of those works without feeling a certain tenderness for the yellow-haired little rascal who used to lean above the magic pages hour after hour, religiously believing every word he read, and no more doubting the reality of Sindbad the Sailor, or the Knight of the Sorrowful Countenance, than he did the existence of his own grandfather.

Against the wall at the foot of the bed hung a single-barrel shotgun—placed there by Grandfather Nutter, who knew what a boy loved, if ever a grandfather did. As the trigger of the gun had been accidentally twisted off, it was not, perhaps, the most dangerous weapon that could be placed in the hands of a youth. In this maimed condition its "bump of destructiveness" was much less than that of my small, brass pocket pistol, which I at once proceeded to suspend from one of the nails supporting the fowling piece, for my vagaries concerning the red man had been entirely dispelled.

Having introduced the reader to the Nutter House, a presentation to the Nutter family naturally follows. The family consisted of my grandfather; his sister, Miss Abigail Nutter; and Kitty Collins, the maid-of-all-work.

Grandfather Nutter was a hale, cheery old gentleman, as straight and as bald as an arrow. He had been a sailor in early life; that is to say, at the age of ten years he fled from the multiplication table, and ran away to sea. A single voyage satisfied him. There never was but one of our family who didn't run away to sea, and this one died at his birth. My grandfather had also been a soldier—a captain of militia in 1812. If I owe the British nation anything, I owe thanks to that particular British soldier who put a musket ball into the fleshy part of Captain Nutter's leg, causing that noble warrior a slight permanent limp, but offsetting the injury by furnishing him with the material for a story which the old gentleman was never weary of telling and I never weary of listening to. The story, in brief, was as follows:

At the breaking out of the war, an English frigate lay for several days off the coast near Rivermouth. A strong fort defended the harbor, and a regiment of minutemen, scattered at various points along shore, stood ready to repel the boats, should the enemy try to effect a landing. Captain Nutter had charge of a slight earth-work just outside the mouth of the river. Late one thick night the sound of oars was heard; the sentinel tried to fire off his gun at half-cock, and couldn't, when Captain Nutter sprung upon the parapet in the pitch darkness, and shouted, "Boat ahoy!" A musket shot immediately embedded itself in the calf of his leg. The Captain tumbled into the fort and the boat, which had probably come in search of water, pulled back to the frigate.

This was my grandfather's only exploit during the war. That his prompt and bold conduct was instrumental in teaching the enemy the hopelessness of attempting to conquer such a people was among the firm beliefs of my boyhood.

At the time I came to Rivermouth my grandfather had retired from active pursuits, and was living at ease on his money, invested principally in shipping. He had been a widower many years; a maiden sister, the aforesaid Miss Abigail, managing his household. Miss Abigail also managed her brother, and her brother's servant, and the visitor at her brother's gate—not in a tyrannical spirit, but from a philanthropic desire to be useful to everybody. In person she was tall and angular; she had a gray complexion, gray eyes, gray eyebrows, and generally wore a gray dress. Her strongest weak point was a belief in the efficacy of "hot drops" as a cure for all known diseases.

If there were ever two people who seemed to dislike each other, Miss Abigail and Kitty Collins were those people. If ever two people really loved each other, Miss Abigail and Kitty Collins were those people also. They were always either skir· mishing or having a cup of tea lovingly together.

Miss Abigail was very fond of me, and so was Kitty; and in the course of their disagreements each let me into the private history of the other.

According to Kitty, it was not originally my grandfather's intention to have Miss Abigail at the head of his domestic establishment. She had swooped down on him (Kitty's own words), with a bandbox in one hand and a faded blue cotton umbrella, still in existence, in the other. Clad in this singular garb —I do not remember that Kitty alluded to any additional peculiarity of dress—Miss Abigail had made her appearance at the door of the Nutter House on the morning of my grandmother's funeral. The small amount of baggage which the lady brought with her would have led the superficial observer to infer that

Miss Abigail's visit was limited to a few days. I run ahead of my story in saying she remained seventeen years! How much longer she would have remained can never be definitely known now, as she died at the expiration of that period.

Whether or not my grandfather was quite pleased by this unlooked-for addition to his family is a problem. He was very kind always to Miss Abigail, and seldom opposed her; though I think she must have tried his patience sometimes, especially when she interfered with Kitty.

Kitty Collins, or Mrs. Catharine, as she preferred to be called, was descended in a direct line from an extensive family of kings who formerly ruled over Ireland. In consequence of various calamities, among which the failure of the potato crop may be mentioned, Miss Kitty Collins, in company with several hundred of her countrymen and countrywomen—also descended from kings—came over to America in an emigrant ship, in the year eighteen hundred and something.

I don't know what freak of fortune caused the royal exile to turn up at Rivermouth; but turn up she did, a few months after arriving in this country, and was hired by my grandmother to do "general housework" for the sum of four shillings and sixpence a week.

Kitty had been living about seven years in my grandfather's family when she unburdened her heart of a secret which had been weighing upon it all that time. It may be said of people, as it is said of nations, "Happy are they that have no history." Kitty had a history, and a pathetic one, I think.

On board the emigrant ship that brought her to America she became acquainted with a sailor, who, being touched by Kitty's forlorn condition, was very good to her. Long before the end of the voyage, which had been tedious and perilous, she was heartbroken at the thought of separating from her kindly protector; but they were not to part just yet, for the sailor returned Kitty's affection, and the two were married on their arrival at port. Kitty's husband—she would never mention his name, but kept it locked in her bosom like some precious relic—had a considerable sum of money when the crew were paid off; and the young couple—for Kitty was young then—lived very happily in a lodging house on South Street, near the docks. This was in New York.

The days flew by like hours, and the stocking in which the little bride kept the funds shrunk and shrunk, until at last there were only three or four dollars left in the toe of it. Then Kitty was troubled; for she knew her sailor would have to go to sea again unless he could get employment on shore. This he endeavored to do, but not with much success. One morning as usual he kissed her good day, and set out in search of work.

4

"Kissed me good-by, and called me his little Irish lass," sobbed Kitty, telling the story—"kissed me good-by, and, Heaven help me! I niver set oi on him nor on the likes of him again."

He never came back. Day after day dragged on, night after night, and then the weary weeks. What had become of him? Had he been murdered? Had he fallen into the docks? Had he deserted her? No! she could not believe that; he was too brave and tender and true. She couldn't believe that. He was dead, dead, or he'd come back to her.

Meanwhile the landlord of the lodging house turned Kitty into the streets, now that "her man" was gone and the payment of the rent doubtful. She got a place as a servant. The family she lived with shortly moved to Boston, and she accompanied them; then they went abroad, but Kitty would not leave America. Somehow she drifted to Rivermouth, and for seven long years never gave speech to her sorrow, until the kindness of strangers, who had become friends to her, unsealed the heroic lips.

Kitty's story, you may be sure, made my grandparents treat her more kindly than ever. In time she grew to be regarded less as a servant than as a friend in the home circle, sharing its joys and sorrows —a faithful nurse, a willing slave, a happy spirit in spite of all. I fancy I hear her singing over her work in the kitchen, pausing from time to time to make some witty reply to Miss Abigail—for Kitty, like all her race, had a vein of unconscious humor. Her bright, honest face comes to me out from the past, the light and life of the Nutter House when I was a boy at Rivermouth.

Chapter VI

LIGHTS AND SHADOWS

THE first shadow that fell upon me in my new home was caused by the return of my parents to New Orleans. Their visit was cut short by business which required my father's presence in Natchez, where he was establishing a branch of the banking houses. When they had gone, a sense of loneliness, such as I had never dreamed of, filled my young breast. I crept away to the stable, and, throwing my arms about Gypsy's neck, sobbed aloud. She too had come from the sunny South, and was now a stranger in a strange land.

The little mare seemed to realize our situation, and gave me all the sympathy I could ask, repeatedly rubbing her soft nose over my face and lapping up my salt tears with evident relish.

When night came, I felt still more lonesome. My grandfather sat in his armchair the greater part of the evening, reading the Rivermouth Barnacle, the local newspaper. There was no gas in those days, and the Captain read by the aid of a small block-tin lamp, which he held in one hand. I observed that he had a habit of dropping off into a doze every three or four minutes, and I forgot my homesickness at intervals in watching him. Two or three times, to my vast amusement, he scorched the edges of the newspaper with the wick of the lamp; and at about half-past eight o'clock I had the satisfaction—I am sorry to confess it was a satisfaction—of seeing the Rivermouth Barnacle in flames.

My grandfather leisurely extinguished the fire with his hands, and Miss Abigail, who sat near a low table, knitting by the light of an astral lamp, did not even look up. She was quite used to this catastrophe.

There was little or no conversation during the evening. In fact, I do not remember that anyone spoke at all, excepting once, when the Captain remarked, in a meditative manner, that my parents "must have reached New York by this time"; at which supposition I nearly strangled myself in attempting to intercept a sob.

The monotonous "click, click" of Miss Abigail's needles made me nervous after a while, and finally drove me out of the sitting room into the kitchen, where Kitty caused me to laugh by saying Miss Abigail thought that what I needed was "a good dose of hot drops"—a remedy she was forever ready to administer in all emergencies. If a boy broke his leg, or lost his mother, I believe Miss Abigail would have given him hot drops.

Kitty laid herself out to be entertaining. She told me several funny Irish stories, and described some of the odd people living in the town; but, in the midst of her comicalities, the tears would involuntarily ooze out of my eyes, though I was not a lad much addicted to weeping. Then Kitty would put her arms around me, and tell me not to mind it—that it wasn't as if I had been left alone in a foreign land with no one to care for me, like a poor girl whom she had once known. I brightened up before long, and told Kitty all about the "Typhoon" and the old sea-man, whose name I tried in vain to recall, and was obliged to fall back on plain Sailor Ben.

I was glad when ten o'clock came, the bedtime for young folks, and old folks too, at the Nutter House. Alone in the hall chamber I had my cry out, once for all, moistening the pillow to such an extent that I was obliged to turn it over to find a dry spot to go to sleep on.

My grandfather wisely concluded to put me to school at once. If I had been permitted to go moon-ing about the house and stables, I should have kept my discontent alive for months. The next morning, accordingly, he took me by the hand and we set forth for the academy, which was located at the farther end of the town.

The Temple School was a two-story brick build-ing, standing in the center of a great, square piece of land, surrounded by a high picket fence. There were three or four sickly trees, but no grass, in this inclosure, which had been worn smooth and hard by the tread of multitudinous feet. I noticed here and there small holes scooped in the ground, indicating that it was the season for marbles. A better playground for baseball couldn't have been devised.

On reaching the schoolhouse door, the Captain inquired for Mr. Grimshaw. The boy who answered our knock ushered us into a side room, and in a few minutes—during which my eye took in forty-two caps hung on forty-two wooden pegs—Mr. Grimshaw made his appearance. He was a slender man, with white, fragile hands and eyes that glanced half a dozen different ways at once—a habit probably acquired from watching the boys.

After a brief consultation, my grandfather patted me on the head and left me in charge of this gentleman, who seated himself in front of me and proceeded to sound the depth, or more properly speaking the shallowness, of my attainments. I suspect my historical information rather startled him. I recollect I gave him to understand that Richard III was the last king of England.

This ordeal over, Mr. Grimshaw rose and bade me follow him. A door opened, and I stood in the blaze of forty-two pairs of upturned eyes. I was a cool hand for my age, but I lacked the boldness to face this battery without wincing. In a sort of dazed way I stumbled after Mr. Grimshaw down a narrow aisle between two rows of desks, and shyly took the seat pointed out to me.

The faint buzz that had floated over the school-room at our entrance died away, and the interrupted lessons were resumed. By degrees I recovered my coolness and ventured to look around me.

The owners of the forty-two caps were seated at small green desks like the one assigned to me. The desks were arranged in six rows, with spaces between just wide enough to prevent the boys whispering. A blackboard set into the wall extended clear across the end of the room; on a raised platform near the door stood the master's table; and directly in front of this was a recitation bench capable of seating fifteen or twenty pupils. A pair of globes, tattooed with dragons and winged horses, occupied a shelf between two windows, which were so high from the floor that nothing but a giraffe could have looked out of them.

Having possessed myself of these details, I scrutinized my new acquaintances with unconcealed curiosity, instinctively selecting my friends and picking out my enemies—and in only two cases did I mistake my man.

A sallow boy with bright, red hair, sitting in the fourth row, shook his fist at me furtively several times during the morning. I had a presentiment I should have trouble with that boy some day—a presentiment subsequently realized.

On my left was a chubby little fellow with a great many freckles (this was Pepper Whitcomb), who made some mysterious motions to me. I didn't understand them, but, as they were clearly of a pacific nature, I winked my eye at him. This appeared to be satisfactory, for he then went on with his studies. At recess he gave me the core of his apple, though there were several applicants for it.

Presently a boy in a loose, olive-green jacket with two rows of brass buttons held up a folded paper behind his slate, intimating that it was intended for me. The paper was passed skilfully from desk to desk until it reached my hands. On opening the scrap, I found that it contained a small piece of molasses candy in an extremely humid state. This was certainly kind. I nodded my acknowledgment, and hastily slipped the delicacy into my mouth. In a second I felt my tongue grow red-hot with cayenne pepper.

My face must have assumed a comical expression, for the boy in the olive-green jacket gave a hysterical laugh, for which he was instantly punished by Mr. Grimshaw. I swallowed the fiery candy, though it brought the water to my eyes, and managed to look so unconcerned that I was the only pupil in the form who escaped questioning as the cause of Marden's misdemeanor. C. Marden was his name.

Nothing else occurred that morning to interrupt the exercises, excepting that a boy in the reading class threw us all into convulsions by calling Absalom *A-bol'som*—"Abolsom, O my son Abolsom!" I laughed as loud as anyone, but I am not sure that I shouldn't have pronounced it Abolsom myself.

At recess several of the scholars came to my desk and shook hands with me, Mr. Grimshaw having previously introduced me to Phil Adams, charging him to see that I got into no trouble. My new acquaintances suggested that we should go to the playground. We were no sooner out of doors than the boy with the red hair thrust his way through the crowd and placed himself at my side.

"I say, youngster, if you're comin' to this school you've got to toe the mark."

I didn't see any mark to toe, and didn't understand what he meant; but I replied politely, that, if it was the custom of the school, I should be happy to toe the mark, if he would point it out to me.

"I don't want any of your sass," said the boy, scowling.

"Look here, Conway!" cried a clear voice from the other side of the playground, "you let young Bailey alone. He's a stranger here, and might be afraid of you, and thrash you. Why do you always throw yourself in the way of getting thrashed?"

I turned to the speaker, who by this time had reached the spot where we stood. Conway slunk off, favoring me with a parting scowl of defiance. I gave my hand to the boy who had befriended me—his name was Jack Harris—and thanked him for his good will.

"I tell you what it is, Bailey," he said, returning my pressure good-naturedly, "you'll have to fight Conway before the quarter ends, or you'll have no rest. That fellow is always hankering after a licking, and of course you'll give him one, by and by; but what's the use of hurrying up an unpleasant job? Let's have some baseball. By the way, Bailey, you were a good kid not to let on to Grimshaw about the candy. Charley Marden would have caught it twice as heavy. He's sorry he played the joke on you, and told me to tell you so. Hallo, Blake! where are the bats?"

This was addressed to a handsome, frank-looking lad of about my own age, who was engaged just then in cutting his initials on the bark of a tree near the schoolhouse. Blake shut up his penknife and went off to get the bats.

During the game which ensued I made the acquaintance of Charley Marden, Binny Wallace, Pepper Whitcomb, Harry Blake, and Fred Langdon. These boys, none of them more than a year or two older than I (Billy Wallace was younger), were ever after my chosen comrades. Phil Adams and Jack Harris were considerably our seniors, and, though they always treated us "kids" very kindly, they generally went with another set. Of course, before long I knew all the Temple boys more or less intimately, but the five I have named were my constant companions.

My first day at the Temple Grammar School was on the whole satisfactory. I had made several warm friends and only two permanent enemies—Conway and his echo, Seth Rodgers; for these two always went together like a deranged stomach and a headache.

Before the end of the week I had my studies well in hand. I was a little ashamed at finding myself at the foot of the various classes, and secretly determined to deserve promotion. The school was an admirable one. I might make this part of my story more entertaining by picturing Mr. Grimshaw as a tyrant with a red nose and a large stick; but unfortunately for the purposes of sensational narrative, Mr. Grimshaw was a quiet, kind-hearted gentleman. Though a rigid disciplinarian, he had a keen sense of justice, was a good reader of character, and the boys respected him. There were two other teachers—a French tutor and a writing master, who visited the school twice a week. On Wednesdays and Saturdays we were dismissed at noon, and these half holidays were the brightest epochs of my existence.

Daily contact with boys, who had not been brought up as gently as I, worked an immediate, and, in some respects, a beneficial change in my character. I had the nonsense taken out of me, as the saying is—some of the nonsense, at least. I became more manly and self-reliant. I discovered that the world was not created exclusively on my account. In New Orleans

I labored under the delusion that it was. Having neither brother nor sister to give up to at home, and being, moreover, the largest pupil at school there, my will had seldom been opposed. At Rivermouth matters were different, and I was not long in adapting myself to the altered circumstances. Of course I got many severe rubs, often unconsciously given; but I had sense to see that I was all the better for them.

My social relations with my new schoolfellows were the pleasantest possible. There was always some exciting excursion on foot—a ramble through the pine woods, a visit to the Devil's Pulpit, a high cliff in the neighborhood—or a surreptitious row on the river, involving an exploration of a group of diminutive islands, upon one of which we pitched a tent and played we were the Spanish sailors who got wrecked there years ago. But the endless pine forest that skirted the town was our favorite haunt. There was a great green pond hidden somewhere in its depths, inhabited by a monstrous colony of turtles. Harry Blake, who had an eccentric passion for carving his name on everything, never let a captured turtle slip through his fingers without leaving his mark engraved on its shell. He must have lettered about two thousand from first to last. We used to call them Harry Blake's sheep.

These turtles were of a discontented and migratory turn of mind, and we frequently encountered two or three of them on the crossroads several miles from

their ancestral mud. Unspeakable was our delight
whenever we discovered one soberly walking off with
Harry Blake's initials! I've no doubt there are, at
this moment, fat ancient turtles wandering about
that gummy woodland with H. B. neatly cut on their
venerable backs.

It soon became a custom among my playmates to
make our barn their rendezvous. Gypsy proved a
strong attraction. Captain Nutter bought me a
little two-wheeled cart, which she drew quite nicely,
after kicking out the dasher and breaking the shafts
once or twice. With our lunch baskets and fishing
tackle stowed away under the seat, we used to start
off early in the afternoon for the seashore, where
there were countless marvels in the shape of shells,
mosses, and kelp. Gypsy enjoyed the sport as keenly
as any of us, even going so far, one day, as to trot
down the beach into the sea where we were bathing.
As she took the cart with her, our provisions were
not much improved. I shall never forget how squash
pie tastes after being soused in the Atlantic Ocean.
Soda crackers dipped in salt water are palatable, but
not squash pie.

There was a good deal of wet weather during those
first six weeks at Rivermouth, and we set ourselves
at work to find some indoor amusement for our
half holidays. It was all very well for Amadis de
Gaul and Don Quixote not to mind the rain; they
had iron overcoats, and were not, from all we can

One day Gypsy trotted down to the beach into the sea, taking the cart
with her

learn, subject to croup and the guidance of their grandfathers. Our case was different.

"Now, boys, what shall we do?" I asked, addressing a thoughtful conclave of seven, assembled in our barn one dismal rainy afternoon.

"Let's have a theater," suggested Binny Wallace. The very thing! But where? The loft of the stable was ready to burst with hay provided for Gypsy, but the long room over the carriage house was unoccupied. The place of all places! My managerial eye saw at a glance its capabilities for a theater. I had been to the play a great many times in New Orleans, and was wise in matters pertaining to the drama. So here, in due time, was set up some extraordinary scenery of my own painting. The curtain, I recollect, though it worked smoothly enough on other occasions, invariably hitched during the performances; and it often required the united energies of the Prince of Denmark, the King, and the Grave-digger, with an occasional hand from "the fair Ophelia" (Pepper Whitcomb in a low-necked dress), to hoist that bit of green cambric.

The theater, however, was a success, as far as it went. I retired from the business with no fewer than fifteen hundred pins, after deducting the headless, the pointless, and the crooked pins with which our doorkeeper frequently got "stuck." From first to last we took in a great deal of this counterfeit money. The price of admission to the "Rivermouth Theater" was twenty pins. I played all the principal parts myself—not that I was a finer actor than the other boys, but because I owned the establishment.

At the tenth representation, my dramatic career was brought to a close by an unfortunate circumstance. We were playing the drama of "William Tell, the Hero of Switzerland." Of course I was William Tell, in spite of Fred Langdon, who wanted to act that character himself. I wouldn't let him, so he withdrew from the company, taking the only bow and arrow we had. I made a crossbow out of a piece of whalebone, and did very well without him. We had reached that exciting scene where Gessler, the Austrian tyrant, commands Tell to shoot the apple from his son's head. Pepper Whitcomb, who played all the juvenile and women parts, was my son. To guard against mischance, a piece of pasteboard was fastened by a handkerchief over the upper portion of Whitcomb's face, while the arrow to be used was sewed up in a strip of flannel. I was a capital marksman, and the big apple, only two yards distant, turned its russet cheek fairly toward me.

I can see poor little Pepper now, as he stood without flinching, waiting for me to perform my great feat. I raised the crossbow amid the breathless silence of the crowded audience consisting of seven boys and three girls, exclusive of Kitty Collins, who insisted on paying her way in with a clothespin. I

5

raised the crossbow, I repeat.   Twang! went the whip-cord; but, alas! instead of hitting the apple the arrow flew right into Pepper Whitcomb's mouth, which happened to be open at the time and destroyed my aim.

I shall never be able to banish that awful moment from my memory.   Pepper's roar, expressive of aston-ishment, indignation, and pain, is still ringing in my ears.   I looked upon him as a corpse, and, glanc-ing not far into the dreary future, pictured myself led forth to execution in the presence of the very same spectators then assembled.

Luckily poor Pepper was not seriously hurt; but Grandfather Nutter, appearing in the midst of the confusion (attracted by the howls of young Tell), issued an injunction against all theatricals there-after, and the place was closed; not, however, without a farewell speech from me, in which I said that this would have been the proudest moment of my life if I hadn't hit Pepper Whitcomb in the mouth.   Where-upon the audience (assisted, I am glad to state, by Pepper) cried, "Hear! hear!"   I then attributed the accident to Pepper himself, whose mouth, being open at the instant I fired, acted upon the arrow much after the fashion of a whirlpool, and drew in the fatal shaft.   I was about to explain how a comparatively small maelstrom could suck in the largest ship, when the curtain fell of its own accord, amid the shouts of the audience.

This was my last appearance on any stage. It was some time, though, before I heard the end of the William Tell business.

Malicious little boys who hadn't been allowed to buy tickets to my theater used to cry out after me in the street:

> "'Who killed Cock Robin?'
> 'I,' said the sparrer,
> 'With my bow and arrer,
> I killed Cock Robin!'"

The sarcasm of this verse was more than I could stand. And it made Pepper Whitcomb pretty mad to be called Cock Robin, I can tell you.

So the days glided on, with fewer clouds and more sunshine than fall to the lot of most boys. Conway was certainly a cloud. Within school bounds he seldom ventured to be aggressive; but whenever we met about town he never failed to brush against me, or pull my cap over my eyes, or drive me distracted by inquiring after my family in New Orleans, always alluding to them as highly respectable colored people.

Jack Harris was right when he said Conway would give me no rest until I fought him. I felt it was ordained ages before our birth that we should meet on this planet and fight. With the view of not running counter to destiny, I quietly prepared myself for the impending conflict. The scene of my dramatic triumphs was turned into a gymnasium for this purpose, though I did not openly avow the fact to the boys. By persistently standing on my head, raising heavy weights, and going hand over hand up a ladder, I developed my muscles until my little body was as tough as a hickory knot and as supple as tripe. I also took occasional lessons in the noble art of self-defense, under the tuition of Phil Adams.

I brooded over the matter until the idea of fighting Conway became a part of me. I fought him in imagination during school hours; I dreamed of fighting with him at night, when he would suddenly expand into a giant twelve feet high, and then as suddenly shrink into a pygmy so small that I couldn't hit him. In this latter shape he would get into my hair, or pop into my waistcoat pocket, treating me with as little ceremony as the Lilliputians showed Captain Lemuel Gulliver—all of which was not pleasant, to be sure. On the whole, Conway was a cloud.

And then I had a cloud at home. It was not Grandfather Nutter, nor Miss Abigail, nor Kitty Collins, though they all helped to compose it. It was a vague, funereal, impalpable something which no amount of gymnastic training would enable me to knock over. It was Sunday. If ever I have a boy to bring up in the way he should go, I intend to make Sunday a cheerful day to him. Sunday was not a cheerful day at the Nutter House. You shall judge for yourself.

It is Sunday morning. I should premise by saying that the deep gloom which has settled over everything set in like a heavy fog early on Saturday evening.

At seven o'clock my grandfather comes smilelessly downstairs. He is dressed in black, and looks as if he had lost all his friends during the night. Miss Abigail, also in black, looks as if she were prepared to bury them, and not indisposed to enjoy the ceremony. Even Kitty Collins has caught the contagious gloom, as I perceive when she brings in the coffee urn—a solemn and sculpturesque urn at any time, but monumental now—and sets it down in front of Miss Abigail. Miss Abigail gazes at the urn as if it held the ashes of her ancestors, instead of a generous quantity of fine old Java coffee. The meal progresses in silence.

Our parlor is by no means thrown open every day. It is open this June morning, and is pervaded by a strong smell of center table. The furniture of the room, and the little China ornaments on the mantelpiece, have a constrained, unfamiliar look. My grandfather sits in a mahogany chair, reading a large Bible covered with green baize. Miss Abigail occupies one end of the sofa, and has her hands crossed stiffly in her lap. I sit in the corner, crushed. Robinson Crusoe and Gil Blas are in close confine-

ment. Baron Trenck, who managed to escape from
the fortress of Glatz, can't for the life of him get out
of our sitting-room closet. Even the Rivermouth
Barnacle is suppressed until Monday. Genial converse, harmless books, smiles, lightsome hearts, all
are banished. If I want to read anything, I can read
Baxter's Saints' Rest. I would die first. So I sit
there kicking my heels, thinking about New Orleans,
and watching a morbid bluebottle fly that attempts
to commit suicide by butting his head against the
windowpane. Listen!—no, yes. It is—it is the robins
singing in the garden—the grateful, joyous robins
singing away like mad, just as if it wasn't Sunday.
Their audacity tickles me.

My grandfather looks up, and inquires in a
sepulchral voice if I am ready for Sabbath school.
It is time to go. I like the Sabbath school; there are
bright young faces there, at all events. When I get
out into the sunshine alone, I draw a long breath; I
would turn a somersault up against Neighbor Pen-
hallow's newly painted fence if I hadn't my best
trousers on, so glad am I to escape from the oppressive
atmosphere of the Nutter House.

Sabbath school over, I go to meeting, joining my
grandfather, who doesn't appear to be any relation
to me this day, and Miss Abigail, in the porch. Our
minister holds out very little hope to any of us of
being saved. Convinced that I am a lost creature,
in common with the human family, I return home

behind my guardians at a snail's pace. We have a dead cold dinner. I saw it laid out yesterday.

There is a long interval between this repast and the second service, and a still longer interval between the beginning and the end of that service; for the Rev. Wibird Hawkins's sermons are none of the shortest, whatever else they may be.

After meeting, my grandfather and I take a walk. We visit—appropriately enough—a neighboring graveyard. I am by this time in a condition of mind to become a willing inmate of the place. The usual evening prayer meeting is postponed for some reason. At half-past eight I go to bed.

This is the way Sunday was observed in the Nutter House, and pretty generally throughout the town, twenty years ago. People who were prosperous and natural and happy on Saturday, became the most rueful of human beings in the brief space of twelve hours. I don't think there was any hypocrisy in this. It was merely the old Puritan austerity cropping out once a week. Many of these people were pure Christians every day in the seven—excepting the seventh. Then they were decorous and solemn to the verge of moroseness.

I should not like to be misunderstood on this point. Sunday is a blessed day, and therefore it should not be made a gloomy one. It is the Lord's day, and I do believe that cheerful hearts and faces are not unpleasant in His sight.

"O day of rest! How beautiful, how fair,
How welcome to the weary and the old!
Day of the Lord! and truce to earthly cares!
Day of the Lord, as all our days should be!
Ah, why will man by his austerities
Shut out the blessed sunshine and the light,
And make of thee a dungeon of despair!"

Chapter VII

ONE MEMORABLE NIGHT

TWO months had elapsed since my arrival at Rivermouth, when the approach of an important celebration produced the greatest excitement among the juvenile population of the town.

There was very little hard study done in the Temple Grammar School the week preceding the Fourth of July. For my part, my heart and brain were so full of firecrackers, Roman candles, rockets, pin wheels, squibs, and gunpowder in various seductive forms, that I wonder I didn't explode under Mr. Grimshaw's very nose. I couldn't tell, for love or money, whether Tallahassee was the capital of Tennessee or of Florida; the present and the pluperfect tenses were inextricably mixed in my memory, and I didn't know a verb from an adjective when I met one. This was not alone my condition, but that of every boy in the school.

Mr. Grimshaw considerately made allowances for our temporary distraction, and sought to fix our interest on the lessons by connecting them directly or indirectly with the coming events. The class in arithmetic, for instance, was requested to state how many boxes of firecrackers, each box measuring sixteen inches square, could be stored in a room of such and such dimensions. He gave us the Declaration of Independence for a parsing exercise, and in geography confined his questions almost exclusively to localities rendered famous in the Revolutionary War.

"What did the people of Boston do with the tea on board the English vessel?" asked our wily instructor.

"Threw it into the river!" shrieked the smaller boys, with an impetuosity that made Mr. Grimshaw smile in spite of himself. One luckless urchin said, "Chucked it," for which happy expression he was kept in at recess.

Notwithstanding these clever stratagems, there was not much solid work done by anybody. The trail of the serpent (an inexpensive but dangerous fire toy) was over us all. We went round deformed by quantities of Chinese crackers artlessly concealed in our trousers pockets; and if a boy whipped out his handerkchief without proper precaution, he was sure to let off two or three torpedoes.

Even Mr. Grimshaw was made a sort of accessory to the universal demoralization. In calling the school to order, he always rapped on the table with a heavy ruler. Under the green baize tablecloth, on the exact spot where he usually struck, a certain boy, whose name I withhold, placed a fat torpedo. The result was a loud explosion, which caused Mr. Grimshaw

to look queer. Charley Marden was at the water
pail, at the time, and directed general attention to
himself by strangling for several seconds and then
squirting a slender thread of water over the blackboard.

Mr. Grimshaw fixed his eyes reproachfully on
Charley, but said nothing. The real culprit (it
wasn't Charley Marden, but the boy whose name I
withhold) instantly regretted his badness, and after
school confessed the whole thing to Mr. Grimshaw,
who heaped coals of fire upon the nameless boy's
head by giving him five cents for the Fourth of July.
If Mr. Grimshaw had caned this unknown youth,
the punishment would not have been half so severe.

On the last day of June the Captain received a
letter from my father, enclosing five dollars "for my
son Tom," which enabled that young gentleman to
make regal preparations for the celebration of our
national independence. A portion of this money,
two dollars, I hastened to invest in fireworks; the
balance I put by for contingencies. In placing the
fund in my possession, the Captain imposed one condition that dampened my ardor considerably—I was
to buy no gunpowder. I might have all the snapping
crackers and torpedoes I wanted; but gunpowder was
out of the question.

I thought this rather hard, for all my young friends
were provided with pistols of various sizes. Pepper
Whitcomb had a horse pistol nearly as large as him-

self; and Jack Harris, though he, to be sure, was a big boy, was going to have a real old-fashioned flintlock musket. However, I didn't mean to let this drawback destroy my happiness. I had one charge of powder stowed away in the little brass pistol which I brought from New Orleans, and was bound to make a noise in the world once, if I never did again.

It was a custom observed from time immemorial for the townsboys to have a bonfire on the Square on the midnight before the Fourth. I didn't ask the Captain's leave to attend this ceremony, for I had a general idea that he wouldn't give it. If the Captain, I reasoned, doesn't forbid me, I break no orders by going. Now this was a specious line of argument, and the mishaps that befell me in consequence of adopting it were richly deserved.

On the evening of the third I retired to bed very early, in order to disarm suspicion. I didn't sleep a wink, waiting for eleven o'clock to come round; and I thought it never would come round, as I lay counting from time to time the slow strokes of the ponderous bell in the steeple of the Old North Church. At length the laggard hour arrived. While the clock was striking I jumped out of bed and began dressing.

My grandfather and Miss Abigail were heavy sleepers, and I might have stolen downstairs and out at the front door undetected; but such a commonplace proceeding did not suit my adventurous disposition. I fastened one end of a rope (it was a few yards nearest the window) and cautiously climbed out on the wide pediment over the hall door. I had neglected to knot the rope; the result was, that, the moment I swung clear of the pediment, I descended like a flash of lightning and warmed both my hands smartly. The rope, moreover, was four or five feet too short; so I got a fall that would have proved serious, had I not tumbled into the middle of one of the big rosebushes growing on either side of the steps.

I scrambled out of that without delay and was congratulating myself on my good luck, when I saw by the light of the setting moon the form of a man leaning over the garden gate. It was one of the town watch, who had probably been observing my operations with curiosity. Seeing no chance of escape, I put a bold face on the matter and walked directly up to him.

"What on airth air you a doin'?" asked the man, grasping the collar of my jacket.

"I live here, sir, if you please," I replied, "and am going to the bonfire. I didn't want to wake up the old folks, that's all."

The man cocked his eyes at me in the most amiable manner, and released his hold.

"Boys is boys," he muttered. He didn't attempt to stop me as I slipped through the gate.

Once beyond his clutches, I took to my heels and soon reached the Square, where I found forty or fifty fellows assembled, engaged in building a pyramid of tar barrels. The palms of my hands still tingled so that I couldn't join in the sport. I stood in the doorway of the Nautilus Bank, watching the workers, among whom I recognized lots of my schoolmates. They looked like a legion of imps, coming and going in the twilight, busy in raising some infernal edifice. What a Babel of voices it was, everybody directing everybody else, and everybody doing everything wrong!

When all was prepared, someone applied a match to the somber pile. A fiery tongue thrust itself out here and there, then suddenly the whole fabric burst into flames, blazing and crackling beautifully. This was a signal for the boys to join hands and dance around the burning barrels, which they did shouting like mad creatures. When the fire had burned down a little, fresh staves were brought and heaped on the pyre. In the excitement of the moment I forgot my tingling palms, and found myself in the thick of the carousal.

Before we were half ready, our combustible material was expended and a disheartening kind of darkness settled down upon us. The boys collected together here and there in knots, consulting as to what should be done. It yet lacked four or five hours of daybreak, and none of us were in the humor to return to bed. I approached one of the groups standing near the town pump, and discovered in the uncertain light of the dying brands the figures of

Jack Harris, Phil Adams, Harry Blake, and Pepper Whitcomb, their faces streaked with perspiration and tar, and their whole appearance suggestive of New Zealand chiefs.

"Hullo! here's Tom Bailey!" shouted Pepper Whitcomb, "he'll join in!"

Of course he would. The sting had gone out of my hands, and I was ripe for anything—none the less ripe for not knowing what was on the tapis. After whispering together for a moment, the boys motioned me to follow them.

We glided out from the crowd and silently wended our way through a neighboring alley, at the head of which stood a tumble-down old barn, owned by one Ezra Wingate. In former days this was the stable of the mail coach that ran between Rivermouth and Boston. When the railroad superseded that primitive mode of travel, the lumbering vehicle was rolled into the barn, and there it stayed. The stage driver, after prophesying the immediate downfall of the nation, died of grief and apoplexy, and the old coach followed in his wake as fast as it could by quietly dropping to pieces. The barn had the reputation of being haunted, and I think we all kept very close together when we found ourselves standing in the black shadow cast by the tall gable. Here, in a low voice, Jack Harris laid bare his plan, which was to burn the ancient stagecoach.

"The old trundle-cart isn't worth twenty-five

cents," said Jack Harris, "and Ezra Wingate ought to thank us for getting the rubbish out of the way. But if any fellow here doesn't want to have a hand in it, let him cut and run, and keep a quiet tongue in his head ever after."

With this he pulled out the staples that held the rusty padlock, and the big barn door swung slowly open. The interior of the stable was pitch-dark, of course. As we made a movement to enter, a sudden scrambling, and the sound of heavy bodies leaping in all directions, caused us to start back in terror.

"Rats!" cried Phil Adams.

"Bats!" exclaimed Harry Blake.

"Cats!" suggested Jack Harris. "Who's afraid?"

Well, the truth is, we were all afraid; and if the pole of the stage had not been lying close to the threshold, I don't believe anything on earth would have induced us to cross it. We seized hold of the pole straps and succeeded with great trouble in dragging the coach out. The two fore wheels had rusted to the axletree, and refused to revolve. It was the merest skeleton of a coach. The cushions had long since been removed, and the leather hangings, where they had not crumbled away, dangled in shreds from the worm-eaten frame. A load of ghosts and a span of phantom horses to drag them would have made the ghastly thing complete.

Luckily for our undertaking, the stable stood at

At this moment a figure was seen leaping wildly from the inside of the blazing coach

the top of a very steep hill. With three boys to push
behind, and two in front to steer, we started the old
coach on its last trip with little or no difficulty. Our
speed increased every moment, and, the fore wheels
becoming unlocked as we arrived at the foot of the
declivity, we charged upon the crowd like a regiment
of cavalry, scattering the people right and left. Before reaching the bonfire, to which someone had
added several bushels of shavings, Jack Harris and
Phil Adams, who were steering, dropped on the ground
and allowed the vehicle to pass over them, which it
did without injuring them; but the boys who were
clinging for dear life to the trunk rack behind fell
over the prostrate steersmen, and there we all lay in
a heap, two or three of us quite picturesque with nosebleed.

The coach, with an intuitive perception of what
was expected of it, plunged into the center of the
kindling shavings, and stopped. The flames sprung
up and clung to the rotten woodwork, which burned
like tinder. At this moment a figure was seen leaping wildly from the inside of the blazing coach. The
figure made three bounds toward us, and tripped over
Harry Blake. It was Pepper Whitcomb, with his
hair somewhat singed and his eyebrows completely
scorched off!

Pepper had slyly ensconced himself on the back
seat before we started, intending to have a neat little
ride downhill, and a laugh at us afterwards. But the

laugh, as it happened, was on our side, or would have been, if half a dozen watchmen had not suddenly pounced down upon us, as we lay scrambling on the ground, weak with mirth over Pepper's misfortune. We were collared and marched off before we well knew what had happened.

The abrupt transition from the noise and light of the Square to the silent, gloomy brick room in the rear of the Meat Market, seemed like the work of enchantment. We stared at each other aghast.

"Well," remarked Jack Harris, with a sickly smile, "this is a go!"

"No go, I should say," whimpered Harry Blake, glancing at the bare brick walls and the heavy iron-plated door.

"Never say die," muttered Phil Adams, dolefully.

The bridewell was a small low-studded chamber built up against the rear end of the Meat Market, and approached from the Square by a narrow passageway. A portion of the room was partitioned off into eight cells, numbered, each capable of holding two persons. The cells were full at the time, as we presently discovered by seeing several hideous faces leering out at us through the gratings of the doors.

A smoky oil lamp in a lantern suspended from the ceiling threw a flickering light over the apartment, which contained no furniture excepting a couple of stout wooden benches. It was a dismal place by night, and only little less dismal by day, for the tall houses surrounding "the lockup" prevented the faintest ray of sunshine from penetrating the ventilator over the door—a long, narrow window opening inward and propped up by a piece of lath.

As we seated ourselves in a row on one of the benches, I imagine that our aspect was anything but cheerful. Adams and Harris looked very anxious, and Harry Blake, whose nose had just stopped bleeding, was mournfully carving his name, by sheer force of habit, on the prison bench. I don't think I ever saw a more "wrecked" expression on any human countenance than Pepper Whitcomb's presented. His look of natural astonishment at finding himself incarcerated in a jail was considerably heightened by his lack of eyebrows.

As for me, it was only by thinking how the late Baron Trenck would have conducted himself under similar circumstances that I was able to restrain my tears.

None of us were inclined to conversation. A deep silence, broken now and then by a startling snore from the cells, reigned throughout the chamber. By and by Pepper Whitcomb glanced nervously toward Phil Adams and said, "Phil, do you think they will hang us?"

"Hang your grandmother!" returned Adams, impatiently, "what I'm afraid of is that they'll keep us locked up until the Fourth is over."

"You ain't smart ef they do!" cried a voice from one of the cells. It was a deep bass voice that sent a chill through me.

"Who are you?" said Jack Harris, addressing the cells in general; for the echoing qualities of the room made it difficult to locate the voice.

"That don't matter," replied the speaker, putting his face close up to the gratings of No. 3, "but ef I was a youngster like you, free an' easy outside ther, this spot wouldn't hold me long."

"That's so!" chimed several of the prison birds, wagging their heads behind the iron lattices.

"Hush!" whispered Jack Harris, rising from his seat and walking on tiptoe to the door of cell No. 3. "What would you do?"

"Do? Why, I'd pile them 'ere benches up agin that 'ere door, an' crawl out of that 'ere winder in no time. That's my advice."

"And werry good adwice it is, Jim," said the occupant of No. 5, approvingly.

Jack Harris seemed to be of the same opinion, for he hastily placed the benches one on the top of another under the ventilator, and, climbing up on the highest bench, peeped out into the passageway.

"If any gent happens to have a ninepence about him," said the man in cell No. 3, "there's a sufferin' family here as could make use of it. Smallest favors gratefully received, an' no questions axed."

This appeal touched a new silver quarter of a

dollar in my trousers pocket; I fished out the coin from a mass of fireworks, and gave it to the prisoner. He appeared to be so good-natured a fellow that I ventured to ask what he had done to get into jail.

"Intirely innocent. I was clapped in here by a rascally nevew as wishes to enjoy my wealth afore I'm dead."

"Your name, sir?" I inquired, with a view of reporting the outrage to my grandfather and having the injured person reinstated in society.

"Git out, you insolent young reptyle!" shouted the man, in a passion.

I retreated precipitately, amid a roar of laughter from the other cells.

"Can't you keep still?" exclaimed Harris, withdrawing his head from the window.

A portly watchman usually sat on a stool outside the door day and night; but on this particular occasion, his services being required elsewhere, the bridewell had been left to guard itself.

"All clear," whispered Jack Harris, as he vanished through the aperture and dropped softly on the ground outside. We all followed him expeditiously —Pepper Whitcomb and myself getting stuck in the window for a moment in our frantic efforts not to be last.

"Now, boys, everybody for himself!"

CHAPTER VIII

THE ADVENTURES OF A FOURTH

THE sun cast a broad column of quivering gold across the river at the foot of our street, just as I reached the doorstep of the Nutter House. Kitty Collins, with her dress tucked about her so that she looked as if she had on a pair of calico trousers, was washing off the sidewalk.

"Arrah, you bad boy!" cried Kitty, leaning on the mop handle, "the Capen has jist been askin' for you. He's gone up town, now. It's a nate thing you done with my clothes line, and it's me you may thank for gettin' it out of the way before the Capen come down."

The kind creature had hauled in the rope, and my escapade had not been discovered by the family; but I knew very well that the burning of the stagecoach, and the arrest of the boys concerned in the mischief, were sure to reach my grandfather's ears sooner or later.

"Well, Thomas," said the old gentleman, an hour or so afterwards, beaming upon me benevolently across the breakfast table, "you didn't wait to be called this morning."

"No, sir," I replied, growing very warm, "I took a little run up town to see what was going on."

79

I didn't say anything about the little run I took home again!

"They had quite a time on the Square last night," remarked Captain Nutter, looking up from the Rivermouth Barnacle, which was always placed beside his coffee cup at breakfast.

I felt that my hair was preparing to stand on end.

"Quite a time," continued my grandfather. "Some boys broke into Ezra Wingate's barn and carried off the old stagecoach. The young rascals! I do believe they'd burn up the whole town if they had their way."

With this he resumed the paper. After a long silence he exclaimed, "Hullo!"—upon which I nearly fell off the chair.

" 'Miscreants unknown,' " read my grandfather, following the paragraph with his forefinger; " 'escaped from the bridewell, leaving no clue to their identity except the letter "H" cut on one of the benches. Five dollars reward offered for the apprehension of the perpetrators.' Sho! I hope Wingate will catch them."

I don't see how I continued to live, for on hearing this the breath went entirely out of my body. I beat a retreat from the room as soon as I could, and flew to the stable with a misty intention of mounting Gypsy and escaping from the place. I was pondering what steps to take, when Jack Harris and Charley Marden entered the yard.

"I say," said Harris, as blithe as a lark, "has old Wingate been here?"

"Been here?" I cried, "I should hope not!"

"The whole thing's out, you know," said Harris, pulling Gypsy's forelock over her eyes and blowing playfully into her nostrils.

"You don't mean it!" I gasped.

"Yes, I do, and we are to pay Wingate three dollars apiece. He'll make rather a good spec out of it."

"But how did he discover that we were the—the miscreants?" I asked, quoting mechanically from the Rivermouth Barnacle.

"Why, he saw us take the old ark, confound him! He's been trying to sell it any time these ten years. Now he has sold it to us. When he found that we had slipped out of the Meat Market, he went right off and wrote the advertisement offering five dollars reward; though he knew well enough who had taken the coach, for he came round to my father's house before the paper was printed to talk the matter over. Wasn't the governor mad, though! But it's all settled, I tell you. We're to pay Wingate fifteen dollars for the old gocart, which he wanted to sell the other day for seventy-five cents, and couldn't. It's a downright swindle. But the funny part of it is to come."

"Oh, there's a funny part to it, is there?" I remarked bitterly.

"Yes. The moment Billy Conway saw the advertisement, he knew it was Harry Blake who cut that letter "H" on the bench; so off he rushes up to Wingate—kind of him, wasn't it?—and claims the reward. 'Too late, young man,' says old Wingate, 'the culprits have been discovered.' You see Slyboots hadn't any intention of paying that five dollars."

Jack Harris's statement lifted a weight from my bosom. The article in the Rivermouth Barnacle had placed the affair before me in a new light. I had thoughtlessly committed a grave offense. Though the property in question was valueless, we were clearly wrong in destroying it. At the same time Mr. Wingate *had* tacitly sanctioned the act by not preventing it when he might easily have done so. He had allowed his property to be destroyed in order that he might realize a large profit.

Without waiting to hear more I went straight to Captain Nutter, and, laying my remaining three dollars on his knee, confessed my share in the previous night's transaction.

The Captain heard me through in profound silence, pocketed the bank notes, and walked off without speaking a word. He had punished me in his own whimsical fashion at the breakfast table, for, at the very moment he was harrowing up my soul by reading the extracts from the Rivermouth Barnacle, he not only knew all about the bonfire, but had paid Ezra Wingate his three dollars. Such was the duplicity of that aged impostor!

I think Captain Nutter was justified in retaining my pocket money, as additional punishment, though the possession of it later in the day would have got me out of a difficult position, as the reader will see further on.

I returned with a light heart and a large piece of punk to my friends in the stable yard, where we celebrated the termination of our trouble by setting off two packs of firecrackers in an empty wine cask. They made a prodigious racket, but failed somehow fully to express my feelings. The little brass pistol in my bedroom suddenly occurred to me. It had been loaded I don't know how many months, long before I left New Orleans, and now was the time, if ever, to fire it off. Muskets, blunderbusses, and pistols were banging away lively all over town, and the smell of gunpowder, floating on the air, set me wild to add something respectable to the universal din.

When the pistol was produced, Jack Harris examined the rusty cap and prophesized that it would not explode.

"Never mind," said I, "let's try it."

I had fired the pistol once, secretly, in New Orleans; and, remembering the noise it gave birth to on that occasion, I shut both eyes tight as I pulled the trigger. The hammer clicked on the cap with a dull, dead sound. Then Harris tried it; then Charley Marden; then I took it again, and after three or four trials was on the point of giving it up as a bad job, when the obstinate thing went off with a tremendous explosion, nearly jerking my arm from the socket. The smoke cleared away, and there I stood with the stock of the pistol clutched convulsively in my hand —the barrel, lock, trigger, and ramrod having vanished into thin air.

"Are you hurt?" cried the boys, in one breath.

"N-no," I replied, dubiously, for the concussion had bewildered me a little.

When I realized the nature of the calamity, my grief was excessive. I can't imagine what led me to do so ridiculous a thing, but I gravely buried the remains of my beloved pistol in our back garden, and erected over the mound a slate tablet to the effect that "Mr. Barker, formerly of new orleans, was Killed accidentally on the Fourth of july, 18—in the second year of his Age."* Binny Wallace, arriving on the spot just after the disaster, and Charley Marden (who enjoyed the obsequies immensely), acted with me as chief mourners. I, for my part, was a very sincere one.

As I turned away in a disconsolate mood from the garden, Charley Marden remarked that he shouldn't be surprised if the pistol butt took root and grew into a mahogany tree or something. He said he

---

* This inscription is copied from a triangular-shaped piece of slate, still preserved in the garret of the Nutter House, together with the pistol butt itself, which was subsequently dug up for a *postmortem* examination.

once planted an old musket stock, and shortly afterwards a lot of shoots sprung up! Jack Harris laughed; but neither I nor Binny Wallace saw Charley's wicked joke.

We were now joined by Pepper Whitcomb, Fred Langdon, and several other desperate characters, on their way to the Square, which was always a busy place when public festivities were going on. Feeling that I was still in disgrace with the Captain, I thought it politic to ask his consent before accompanying the boys.

He gave it with some hesitation, advising me to be careful not to get in front of the firearms. Once he put his fingers mechanically into his vest pocket and half drew forth some dollar bills, then slowly thrust them back again as his sense of justice overcame his genial disposition. I guess it cut the old gentleman to the heart to be obliged to keep me out of my pocket money. I know it did me. However, as I was passing through the hall, Miss Abigail, with a very severe cast of countenance, slipped a brand new quarter into my hand. We had silver currency in those days, thank Heaven!

Great were the bustle and confusion on the Square. By the way, I don't know why they called this large open space a square, unless because it was an oval— an oval formed by the confluence of half a dozen streets, now thronged by crowds of smartly dressed townspeople and country folks; for Rivermouth on the Fourth was the center of attraction to the inhabitants of the neighboring villages.

On one side of the Square were twenty or thirty booths arranged in a semicircle, gay with the little flags and seductive with lemonade, ginger beer, and seed cakes. Here and there were tables at which could be purchased the smaller sort of fireworks, such as pin wheels, serpents, double headers, and punk warranted not to go out. Many of the adjacent houses made a pretty display of bunting, and across each of the streets opening on the Square was an arch of spruce and evergreen, blossoming all over with patriotic mottoes and paper roses.

It was a noisy, merry, bewildering scene as we came upon the ground. The incessant rattle of small arms, the booming of the twelve pounder firing on the Mill Dam, and the silvery clangor of the church bells ringing simultaneously—not to mention an ambitious brass band that was blowing itself to pieces on a balcony—was enough to drive one distracted. We amused ourselves for an hour or two, darting in and out among the crowd and setting off our crackers. At one o'clock the Hon. Hezekiah Elkins mounted a platform in the middle of the Square and delivered an oration, to which his "feller citizens" didn't pay much attention, having all they could do to dodge the squibs that were set loose upon them by mischievous boys stationed on the surrounding housetops.

We amused ourselves for an hour or more, darting in and out among
the crowd and setting off our crackers

Our little party which had picked up recruits here and there, not being swayed by eloquence, withdrew to a booth on the outskirts of the crowd, where we regaled ourselves with root beer at two cents a glass. I recollect being much struck by the placard surmounting this tent:

ROOT BEER
SOLD HERE

It seemed to me the perfection of pith and poetry. What could be more terse? Not a word to spare, and yet everything fully expressed. Rime and rhythm faultless. It was a delightful poet who made those verses. As for the beer itself—that, I think, must have been made from the root of all evil! A single glass of it insured an uninterrupted pain for twenty-four hours.

The influence of my liberality working on Charley Marden—for it was I who paid for the beer—he presently invited us all to take an ice cream with him at Pettingil's saloon. Pettingil was the Delmonico of Rivermouth. He furnished ices and confectionery for aristocratic balls and parties, and didn't disdain to officiate as leader of the orchestra at the same; for Pettingil played on the violin, as Pepper Whitcomb described it, "like Old Scratch."

Pettingil's confectionery store was on the corner of Willow and High Streets. The saloon, separated from the shop by a flight of three steps leading to a door hung with faded red drapery, had about it an air of mystery and seclusion quite delightful. Four windows, also draped, faced the side street, affording an unobstructed view of Marm Hatch's back yard, where a number of inexplicable garments on a clothes line were always to be seen careening in the wind.

There was a lull just then in the ice-cream business, it being dinner time, and we found the saloon unoccupied. When we had seated ourselves around the largest marble-topped table, Charley Marden in a manly voice ordered twelve sixpenny ice creams, "strawberry and verneller mixed."

It was a magnificent sight, those twelve chilly glasses entering the room on a waiter, the red and white custard rising from each glass like a church steeple, and the spoon handle shooting up from the apex like a spire. I doubt if a person of the nicest palate could have distinguished, with his eyes shut, which was the vanilla and which the strawberry; but if I could at this moment obtain a cream tasting as that did, I would give five dollars for a very small quantity.

We fell to with a will, and so evenly balanced were our capabilities that we finished our creams together, the spoons clinking in the glasses like one spoon.

"Let's have some more!" cried Charley Marden, with the air of Aladdin ordering up a fresh hogshead of pearls and rubies. "Tom Bailey, tell Pettingil to send in another round."

Could I credit my ears? I looked at him to see if he were in earnest. He meant it. In a moment more I was leaning over the counter giving directions for a second supply. Thinking it would make no difference to such a gorgeous young sybarite as Marden, I took the liberty of ordering ninepenny creams this time.

On returning to the saloon, what was my horror at finding it empty!

There were twelve cloudy glasses, standing in a circle on the sticky marble slab, and not a boy to be seen. A pair of hands letting go their hold on the window sill outside explained matters. I had been made a victim.

I couldn't stay and face Pettingil, whose peppery temper was well known among the boys. I hadn't a cent in the world to appease him. What should I do? I heard the clink of approaching glasses—the ninepenny creams. I rushed to the nearest window. It was only five feet to the ground. I threw myself out as if I had been an old hat.

Landing on my feet, I fled breathlessly down High Street, through Willow, and was turning into Brierwood Place when the sound of several voices, calling to me in distress, stopped my progress.

"Look out, you fool! the mine! the mine!" yelled the warning voices.

Several men and boys were standing at the head

7

of the street, making insane gestures to me to avoid something. But I saw no mine, only in the middle of the road in front of me was a common flour barrel, which, as I gazed at it, suddenly rose into the air with a terrific explosion. I felt myself thrown violently off my feet. I remember nothing else, excepting that, as I went up, I caught a momentary glimpse of Ezra Wingate leering through his shop window like an avenging spirit.

The mine that had wrought me woe was not properly a mine at all, but merely a few ounces of powder placed under an empty keg or barrel and fired with a slow match. Boys who didn't happen to have pistols or cannon generally burned their powder in this fashion.

For an account of what followed I am indebted to hearsay, for I was insensible when the people picked me up and carried me home on a shutter borrowed from the proprietor of Pettingil's saloon. I was supposed to be killed, but happily (happily for me at least) I was merely stunned. I lay in a semi-unconscious state until eight o'clock that night, when I attempted to speak. Miss Abigail who watched by the bedside, put her ear down to my lips and was saluted with these remarkable words:

"Strawberry and verneller mixed!"

"Mercy on us! what is the boy saying?" cried Miss Abigail.

"ROOTBEERSOLDHERE!"

Chapter IX

I BECOME AN R. M. C.

IN the course of ten days I recovered sufficiently from my injuries to attend school, where, for a little while, I was looked upon as a hero, on account of having been blown up. What don't we make a hero of? The distraction which prevailed in the classes the week preceding the Fourth had subsided, and nothing remained to indicate the recent festivities, excepting a noticeable want of eyebrows on the part of Pepper Whitcomb and myself.

In August we had two weeks' vacation. It was about this time that I became a member of the Rivermouth Centipedes, a secret society composed of twelve of the Temple Grammar School boys. This was an honor to which I had long aspired, but, being a new boy, I was not admitted to the fraternity until my character had fully developed itself.

It was a very select society, the object of which I never fathomed, though I was an active member of the body during the remainder of my residence at Rivermouth, and at one time held the onerous position of F. C.—First Centipede. Each of the elect wore a copper cent (some occult association being established between a cent apiece and a centipede!)

suspended by a string round his neck. The medals were worn next the skin, and it was while bathing one day at Grave Point, with Jack Harris and Fred Langdon, that I had my curiosity roused to the highest pitch by a sight of these singular emblems. As soon as I ascertained the existence of a boys' club, of course I was ready to die to join it. And eventually I was allowed to join.

The initiation ceremony took place in Fred Langdon's barn, where I was submitted to a series of trials not calculated to soothe the nerves of a timorous boy. Before being led to the Grotto of Enchantment—such was the modest title given to the loft over my friend's woodhouse—my hands were securely pinioned, and my eyes covered with a thick silk handkerchief. At the head of the stairs I was told in an unrecognizable, husky voice that it was not yet too late to retreat if I felt myself physically too weak to undergo the necessary tortures. I replied that I was not too weak, in a tone which I intended to be resolute, but which, in spite of me, seemed to come from the pit of my stomach.

"It is well!" said the husky voice.

I did not feel so sure about that; but, having made up my mind to be a Centipede, a Centipede I was bound to be. Other boys had passed through the ordeal and lived, why should not I?

A prolonged silence followed this preliminary examination, and I was wondering what would come next, when a pistol fired off close by my ear deafened me for a moment. The unknown voice then directed me to take ten steps forward and stop at the word halt. I took ten steps, and halted.

"Stricken mortal," said a second husky voice, more husky, if possible, than the first, "if you had advanced another inch, you would have disappeared down an abyss three thousand feet deep."

I naturally shrunk back at this friendly piece of information. A prick from some two-pronged instrument, evidently a pitchfork, gently checked my retreat. I was then conducted to the brink of several other precipices, and ordered to step over many dangerous chasms, where the result would have been instant death if I had committed the least mistake. I have neglected to say that my movements were occompanied by dismal groans from different parts of the grotto.

Finally, I was led up a steep plank to what appeared to me an incalculable height. Here I stood breathless while the by-laws were read aloud. A more extraordinary code of laws never came from the brain of man. The penalties attached to the abject being who should reveal any of the secrets of the society were enough to make the blood run cold. A second pistol shot was heard, the something I stood on sunk with a crash beneath my feet, and I fell two miles, as nearly as I could compute it. At the same instant the handkerchief was whisked from my eyes, and I found myself standing in an empty hogshead surrounded by twelve masked figures fantastically dressed. One of the conspirators was really appalling with a tin saucepan on his head, and a tigerskin sleigh robe thrown over his shoulders. I scarcely need say that there were no vestiges to be seen of the fearful gulfs over which I had passed so cautiously. My ascent had been to the top of the hogshead, and my descent to the bottom thereof. Holding one another by the hand, and chanting a low dirge, the Mystic Twelve revolved about me. This concluded the ceremony. With a merry shout the boys threw off their masks, and I was declared a regularly installed member of the R. M. C.

I afterwards had a good deal of sport out of the club, for these initiations, as you may imagine, were sometimes very comical spectacles, especially when the aspirant for centipedal honors happened to be of a timid disposition. If he showed the slightest terror, he was certain to be tricked unmercifully. One of our subsequent devices—a humble invention of my own—was to request the blindfolded candidate to put out his tongue, whereupon the First Centipede would say, in a low tone, as if not intended for the ear of the victim, "Diabolus, fetch me the red-hot iron!" The expedition with which that tongue would disappear was simply ridiculous.

Our meetings were held in various barns, at no stated periods, but as circumstances suggested. Any member had a right to call a meeting. Each boy who failed to report himself was fined one cent. Whenever a member had reasons for thinking that another member would be unable to attend, he called a meeting. For instance, immediately on learning the death of Harry Blake's great-grandfather, I issued a call. By these simple and ingenious measures we kept our treasury in a flourishing condition, sometimes having on hand as much as a dollar and a quarter.

I have said that the society had no especial object. It is true, there was a tacit understanding among us that the Centipedes were to stand by one another on all occasions, though I don't remember that they did; but further than this we had no purpose, unless it was to accomplish as a body the same amount of mischief which we were sure to do as individuals. To mystify the staid and slow-going Rivermouthians was our frequent pleasure. Several of our pranks won us such a reputation among the townsfolk that we were credited with having a large finger in whatever went amiss in the place.

One morning, about a week after my admission into the secret order, the quiet citizens awoke to find that the signboards of all the principal streets had changed places during the night. People who went trustfully to sleep in Currant Square opened their eyes in Honeysuckle Terrace. Jones's Avenue at the north end had suddenly become Walnut Street, and

Peanut Street was nowhere to be found. Confusion reigned. The town authorities took the matter in hand without delay, and six of the Temple Grammar School boys were summoned to appear before Justice Clapham.

Having tearfully disclaimed to my grandfather all knowledge of the transaction, I disappeared from the family circle, and was not apprehended until late in the afternoon, when the Captain dragged me ignominiously from the haymow and conducted me, more dead than alive, to the office of Justice Clapham. Here I encountered five other pallid culprits, who had been fished out of divers coal bins, garrets, and chicken coops, to answer the demands of the outraged laws. (Charley Marden had hidden himself in a pile of gravel behind his father's house, and looked like a recently exhumed mummy.)

There was not the least evidence against us; and, indeed, we were wholly innocent of the offense. The trick, as was afterwards proved, had been played by a party of soldiers stationed at the fort in the harbor. We were indebted for our arrest to Master Conway, who had slyly dropped a hint, within the hearing of Selectman Mudge, to the effect that "young Bailey and his five cronies could tell something about them signs." When he was called upon to make good his assertion, he was considerably more terrified than the Centipedes, though they were ready to sink into their shoes.

At our next meeting it was unanimously resolved that Conway's animosity should not be quietly submitted to. He had sought to inform against us in the stagecoach business; he had volunteered to carry Pettingil's "little bill" for twenty-four ice creams to Charley Marden's father; and now he had caused us to be arraigned before Justice Clapham on a charge equally groundless and painful. After much noisy discussion a plan of retaliation was agreed upon.

There was a certain slim, mild apothecary in the town, by name of Meeks. It was generally given out that Mr. Meeks had a vague desire to get married, but, being a shy and timorous youth, lacked the moral courage to do so. It was also well known that the Widow Conway had not buried her heart with the late lamented. As to her shyness, that was not so clear. Indeed, her attentions to Mr. Meeks, whose mother she might have been, were of a nature not to be misunderstood, and were not misunderstood by anyone but Mr. Meeks himself.

The widow carried on a dressmaking establishment at her residence on the corner opposite Meek's drug store, and kept a wary eye on all the young ladies from Miss Dorothy Gibb's Female Institute who patronized the shop for soda water, acid drops, and slate pencils. In the afternoon the widow was usually seen seated, smartly dressed, at her window upstairs, casting destructive glances across the street, the artificial roses in her cap and her whole languishing manner saying as plainly as a label on a prescription, "To Be Taken Immediately!" But Mr. Meeks didn't take.

The lady's fondness, and the gentleman's blindness, were topics ably handled at every sewing circle in the town. It was through these two luckless individuals that we proposed to strike a blow at the common enemy. To kill less than three birds with one stone did not suit our sanguinary purpose. We disliked the widow not so much for her sentimentality as for being the mother of Bill Conway; we disliked Mr. Meeks not because he was insipid, like his own sirups, but because the widow loved him; Bill Conway we hated for himself.

Late one dark Saturday night in September we carried our plan into effect. On the following morning, as the orderly citizens wended their way to church past the widow's abode, their sober faces relaxed at beholding over her front door the well-known gilt Mortar and Pestle which usually stood on the top of a pole on the opposite corner; while the passers on that side of the street were equally amused and scandalized at seeing a placard bearing the following announcement tacked to the druggist's window shutters:

Wanted a Semptress!

The naughty cleverness of the joke (which I should be sorry to defend) was recognized at once. It spread

like wildfire over the town, and, though the mortar
and the placard were speedily removed, our triumph
was complete. The whole community was on the
broad grin, and our participation in the affair seemingly unsuspected.

It was those wicked soldiers at the fort!

Chapter X

I FIGHT CONWAY

THERE was one person, however, who cherished a strong suspicion that the Centipedes had had a hand in the business, and that person was Conway. His red hair seemed to change to a livelier red, and his sallow cheeks to a deeper sallow, as we glanced at him stealthily over the tops of our slates the next day in school. He knew we were watching him, and made sundry mouths and scowled in the most threatening way over his sums.

Conway had an accomplishment peculiarly his own—that of throwing his thumbs out of joint at will. Sometimes while absorbed in study, or on becoming nervous at recitation, he performed the feat unconsciously. Throughout this entire morning his thumbs were observed to be in a chronic state of dislocation, indicating great mental agitation on the part of the owner. We fully expected an outbreak from him at recess; but the intermission passed off tranquilly, somewhat to our disappointment.

At the close of the afternoon session it happened that Binny Wallace and myself, having got swamped in our Latin exercise, were detained in school for the purpose of refreshing our memories with a page of

Mr. Andrews's perplexing irregular verbs. Binny
Wallace, finishing his task first, was dismissed. I
followed shortly after, and, on stepping into the playground, saw my little friend plastered, as it were, up
against the fence, and Conway standing in front of
him ready to deliver a blow on the upturned, unpro-
tected face, whose gentleness would have stayed any
arm but a coward's.

Seth Rodgers, with both hands in his pockets, was
leaning against the pump lazily enjoying the sport;
but on seeing me sweep across the yard, whirling my
strap of books in the air like a sling, he called out
lustily, "Lay low, Conway! here's young Bailey!"

Conway turned just in time to catch on his shoulder the blow intended for his head. He reached forward one of his long arms—he had arms like a wind-
mill, that boy—and, grasping me by the hair, tore out
quite a respectable handful. The tears flew to my
eyes, but they were not the tears of defeat; they were
merely the involuntary tribute which nature paid to
the departed tresses.

In a second my little jacket lay on the ground, and
I stood on guard, resting lightly on my right leg and
keeping my eye fixed steadily on Conway's—in all of
which I was faithfully following the instructions of
Phil Adams, whose father subscribed to a sporting
journal.

Conway also threw himself into a defensive attitude, and there we were, glaring at each other, mo-

tionless, neither of us disposed to risk an attack, but both on the alert to resist one. There is no telling how long we might have remained in that absurd position, had we not been interrupted.

It was a custom with the larger pupils to return to the playground after school, and play baseball until sundown. The town authorities had prohibited ball playing on the Square, and, there being no other available place, the boys fell back perforce on the school yard. Just at this crisis a dozen or so of the Templars entered the gate, and, seeing at a glance the belligerent status of Conway and myself, dropped bat and ball, and rushed to the spot where we stood.

"Is it a fight?" asked Phil Adams, who saw by our freshness that we had not yet got to work.

"Yes, it's a fight," I answered, "unless Conway will ask Wallace's pardon, promise never to hector me in future—and put back my hair!"

This last condition was rather a staggerer.

"I shan't do nothing of the sort," said Conway, sulkily.

"Then the thing must go on," said Adams, with dignity. "Rodgers, as I understand it, is your second, Conway? Bailey, come here. What's the row about?"

"He was thrashing Binny Wallace."

"No, I wasn't," interrupted Conway, "but I was going to, because he knows who put Meeks's mortar over our door. And I know well enough who did it; it was that sneaking little mulatter!"—pointing at me.

"Oh, by George!" I cried, reddening at the insult.

"Cool is the word," said Adams, as he bound a handkerchief round my head, and carefully tucked away the long straggling locks that offered a tempting advantage to the enemy. "Who ever heard of a fellow with such a head of hair going into action!" muttered Phil, twitching the handkerchief to ascertain if it were securely tied. He then loosened my gallowses (braces), and buckled them tightly above my hips. "Now, then, bantam, never say die!"

Conway regarded these business-like preparations with evident misgiving, for he called Rodgers to his side, and had himself arrayed in a similar manner, though his hair was cropped so close that you couldn't have taken hold of it with a pair of tweezers.

"Is your man ready?" asked Phil Adams, addressing Rodgers.

"Ready!"

"Keep your back to the gate, Tom," whispered Phil in my ear, "and you'll have the sun in his eyes."

Behold us once more face to face, like David and the Philistine. Look at us as long as you may, for this is all you shall see of the combat. According to my thinking, the hospital teaches a better lesson than the battle field. I shall tell you about my black

eye, and my swollen lip, if you will. but not a word of
the fight.

You'll get no description of it from me, simply
because I think it would prove very poor reading,
and not because I consider my revolt against Conway's tyranny unjustifiable.

I had borne Conway's persecutions for many
months with lamblike patience. I might have
shielded myself by appealing to Mr. Grimshaw; but
no boy in the Temple Grammar School could do that
without losing caste. Whether this was just or not
doesn't matter a pin, since it was so—a traditionary
law of the place. The personal inconvenience I suffered
from my tormentor was nothing to the pain he inflicted on me indirectly by his persistent cruelty to
little Binny Wallace. I should have lacked the spirit
of a hen if I had not resented it finally. I am glad
that I faced Conway, and asked no favors, and got
rid of him forever. I am glad that Phil Adams taught
me to box, and I say to all youngsters: Learn to
box, to ride, to pull an oar, and to swim. The occasion may come round when a decent proficiency in
one or the rest of these accomplishments will be of
service to you.

In one of the best books* ever written for boys
are these words:

"Learn to box, then, as you learn to play cricket
and football. Not one of you will be the worse, but
* ("Tom Brown's School Days at Rugby.")

very much the better, for learning to box well. Should you never have to use it in earnest, there's no exercise in the world so good for the temper, and for the muscles of the back and legs.

"As for fighting, keep out of it, if you can, by all means. When the time comes, if ever it should, that you have to say 'Yes' or 'No' to a challenge to fight, say 'No' if you can—only take care you make it plain to yourself why you say 'No.' It's a proof of the highest courage, if done from true Christian motives. It's quite right and justifiable, if done from a simple aversion to physical pain and danger. But don't say 'No' because you fear God, for that's neither Christian nor honest. And if you do fight, fight it out; and don't give in while you can stand and see."

And don't give in when you can't! say I. For I could stand very little, and see not at all (having pummelled the school pump for the last twenty seconds), when Conway retired from the field. As Phil Adams stepped up to shake hands with me, he received a telling blow in the stomach; for all the fight was not out of me yet, and I mistook him for a new adversary.

Convinced of my error, I accepted his congratulations, with those of the other boys, blandly and blindly. I remember that Binny Wallace wanted to give me his silver pencil case. The gentle soul had stood throughout the contest with his face turned to the fence, suffering untold agony.

8

A good wash at the pump, and a cold key applied to my eye, refreshed me amazingly. Escorted by two or three of the schoolfellows, I walked home through the pleasant autumn twilight, battered but triumphant. As I went along, my cap cocked on one side to keep the chilly air from my eye, I felt that I was not only following my nose, but following it so closely that I was in some danger of treading on it. I seemed to have nose enough for the whole party. My left cheek, also, was puffed out like a dumpling. I couldn't help saying to myself, "If this is victory, how about that other fellow?"

"Tom," said Harry Blake, hesitating.

"Well?"

"Did you see Mr. Grimshaw looking out of the recitation room window just as we left the yard?"

"No; was he, though?"

"I am sure of it."

"Then he must have seen all the row."

"Shouldn't wonder."

"No, he didn't," broke in Adams, "or he would have stopped it short meter; but I guess he saw you pitching into the pump—which you did uncommonly strong, and of course he smelled mischief directly."

"Well, it can't be helped now," I reflected.

"—As the monkey said when he fell out of the coconut tree," added Charley Marden, trying to make me laugh.

It was early candlelight when we reached the

"Ah, you rascal!" cried Captain Nutter, after hearing my story

house. Miss Abigail, opening the front door, started back at my hilarious appearance. I tried to smile upon her sweetly, but the smile, rippling over my swollen cheek, and dying away like a spent wave on my nose, produced an expression of which Miss Abigail declared she had never seen the like excepting on the face of a Chinese idol.

She hustled me unceremoniously into the presence of my grandfather in the sitting room. Captain Nutter, as the recognized professional warrior of our family, could not consistently take me to task for fighting Conway, nor was he disposed to do so; for the Captain was well aware of the long-continued provocation I had endured.

"Ah, you rascal!" cried the old gentleman, after hearing my story, "just like me when I was young— always in one kind of trouble or another. I believe it runs in the family."

"I think," said Miss Abigail, without the faintest expression on her countenance. "that a tablespoonful of hot dro—"

The Captain interrupted Miss Abigail peremptorily, directing her to make a shade out of cardboard and black silk to tie over my eye. Miss Abigail must have been possessed with the idea that I had taken up pugilism as a profession, for she turned out no fewer than six of these blinders.

"They'll be handy to have in the house." says Miss Abigail, grimly.

Of course, so great a breach of discipline was not to be passed over by Mr. Grimshaw. He had, as we suspected, witnessed the closing scene of the fight from the schoolroom window, and the next morning, after prayers, I was not wholly unprepared when Master Conway and myself were called up to the desk for examination. Conway, with a piece of court-plaster in the shape of a Maltese cross on his right cheek, and I with the silk patch over my left eye, caused a general titter through the room.

"Silence!" said Mr. Grimshaw, sharply.

As the reader is already familiar with leading points in the case of Bailey *versus* Conway, I shall not report the trial further than to say that Adams, Marden, and several other pupils testified to the fact that Conway had imposed on me ever since my first day at the Temple School. Their evidence also went to show that Conway was a quarrelsome character generally. Bad for Conway. Seth Rodgers, on the part of his friend, proved that I had struck the first blow. That was bad for me.

"If you please, sir," said Binny Wallace, holding up his hand for permission to speak, "Bailey didn't fight on his own account; he fought on my account, and, if you please, sir, I am the boy to be blamed, for I was the cause of the trouble."

This drew out the story of Conway's harsh treatment of the smaller boys. As Binny related the wrongs of his playfellows, saying very little of his own grievances, I noticed that Mr. Grimshaw's hand, unknown to himself perhaps, rested lightly from time to time on Wallace's sunny hair. The examination finished, Mr. Grimshaw leaned on the desk thoughtfully for a moment, and then said:

"Every boy in this school knows that it is against the rules to fight. If one boy maltreats another, within school bounds or within school hours, that is a matter for me to settle. The case should be laid before me. I disapprove of tale bearing, I never encourage it in the slightest degree; but when one pupil systematically persecutes a schoolmate, it is the duty of some head boy to inform me. No pupil has a right to take the law into his own hands. If there is any fighting to be done, I am the person to be consulted. I disapprove of boys' fighting; it is unnecessary and unchristian. In the present instance, I consider every large boy in this school at fault; but as the offense is one of omission rather than commission, my punishment must rest only on the two boys convicted of misdemeanor. Conway loses his recess for a month, and Bailey has a page added to his Latin lessons for the next four recitations. I now request Bailey and Conway to shake hands in the presence of the school and acknowledge their regret at what has occurred."

Conway and I approached each other slowly and cautiously, as if we were bent upon another hostile collision. We clasped hands in the tamest manner imaginable, and Conway mumbled, "I'm sorry I fought with you."

"I think you are," I replied, dryly, "and I'm sorry I had to thrash you."

"You can go to your seats," said Mr. Grimshaw, turning his face aside to hide a smile. I am sure my apology was a very good one.

I never had any more trouble with Conway. He and his shadow, Seth Rodgers, gave me a wide berth for many months. Nor was Binny Wallace subjected to further molestation. Miss Abigail's sanitary stores, including a bottle of opodeldoc, were never called into requisition. The six black silk patches, with their elastic strings, are still dangling from a beam in the garret of the Nutter House, waiting for me to get into fresh difficulties.

Chapter XI

ALL ABOUT GYPSY

THIS record of my life at Rivermouth would be strangely incomplete did I not devote an entire chapter to Gypsy. I had other pets, of course, for what healthy boy could long exist without numerous friends in the animal kingdom? I had two white mice that were forever gnawing their way out of a pasteboard *chateau* and crawling over my face when I lay asleep. I used to keep the pink-eyed little beggars in my bedroom, greatly to the annoyance of Miss Abigail, who was constantly fancying that one of the mice had secreted itself somewhere about her person.

I also owned a dog, a terrier, who managed in some inscrutable way to pick a quarrel with the moon, and on bright nights kept up such a ki-yi-ing in our back garden that we were finally forced to dispose of him at private sale. He was purchased by Mr. Oxford, the butcher. I protested against the arrangement, and even afterward, when we had sausages from Mr. Oxford's shop, I made believe I detected in them certain evidences that Cato had been foully dealt with.

Of birds, I had no end—robins, purple martins,

wrens, bulfinches, bobolinks, ringdoves, and pigeons. At one time I took solid comfort in the iniquitous society of a dissipated old parrot, who talked so terribly, that the Rev. Wilbird Hawkins, happening to get a sample of Poll's vituperative powers, pronounced him "a benighted heathen," and advised the Captain to get rid of him. A brace of turtles supplanted the parrot in my affections; the turtles gave way to rabbits; and the rabbits in turn yielded to the superior charms of a small monkey, which the Captain bought of a sailor lately from the coast of Africa.

But Gypsy was the prime favorite, in spite of many rivals. I never grew weary of her. She was the most knowing little thing in the world. Her proper sphere in life—and the one to which she ultimately attained—was the sawdust arena of a traveling circus. There was nothing short of the three R's, reading, 'riting, and 'rithmetic, that Gypsy couldn't be taught. The gift of speech was not hers, but the faculty of thought was.

My little friend, to be sure, was not exempt from certain graceful weaknesses, inseparable perhaps from the female character. She was very pretty, and she knew it. She was also passionately fond of dress— by which I mean her best harness. When she had this on, her curvetings and prancings were laughable, though in ordinary tackle she went along demurely enough. There was something in the enameled

leather and the silver-washed mountings that chimed
with her artistic sense. To have her mane braided,
and a rose or a pansy stuck in her forelock, was to
make her too conceited for anything.

She had another trait not rare among her sex.
She liked the attentions of young gentlemen, while
the society of girls bored her. She would drag them,
sulkily, in the cart; but as for permitting one of them
in the saddle, the idea was preposterous. Once when
Pepper Whitcomb's sister, in spite of our remon-
strances, ventured to mount her, Gypsy gave a little
indignant neigh, and tossed the gentle Emma heels
over head in no time. But with any of the boys the
mare was as docile as a lamb.

Her treatment of the several members of the family
was comical. For the Captain she entertained a
wholesome respect, and was always on her good behavior when he was around. As to Miss Abigail,
Gypsy simply laughed at her—literally laughed, contracting her upper lip and displaying all her snow-
white teeth, as if something about Miss Abigail
struck her, Gypsy, as being extremely ridiculous.

Kitty Collins, for some reason or another, was
afraid of the pony, or pretended to be. The sagacious
little animal knew it, of course, and frequently, when
Kitty was hanging out clothes near the stable, the
mare being loose in the yard, would make short
plunges at her. Once Gypsy seized the basket of
clothespins with her teeth, and rising on her hind

Once Gypsy seized the basket of clothespins with her teeth, and rising on her hind feet followed Kitty up the scullery steps

legs, pawing the air with her fore feet followed Kitty clear up to the scullery steps.

That part of the yard was shut off from the rest by a gate; but no gate was proof against Gypsy's ingenuity. She could let down bars, lift up latches, draw bolts, and turn all sorts of buttons. This accomplishment rendered it hazardous for Miss Abigail near the window. On one occasion Gypsy put in her head and lapped up six custard pies that had been placed by the casement to cool.

An account of my young lady's various pranks would fill a thick volume. A favorite trick of hers, on being requested to "walk like Miss Abigail," was to assume a little skittish gait so true to nature that Miss Abigail herself was obliged to admit the cleverness of the imitation.

The idea of putting Gypsy through a systematic course of instruction was suggested to me by a visit to the circus which gave an annual performance in Rivermouth. This show embraced among its attractions a number of trained Shetland ponies, and I determined that Gypsy should likewise have the benefit of a liberal education. I succeeded in teaching her to waltz, to fire a pistol by tugging at a string tied to the trigger, to lie down dead, to wink one eye, and to execute many other feats of a difficult nature. She took to her studies admirably, and enjoyed the whole thing as much as anyone.

The monkey was a perpetual marvel to Gypsy.

They became bosom friends in an incredibly brief period, and were never easy out of each other's sight. Prince Zany—that's what Pepper Whitcomb and I christened him one day, much to the disgust of the monkey, who bit a piece out of Pepper's nose—resided in the stable, and went to roost every night on the pony's back, where I usually found him in the morning. Whenever I rode out, I was obliged to secure his Highness the Prince with a stout cord to the fence, he chattering all the time like a madman.

One afternoon as I was cantering through the crowded part of the town, I noticed that the people in the street stopped, stared at me, and fell to laughing. I turned round in the saddle, and there was Zany, with a great burdock leaf in his paw, perched up behind me on the crupper, as solemn as a judge.

After a few months, poor Zany sickened mysteriously and died. The dark thought occurred to me then, and comes back to me now with redoubled force, that Miss Abigail must have given him some hot drops. Zany left a large circle of sorrowing friends, if not relatives. Gypsy, I think, never entirely recovered from the shock occasioned by his early demise. She became fonder of me, though; and one of her cunningest demonstrations was to escape from the stable yard, and trot up to the door of the Temple Grammar School, where I would discover her at recess patiently waiting for me, with her fore feet on the second step, and wisps of straw standing out all over her like quills upon the fretful porcupine.

I should fail if I tried to tell you how dear the pony was to me. Even hard, unloving men become attached to the horses they take care of; so I, who was neither unloving nor hard, grew to love every glossy hair of the pretty little creature that depended on me for her soft straw bed and her daily modicum of oats. In my prayer at night I never forgot to mention Gypsy with the rest of the family—generally setting forth her claims first.

Whatever relates to Gypsy belongs properly to this narrative; therefore I offer no apology for rescuing from oblivion, and boldly printing here a short composition which I wrote in the early part of my first quarter at the Temple Grammar School. It is my maiden effort in a difficult art, and is, perhaps, lacking in those graces of thought and style which are reached only after the severest practice.

Every Wednesday morning, on entering school, each pupil was expected to lay his exercise on Mr. Grimshaw's desk; the subject was usually selected by Mr. Grimshaw himself, the Monday previous. With a humor characteristic of him, our teacher had instituted two prizes, one for the best and the other for the worst composition of the month. The first prize consisted of a penknife, or a pencil case, or some such article dear to the heart of youth; the second prize entitled the winner to wear for an hour or two a sort of conical paper cap, on the front of which was written, in tall letters, this modest admission: I AM A DUNCE! The competitor who took prize No. 2 wasn't generally an object of envy.

My pulse beat high with pride and expectation that Wednesday morning, as I laid my essay, neatly folded, on the master's table. I firmly decline to say which prize I won; but here's the composition to speak for itself:

The horse

the horse is a useful animal He is nice to have. i have one. her name is gipsey. She bites, her main is very long. one Day i was washing her front Foot when she bent down her head and lifted me up by the trouser and tumbled me into the water Pale that was standing near by. i hit her six times with a peace of hoop—the way of the transgressor is hard.

T. Bailey

It is no small-author vanity that induces me to publish this stray leaf of natural history. I lay it before our young folks, not for their admiration, but for their criticism. Let each reader take his lead pencil and remorselessly correct the orthography, the capitalization, and the punctuation of the essay. I shall not feel hurt at seeing my treatise cut all to pieces; though I think highly of the production, not on account of its literary excellence, which I candidly admit is not overpowering, but because it was written

years and years ago about Gypsy, by a little fellow
who, when I strive to recall him, appears to me like
a reduced ghost of my present self.

I am confident that any reader who has ever had
pets, birds or animals, will forgive me for this brief
digression.

Chapter XII

WINTER AT RIVERMOUTH

"I GUESS we're going to have a regular old-fashioned snowstorm," said Captain Nutter, one bleak December morning, casting a peculiarly nautical glance skyward.

The Captain was always hazarding prophecies about the weather, which somehow never turned out according to his prediction. The vanes on the church steeples seemed to take fiendish pleasure in humiliating the dear old gentleman. If he said it was going to be a clear day, a dense sea fog was pretty certain to set in before noon. Once he caused a protracted drought by assuring us every morning, for six consecutive weeks, that it would rain in a few hours. But, sure enough, that afternoon it began snowing.

Now I had not seen a snowstorm since I was eighteen months old, and, of course, remembered nothing about it. A boy familiar from his infancy with the rigors of new England winters can form no idea of the impression made on me by this natural phenomenon. My delight and surprise were as boundless as if the heavy gray sky had let down a shower of pond lilies and white roses, instead of snowflakes. It happened to be a half holiday, so I had nothing to do but watch the feathery crystals whirling hither and thither through the air. I stood by the sitting-room window gazing at the wonder until twilight shut out the novel scene.

We had had several slight flurries of hail and snow before, but this was a regular nor'easter.

Several inches of snow had already fallen. The rosebushes at the door dropped with the weight of their magical blossoms, and the two posts that held the garden gate were transformed into stately Turks, with white turbans, guarding the entrance to the Nutter House.

The storm increased at sundown, and continued with unabated violence through the night. The next morning, when I jumped out of bed, the sun was shining brightly, the cloudless heavens wore the tender azure of June, and the whole earth lay muffled up to the eyes, as it were, in a thick mantle of milk-white down.

It was a very deep snow. The Oldest Inhabitant (what would become of a New England town or village without its oldest inhabitant?) overhauled his almanacs and pronounced it the deepest snow we had had for twenty years. It couldn't have been much deeper without smothering us all. Our street was a sight to be seen, or, rather, it was a sight not to be seen, for very little street was visible. One huge drift completely banked up our front door and half-covered my bedroom window.

There was no school that day, for all the thorough-fares were impassable. By twelve o'clock, however, the great snowplows, each drawn by four yoke of oxen, broke a wagon path through the principal streets; but the foot passengers had a hard time of it floundering in the arctic drifts.

The Captain and I cut a tunnel, three feet wide and six feet high, from our front door to the sidewalk opposite. It was a beautiful cavern, with its walls and roof inlaid with mother-of-pearl and diamonds. I am sure the ice palace of the Russian Empress, in Cowper's poem, was not a more superb piece of archi-tecture.

The thermometer began falling shortly before sunset, and we had the bitterest cold night I ever experienced. This brought out the Oldest Inhabitant again the next day—and what a gay old boy he was for deciding everything!   Our tunnel was turned into solid ice. A crust thick enough to bear men and horses had formed over the snow everywhere, and the air was alive with merry sleigh bells. Icy stalactites, a yard long, hung from the eaves of the house, and the Turkish sentinels at the gate looked as if they had given up all hopes of ever being relieved from duty.

So the winter set in cold and glittering. Every-thing out of doors was sheathed in silver mail. To quote from Charley Marden, it was "cold enough to freeze the tail off a brass monkey"—an observation which seemed to me extremely happy, though I knew little or nothing concerning the endurance of brass monkeys, having never seen one.

I had looked forward to the advent of the season with grave apprehensions, nerving myself to meet dreary nights and monotonous days; but summer itself was not more jolly than winter at Rivermouth. Snowballing at school, skating on the Mill Pond, coasting by moonlight, long rides behind Gypsy in a brand-new little sleigh built expressly for her, were sports no less exhilarating than those which belonged to the sunny months. And then Thanksgiving! The nose of Memory—why shouldn't Memory have a nose?—dilates with pleasure over the rich perfume of Miss Abigail's forty mince pies, each one more delightful than the other, like the Sultan's forty wives. Christmas was another red-letter day, though it was not so generally observed in New England as it is now.

The great wood fire in the tiled chimney place made our sitting room very cheerful of winter nights. When the north wind howled about the eaves, and the sharp fingers of the sleet tapped against the windowpanes, it was nice to be so warmly sheltered from the storm. A dish of apples and a pitcher of chilly cider were always served during the evening. The Captain had a funny way of leaning back in the chair, and eating his apple with his eyes closed. Sometimes I played dominos with him, and sometimes Miss Abigail read aloud to us, pronouncing "to" *toe*, and sounding all the *eds*.

In a former chapter I alluded to Miss Abigail's managing propensities. She had affected many changes in the Nutter House before I came there to live; but there was one thing against which she had long contended without being able to overcome. This was the Captain's pipe. On first taking command of the household she prohibited smoking in the sitting room, where it had been the old gentleman's custom to take a whiff or two of the fragrant weed after meals. The edict went forth—and so did the pipe. An excellent move, no doubt; but then the house was his, and if he saw fit to keep a tub of tobacco burning in the middle of the parlor floor, he had a perfect right to do so. However, he humored her in this as in other matters, and smoked by stealth, like a guilty creature, in the barn, or about the gardens. That was practicable in summer, but in winter the Captain was hard put to it. When he couldn't stand it longer, he retreated to his bedroom and barricaded the door. Such was the position of affairs at the time of which I write.

One morning, a few days after the great snow, as Miss Abigail was dusting the chronometer in the hall, she beheld Captain Nutter slowly descending the staircase, with a long clay pipe in his mouth. Miss Abigail could hardly credit her own eyes.

"Dan'el!" she gasped, retiring heavily on the hat rack.

The tone of reproach with which this word was

uttered failed to produce the slightest effect on the Captain, who merely removed the pipe from his lips for an instant, and blew a cloud into the chilly air. The thermometer stood at two degrees below zero in our hall.

"Dan'el!" cried Miss Abigail, hysterically—"Dan'el, don't come near me!" Whereupon she fainted away; for the smell of tobacco smoke always made her deadly sick.

Kitty Collins rushed from the kitchen with a basin of water, and set to work bathing Miss Abigail's temples and chafing her hands. I thought my grandfather rather cruel, as he stood there with a half-smile on his countenance, complacently watching Miss Abigail's sufferings. When she was "brought to," the Captain sat down beside her, and, with a lovely twinkle in his eye, said softly:

"Abigail, my dear, *there wasn't any tobacco in that pipe!* It was a new pipe. I fetched it down for Tom to blow soap bubbles with."

At these words Kitty Collins hurried away, her features working strangely. Several minutes later I came upon her in the scullery with the greater portion of a crash towel stuffed into her mouth. "Miss Abigail smelt the terbecca with her oi!" cried Kitty, partially removing the cloth, and then immediately stopping herself up again.

The Captain's joke furnished us—that is, Kitty and me—with mirth for many a day; as to Miss

Abigail, I think she never wholly pardoned him. After this Captain Nutter gradually gave up smoking, which is an untidy, injurious, disgraceful, and highly pleasant habit.

A boy's life in a secluded New England town in winter does not afford many points for illustration. Of course he gets his ears or toes frostbitten; of course he smashes his sled against another boy's; of course he bangs his head on the ice; and he's a lad of no enterprise whatever if he doesn't manage to skate into an eel hole and be brought home half-drowned. All these things happened to me; but, as they lack novelty, I pass them over, to tell you about the famous snow fort which we built on Slatter's Hill.

Chapter XIII

THE SNOW FORT ON SLATTER'S HILL

THE memory of man, even that of the Oldest Inhabitant, runneth not back to the time when there did not exist a feud between the North End and the South End boys of Rivermouth. The origin of the feud is involved in mystery; it is impossible to say which party was the first aggressor in the far-off ante-revolutionary ages; but the fact remains that the youngsters of those antipodal sections entertained a mortal hatred for each other, and that this hatred had been handed down from generation to generation, like Miles Standish's punch bowl.

I know not what laws, natural or unnatural, regulated the warmth of the quarrel, but at some seasons it raged more violently than at others. This winter both parties were unusually lively and antagonistic. Great was the wrath of the South-Enders, when they discovered that the North-Enders had thrown up a fort on the crown of Slatter's Hill.

Slatter's Hill, or No-man's-land, as it was generally called, was a rise of ground covering, perhaps, an acre and a quarter, situated on an imaginary line, marking the boundary between the two districts.

An immense stratum of granite, which here and there thrust out a wrinkled bowlder, prevented the site from being used for building purposes. The street ran on either side of the hill, from one part of which a quantity of rock had been removed to form the under-pinning of the new jail. This excavation made the approach from that point all but impossible, especially when the ragged ledges were a-glitter with ice. You see what a spot it was for a snow fort.

One evening twenty or thirty of the North-Enders quietly took possession of Slatter's Hill, and threw up a strong line of breastworks, something after this shape:

The rear of the intrenchment, being protected by the quarry, was left open. The walls were four feet high and twenty-two inches thick, strengthened at the angles by stakes driven firmly into the ground.

Fancy the rage of the South-Enders the next day when they spied our snowy citadel, with Jack Harris's red silk pocket handkerchief floating defiantly from the flagstaff.

In less than an hour it was known all over town, in military circles at least, that the "Puddle-dockers" and the "River-rats" (these were the derisive subtitles bestowed on our South-End foes) intended to attack the fort that Saturday afternoon.

At two o'clock all the fighting boys of the Temple Grammar School, and as many recruits as we could muster, lay behind the walls of Fort Slatter, with three hundred compact snowballs piled up in pyramids, awaiting the approach of the enemy. The enemy was not slow in making his approach—fifty strong, headed by one Mat Ames. Our forces were under the command of General J. Harris.

Before the action commenced, a meeting was arranged between the rival commanders, who drew up and signed certain rules and regulations respecting the conduct of the battle.

As it was impossible for the North-Enders to occupy the fort permanently, it was stipulated that the South-Enders should assault it only on Wednesday and Saturday afternoons between the hours of two and six. For them to take possession of the place at any other time was not to constitute a capture, but on the contrary was to be considered a dishonorable and cowardly act.

The North-Enders, on the other hand, agreed to give up the fort whenever ten of the storming party succeeded in obtaining at one time a footing on the parapet, and were able to hold the same for the space of two minutes. Both sides were to abstain from putting pebbles into their snowballs, nor was it permissible to use frozen ammunition. A snowball soaked in water and left out to cool was a projectile which in previous years had been resorted to with disastrous results.

These preliminaries settled, the commanders retired to their respective corps. The interview had taken place on the hillside between the opposing lines.

General Harris divided his men into two bodies: the first comprised the most skilful marksmen, or gunners; the second, the reserve force, was composed of the strongest boys, whose duty it was to repel the scaling parties, and to make occasional sallies for the purpose of capturing prisoners, who were bound by the articles of treaty to serve faithfully under our flag until they were exchanged at the close of the day.

The repellers were called light infantry; but when they carried on operations beyond the fort they became cavalry. It was also their duty, when not otherwise engaged, to manufacture snowballs. The General's staff consisted of five Templars (I among the number, with the rank of Major), who carried the General's orders and looked after the wounded.

General Mat Ames, a veteran commander, was no less wide-awake in the disposition of his army. Five companies, each numbering but six men, in order not to present too big a target to our sharpshooters, were to charge the fort from different points, their advance being covered by a heavy fire from the gunners posted in the rear. Each scaler was provided with only two rounds of ammunition, which were not to be used until he had mounted the breastwork and could deliver his shots on our heads.

The following cut represents the interior of the fort just previous to the assault. Nothing on earth could represent the state of things after the first volley.

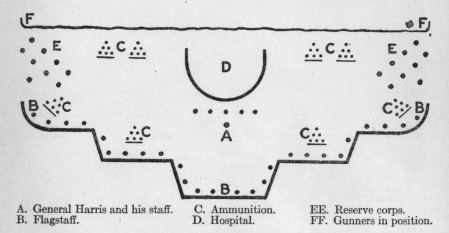

A. General Harris and his staff.   C. Ammunition.   EE. Reserve corps.
B. Flagstaff.   D. Hospital.   FF. Gunners in position.

The enemy was posted thus:

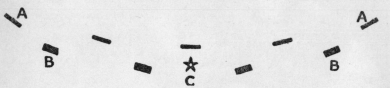

AA. The five attacking columns.   BB. Artillery.   C. General Ames's headquarters.

The thrilling moment had now arrived. If I had been going into a real engagement I could not have been more deeply impressed by the importance of the occasion.

The fort opened fire first—a single ball from the

A cheer went up from Fort Slatter and in an instant the air was thick
with flying missiles

dexterous hand of General Harris taking General
Ames in the very pit of his stomach. A cheer went up
from Fort Slatter. In an instant the air was thick
with flying missiles, in the midst of which we dimly
described the storming parties sweeping up the hill,
shoulder to shoulder. The shouts of the leaders, and
the snowballs bursting like shells about our ears,
made it very lively.

Not more than a dozen of the enemy succeeded
in reaching the crest of the hill; five of these clambered
upon the icy walls, where they were instantly grabbed
by the legs and jerked into the fort. The rest retired,
confused and blinded by our well-directed fire.

When General Harris (with his right eye bunged
up) said, "Soldiers, I am proud of you!" my heart
swelled in my bosom.

The victory, however, had not been without its
price. Six North-Enders, having rushed out to har-
ass the discomfited enemy, were gallantly cut off by
General Ames and captured. Among these were
Lieutenant P. Whitcomb (who had no business to
join in the charge, being weak in the knees), and
Captain Fred Langdon, of General Harris's staff.
Whitcomb was one of the most notable shots on our
side, though he was not much to boast of in a rough-
and-tumble fight, owing to the weakness before mentioned. General Ames put him among the gunners,
and we were quickly made aware of the loss we had
sustained, by receiving a frequent artful ball which

seemed to light with unerring instinct on any nose that was the least bit exposed. I have known one of Pepper's snowballs, fired point-blank, to turn a corner and hit a boy who considered himself absolutely safe.

But we had not time for vain regrets. The battle raged. Already there were two bad cases of black eye, and one of nosebleed, in the hospital.

It was glorious excitement, those pell-mell on-slaughts and hand-to-hand struggles. Twice we were within an ace of being driven from our stronghold, when General Harris and his staff leaped recklessly upon the ramparts and hurled the besiegers heels over head downhill.

At sunset the garrison of Fort Slatter was still unconquered, and the South-Enders, in a solid pha-lanx, marched off whistling "Yankee Doodle," while we cheered and jeered them until they were out of hearing.

General Ames remained behind to effect an ex-change of prisoners. We held thirteen of his men, and he eleven of ours. General Ames proposed to call it an even thing, since many of his eleven prisoners were officers, while nearly all our thirteen captives were privates. A dispute arising on this point, the two noble generals came to fisticuffs, and in the fracas our brave commander got his remaining well eye badly damaged. This didn't prevent him from writ-ing a general order the next day, on a slate, in which he complimented the troops on their heroic behavior.

On the following Wednesday the siege was renewed. I forget whether it was on that afternoon or the next that we lost Fort Slatter; but lose it we did, with much valuable ammunition and several men. After a series of desperate assaults, we forced General Ames to capitulate; and he, in turn, made the place too hot to hold us. So from day to day the tide of battle surged to and fro, sometimes favoring our arms, and sometimes those of the enemy.

General Ames handled his men with great skill; his deadliest foe could not deny that. Once he out-generalled our commander in the following manner: He massed his gunners on our left and opened a brisk fire, under cover of which a single company (six men) advanced on that angle of the fort. Our reserves on the right rushed over to defend the threatened point. Meanwhile, four companies of the enemy's scalers made a detour round the foot of the hill, and dashed into Fort Slatter without opposition. At the same moment General Ames's gunners closed in on our left, and there we were between two fires. Of course we had to vacate the fort. A cloud rested on General Harris's military reputation until his superior tactics enabled him to dispossess the enemy.

As the winter wore on, the war spirit waxed fiercer and fiercer. At length the provision against using heavy substances in the snowballs was disregarded. A ball stuck full of sand-bird shot came tearing into

Fort Slatter. In retaliation, General Harris ordered a broadside of shells, *i. e.*, snowballs containing marbles. After this both sides never failed to freeze their ammunition.

It was no longer child's play to march up to the walls of Fort Slatter, nor was the position of the besieged less perilous. At every assault three or four boys on each side were disabled. It was not an infrequent occurrence for the combatants to hold up a flag of truce while they removed some insensible comrade.

Matters grew worse and worse. Seven North-Enders had been seriously wounded, and a dozen South-Enders were reported on the sick list. The selectmen of the town awoke to the fact of what was going on, and detailed a posse of police to prevent further disturbance. The boys at the foot of the hill, South-Enders as it happened, finding themselves assailed in the rear and on the flank, turned round and attempted to beat off the watchmen. In this they were sustained by numerous volunteers from the fort, who looked upon the interference as tyrannical.

The watch were determined fellows, and charged the boys valiantly, driving them all into the fort, where we made common cause fighting side by side like the best of friends. In vain the four guardians of the peace rushed up the hill, flourishing their clubs and calling upon us to surrender. They could not get within ten yards of the fort, our fire was so

destructive. In one of the onsets a man named
Mugridge, more valorous than his peers, threw himself upon the parapet, when he was seized by twenty
pairs of hands and dragged inside the breastwork,
where fifteen boys sat down on him to keep him
quiet.

Perceiving that it was impossible with their small
number to dislodge us, the watch sent for reënforce-
ments. Their call was responded to, not only by the
whole constabulary force (eight men), but by a numerous body of citizens, who had become alarmed
at the prospect of a riot. This formidable array
brought us to our senses; we began to think that
maybe discretion was the better part of valor. General Harris and General Ames, with their respective
staffs, held a council of war in the hospital, and a
backward movement was decided on. So, after one
grand farewell volley, we fled, sliding, jumping, rolling, tumbling down the quarry at the rear of the fort,
and escaped without losing a man.

But we lost Fort Slatter forever. Those battle-
scarred ramparts were razed to the ground, and humiliating ashes sprinkled over the historic spot, near
which a solitary lynx-eyed policeman was seen prowling from time to time during the rest of the winter.

The event passed into a legend, and afterwards,
when later instances of pluck and endurance were
spoken of, the boys would say, "By golly! you ought
to have been at the fights on Slatter's Hill!"

10

Chapter XIV

THE CRUISE OF THE "DOLPHIN"

IT was spring again. The snow had faded away like a dream, and we were awakened, so to speak, by the sudden chirping of robins in our back garden. Marvelous transformation of snow-drifts into lilacs, wondrous miracle of the unfolding leaf! We read in the Holy Book how our Saviour, at the marriage feast, changed the water into wine; we pause and wonder; but every hour a greater miracle is wrought at our very feet, if we have but eyes to see it.

I had now been a year at Rivermouth. If you do not know what sort of boy I was, it is not because I haven't been frank with you. Of my progress at school I say little; for this is a story, pure and simple, and not a treatise on education. Behold me, however, well up in most of the classes. I have worn my Latin grammar into tatters, and am in the first book of Vergil. I interlard my conversation at home with easy quotations from that poet, and impress Captain Nutter with a lofty notion of my learning. I am likewise translating Les Adventures de Télé-maque from the French, and shall tackle Blair's Lectures the next term. I am ashamed of my crude composition about The Horse, and can do better now. Sometimes my head almost aches with the variety of my knowledge. I consider Mr. Grimshaw the greatest scholar that ever lived, and I don't know which I would rather be—a learned man like him or a circus rider.

My thoughts revert to this particular spring more frequently than to any other period of my boyhood, for it was marked by an event that left an indelible impression on my memory. As I pen these pages, I feel that I am writing of something which happened yesterday, so vividly it all comes back to me.

Every Rivermouth boy looks upon the sea as being in some way mixed up with his destiny. While he is yet a baby lying in his cradle, he hears the dull, far-off boom of the breakers; when he is older he wanders by the sandy shore, watching the waves that come plunging up the beach like white-maned sea horses, as Thoreau calls them; his eye follows the lessening sail as it fades into the blue horizon, and he burns for the time when he shall stand on the quarter-deck of his own ship, and go sailing proudly across that mysterious waste of waters.

Then the town itself is full of hints and flavors of the sea. The gables and roofs of the houses facing eastward are covered with red rust, like the flukes of old anchors; a salty smell pervades the air, and dense, gray fogs, the very breath of Ocean, periodically creep up into the quiet streets and envelop everything. The terrific storms that lash the coast; the kelp and spars, and sometimes the bodies of drowned men, tossed on shore by the scornful waves; the shipyards, the wharves, and the tawny fleet of fishing smacks yearly fitted out at Rivermouth—these things, and a hundred other, feed the imagination and fill the brain of every healthy boy with dreams of adventure. He learns to swim almost as soon as he can walk; he draws in with his mother's milk the art of handling an oar; he is born a sailor, whatever he may turn out to be afterwards.

To own the whole or a portion of a rowboat is his earliest ambition. No wonder that I, born to this life, and coming back to it with freshest sympathies, should have caught the prevailing infection. No wonder I longed to buy a part of the trim little sailboat "Dolphin," which chanced just then to be in the market. This was in the latter part of May.

Three shares, at five or six dollars each, I forget which, had already been taken by Phil Adams, Fred Langdon, and Binny Wallace. The fourth and remaining share hung fire. Unless a purchaser could be found for this the bargain was to fall through.

I am afraid I required but slight urging to join in the investment. I had four dollars and fifty cents on hand, and the treasurer of the Centipedes advanced me the balance, receiving my silver pencil case as ample security. It was a proud moment when I stood on the wharf with my partners inspecting the "Dolphin," moored at the foot of a very slippery flight of steps. She was painted white with a green stripe outside, and on the stern a yellow dolphin, with its scarlet mouth wide open, stared with a surprised expression at its own reflection in the water. The boat was a great bargain.

I whirled my cap in the air and ran to the stairs leading down from the wharf, when a hand was laid gently on my shoulder. I turned and faced Captain Nutter. I never saw such an old sharp eye as he was in those days.

I knew he wouldn't be angry with me for buying a rowboat; but I also knew that the little bowsprit suggesting a jib, and the tapering mast ready for its few square feet of canvas, were trifles not likely to meet his approval. As far as rowing on the river, among the wharves, was concerned, the Captain had long since withdrawn his decided objections, having convinced himself, by going out with me several times, that I could manage a pair of sculls as well as anybody.

I was right in my surmises. He commanded me, in the most emphatic terms, never to go out in the "Dolphin" without leaving the mast in the boathouse. This curtailed my anticipated sport, but the pleasure of having a pull whenever I wanted it remained. I never disobeyed the Captain's orders touching the sail, though I sometimes extended my row beyond the points he had indicated.

The river was dangerous for sailboats. Squalls, without the slightest warning, were of frequent occurrence; scarcely a year passed that six or seven persons were not drowned under the very windows of the town, and these, oddly enough, were generally sea captains, who either did not understand the river, or lacked the skill to handle a small craft.

A knowledge of such disasters, one of which I witnessed, consoled me somewhat when I saw Phil Adams skimming over the water in a spanking breeze with every stitch of canvas set. There were few better yachtsmen than Phil Adams. He usually went sailing alone, for both Fred Langdon and Binny Wallace were under the same restrictions I was.

Not long after the purchase of the boat we planned an excursion to Sandpeep Island, the last of the islands in the harbor. We proposed to start early in the morning, and return with the tide in the moonlight. Our only difficulty was to obtain a whole day's exemption from school, the customary half holiday not being long enough for our picnic. Somehow, we couldn't work it, but fortune arranged it for us. I may say here, that, whatever else I did, I never played truant ("hookey" we called it) in my life.

One afternoon the four owners of the "Dolphin" exchanged significant glances when Mr. Grimshaw announced from the desk that there would be no school the following day, he having just received intelligence of the death of his uncle in Boston. I was sincerely attached to Mr. Grimshaw, but I am afraid that the death of his uncle did not affect me as it ought to have done.

We were up before sunrise the next morning, in order to take advantage of the flood tide, which waits for no man. Our preparations for the cruise were made the previous evening. In the way of eatables and drinkables, we had stored in the stern of the "Dolphin" a generous bag of hardtack (for the chowder), a piece of pork to fry the cunners in, three gigantic apple pies (bought at Pettingil's), half a dozen lemons, and a keg of spring water—the last-named article we slung over the side, to keep it cool, as soon as we got under way. The crockery and the bricks for our camp stove we placed in the bows with the groceries, which included sugar, pepper, salt, and a bottle of pickles. Phil Adams contributed to the outfit a small tent of unbleached cotton cloth, under which we intended to take our nooning.

We unshipped the mast, threw in an extra oar, and were ready to embark. I do not believe that Christopher Columbus, when he started on his rather successful voyage of discovery, felt half the responsibility and importance that weighed upon me as I sat on the middle seat of the "Dolphin," with my oar resting in the rowlock. I wonder if Christopher Columbus quietly slipped out of the house without letting his estimable family know what he was up to?

Charley Marden, whose father had promised to

cane him if he ever stepped foot on sail or rowboat, came down to the wharf in a sour-grape humor to see us off. Nothing would tempt him to go out on the river in such a crazy clam-shell of a boat. He pretended that he did not expect to behold us alive again, and tried to throw a wet blanket over the expedition.

"Guess you'll have a squally time of it," said Charley, casting off the painter. "I'll drop in at old Newbury's" (Newbury was the parish undertaker) "and leave word, as I go along!"

"Bosh!" muttered Phil Adams, sticking the boat hook into the stringpiece of the wharf, and sending the "Dolphin" half a dozen yards toward the current.

How calm and lovely the river was! Not a ripple stirred on the glassy surface, broken only by the sharp cutwater of our tiny craft. The sun, as round and red as an August moon, was by this time peering above the water line.

The town had drifted behind us, and we were entering among the group of islands. Sometimes we could almost touch with our boat hook the shelving banks on either side. As we neared the mouth of the harbor, a little breeze now and then wrinkled the blue water, shook the spangles from the foliage, and gently lifted the spiral mist wreaths that still clung along shore. The measured dip of our oars and the drowsy twitterings of the birds seemed to mingle

It took us an hour or two to transport our stores to the spot selected for the encampment

with, rather than break, the enchanted silence that reigned about us.

The scent of the new clover comes back to me now, as I recall that delicious morning when we floated away in a fairy boat down a river like a dream!

The sun was well up when the nose of the "Dolphin" nestled against the snow-white bosom of Sandpeep Island. This island, as I have said before, was the last of the cluster, one side of it being washed by the sea. We landed on the river side, the sloping sands and quiet water affording us a good place to moor the boat.

It took us an hour or two to transport our stores to the spot selected for the encampment. Having pitched our tent, using the five oars to support the canvas, we got out our lines and went down the rocks seaward to fish. It was early for cunners, but we were lucky enough to catch as nice a mess as ever you saw. A cod for the chowder was not so easily secured. At last Binny Wallace hauled in a plump little fellow, crusted all over with flaky silver.

To skin the fish, build our fireplace, and cook the chowder kept us busy the next two hours. The fresh air and the exercise had given us the appetites of wolves, and we were about famished by the time the savory mixture was ready for our clam-shell saucers.

I shall not insult the rising generation on the seaboard by telling them how delectable is a chowder compounded and eaten in this Robinson Crusoe fashion. As for the boys who live inland, and know naught of such marine feasts, my heart is full of pity for them. What wasted lives! Not to know the delights of a clambake, not to love chowder, to be ignorant of lobscouse!

How happy we were, we four, sitting cross-legged in the crisp, salt grass, with the invigorating sea breeze blowing gratefully through our hair! What a joyous thing was life, and how far off seemed death —death, that lurks in all pleasant places, and was so near!

The banquet finished, Phil Adams drew from his pocket a handful of sweet-fern cigars; but as none of the party could indulge without imminent risk of becoming sick, we all, on one pretext or another, declined, and Phil smoked by himself.

The wind had freshened by this, and we found it comfortable to put on the jackets which had been thrown aside in the heat of the day. We strolled along the beach and gathered large quantities of the fairy-woven Iceland moss, which, at certain seasons, is washed to these shores; then we played at ducks and drakes, and then, the sun being sufficiently low, we went in bathing.

Before our bath was ended a slight change had come over the sky and sea; fleecy-white clouds scudded here and there, and a muffled moan from the breakers caught our ears from time to time. While we were dressing, a few hurried drops of rain came lisping down, and we adjourned to the tent to await the passing of the squall.

"We're all right, anyhow," said Phil Adams. "It won't be much of a blow, and we'll be as snug as a bug in a rug, here in the tent, particularly if we have that lemonade which some of you fellows were going to make."

By an oversight, the lemons had been left in the boat. Binny Wallace volunteered to go for them.

"Put an extra stone on the painter, Binny," said Adams, calling after him, "it would be awkward to have the 'Dolphin' give us the slip and return to port minus her passengers."

"That it would," answered Binny, scrambling down the rocks.

Sandpeep Island is diamond-shaped—one point running out into the sea, and the other looking toward the town. Our tent was on the river side. Though the "Dolphin" was also on the same side, it lay out of sight by the beach at the farther extremity of the island.

Binny Wallace had been absent five or six minutes, when we heard him calling our several names in tones that indicated distress or surprise, we could not tell which. Our first thought was, "The boat has broken adrift!"

We sprang to our feet and hastened down to the beach. On turning the bluff which hid the mooring place from our view, we found the conjecture correct.

Not only was the "Dolphin" afloat, but poor little Binny Wallace was standing in the bows with his arms stretched helplessly toward us—*drifting out to sea!*

"Head the boat in shore," shouted Phil Adams.

Wallace ran to the tiller; but the slight cockle-shell merely swung round and drifted broadside on. Oh, if we had but left a single scull in the "Dolphin!"

"Can you swim it?" cried Adams, desperately, using his hand as a speaking trumpet, for the distance between the boat and the island widened momently.

Binny Wallace looked down at the sea, which was covered with whitecaps, and made a despairing gesture. He knew, and we knew, that the stoutest swimmer could not live forty seconds in those angry waters.

A wild, insane light came into Phil Adams's eyes, as he stood knee-deep in the boiling surf, and for an instant I think he meditated plunging into the ocean after the receding boat.

The sky darkened, and an ugly look stole rapidly over the broken surface of the sea.

Binny Wallace half rose from his seat in the stern, and waved his hand to us in token of farewell. In spite of the distance, increasing every instant, we could see his face plainly. The anxious expression it bore at first had passed. It was pale and meek now, and I love to think there was a kind of halo about it, like that which painters place around the forehead of a saint. So he drifted away.

The sky grew darker and darker. It was only by straining our eyes through the unnatural twilight that we could keep the "Dolphin" in sight. The figure of Binny Wallace was no longer visible, for the boat itself had dwindled to a mere white dot on the black water. Now we lost it, and our hearts stopped throbbing; and now the speck appeared again, for an instant, on the crest of a high wave.

Finally, it went out like a spark, and we saw it no more. Then we gazed at each other, and dared not speak.

Absorbed in following the course of the boat, we had scarcely noticed the huddled, inky clouds that sagged down all around us. From these threatening masses, seamed at intervals with pale lightning, there now burst a heavy peal of thunder that shook the ground under our feet. A sudden squall struck the sea, plowing deep, white furrows into it, and at the same instant a single, piercing shriek rose above the tempest—the frightened cry of a gull swooping over the island. How it startled us!

It was impossible any longer to keep our footing on the beach. The wind and the breakers would have swept us into the ocean if we had not clung to each other with the desperation of drowning men. Taking advantage of a momentary lull, we crawled up the sands on our hands and knees, and, pausing in the lee of the granite ledge to gain breath returned to the camp, where we found that the gale had snapped all the fastenings of the tent but one. Held by this, the puffed-out-canvas swayed in the wind like a balloon. It was a task of some difficulty to secure it, which we did by beating down the canvas with the oars·

After several trials, we succeeded in setting up the tent on the leeward side of the ledge. Blinded by the vivid flashes of lightning, and drenched by the rain, which fell in torrents, we crept, half dead with fear and anguish, under our flimsy shelter. Neither the anguish nor the fear was on our own account, for we were comparatively safe, but for poor little Binny Wallace, driven out to sea in the merciless gale. We shuddered to think of him in that frail shell, drifting on and on to his grave, the sky rent with lightning over his head, and the green abysses yawning beneath him. We fell to crying, the three of us, and cried I know not how long.

Meanwhile the storm raged with augmented fury. We were obliged to hold on to the ropes of the tent to prevent it blowing away. The spray from the river leaped several yards up the rocks and clutched at us malignantly. The very island trembled with the concussions of the sea beating upon it, and at times I fancied that it had broken loose from its foundation, and was floating off with us. The breakers, streaked with angry phosphorus, were fearful to look at.

The wind rose higher and higher, cutting long slits in the tent, through which the rain poured incessantly. To complete the sum of our miseries, the night was at hand. It came down suddenly, at last, like a curtain, shutting in Sandpeep Island from all the world.

It was a dirty night, as the sailors say. The darkness was something that could be felt as well as seen—it pressed down upon one with a cold, clammy touch. Gazing into the hollow blackness, all sorts of imaginable shapes seemed to start forth from vacancy, brilliant colors, stars, prisms, and dancing lights. What boy, lying awake at night, has not amused or terrified himself by peopling the spaces around his bed with these phenomena of his own eyes?

"I say," whispered Fred Langdon, at length clutching my hand, "don't you see things—out there—in the dark?"

"Yes, yes, Binny Wallace's face!"

I added to my own nervousness by making this avowal; though for the last ten minutes I had seen little besides that star-pale face with its angelic hair and brows. First a slim, yellow circle, like the nimbus round the moon, took shape and grew sharp against the darkness; then this faded gradually, and there was the Face, wearing the same sad, sweet look it wore when he waved his hand to us across the awful water. This optical illusion kept repeating itself.

"And I, too," said Adams. "I see it every now and then, outside there. What wouldn't I give if it really was poor little Wallace looking in at us! O boys, how shall we dare to go back to the town without him? I've wished a hundred times, since we've been sitting here, that I was in his place, alive or dead!"

We dreaded the approach of morning as much as we longed for it. The morning would tell us all. Was it possible for the "Dolphin" to outride such a storm? There was a lighthouse on Mackerel Reef, which lay directly in the course the boat had taken, when it disappeared. If the "Dolphin" had caught on this reef, perhaps Binny Wallace was safe. Perhaps his cries had been heard by the keeper of the light. The man owned a lifeboat, and had rescued several people. Who could tell?

Such were the questions we asked ourselves again and again, as we lay in each other's arms waiting for daybreak. What an endless night it was! I have know months that did not seem so long.

Our position was irksome rather than perilous; for the day was certain to bring us relief from the town, where our prolonged absence, together with the storm, had no doubt excited the liveliest alarm for our safety. But the cold, the darkness, and the suspense were hard to bear.

Our soaked jackets had chilled us to the bone. To keep warm, we lay huddled together so closely

11

that we could hear our hearts beat above the tumult of sea and sky.

After awhile we grew very hungry, not having broken our fast since early in the day. The rain had turned the hardtack into a sort of dough; but it was better than nothing.

We used to laugh at Fred Langdon for always carrying in his pocket a small vial of essence of peppermint or sassafras, a few drops of which, sprinkled on a lump of loaf sugar, he seemed to consider a great luxury. I don't know what would have become of us at this crisis, if it hadn't been for that omnipresent bottle of hot stuff. We poured the stinging liquid over our sugar, which had kept dry in a sardine box, and warmed ourselves with frequent doses.

After four or five hours the rain ceased, the wind died away to a moan, and the sea—no longer raging like a maniac—sobbed and sobbed with a piteous human voice all along the coast. And well it might, after that night's work. Twelve sail of the Gloucester fishing fleet had gone down with every soul on board, just outside of Whale's-back Light. Think of the wide grief that follows in the wake of one wreck; then think of the despairing women who wrung their hands and wept, the next morning, in the streets of Gloucester, Marblehead, and Newcastle!

Though our strength was nearly spent, we were too cold to sleep. Once I sunk into a troubled doze, when I seemed to hear Charley Marden's parting words, only it was the sea that said them. After that I threw off the drowsiness whenever it threatened to overcome me.

Fred Langdon was the earliest to discover a filmy, luminous streak in the sky, the first glimmering of sunrise.

"Look, it is nearly daybreak!"

While we were following the direction of his finger, a sound of distant oars fell on our ears.

We listened breathlessly, and as the dip of the blades became more audible, we discerned two foggy lights, like will-o'-the-wisps, floating on the river.

Running down to the water's edge, we hailed the boats with all our might. The call was heard, for the oars rested a moment in the rowlocks, and then pulled in toward the island.

It was two boats from the town, in the foremost of which we could now make out the figures of Captain Nutter and Binny Wallace's father. We shrunk back on seeing him.

"Thank God!" cried Mr. Wallace, fervently, as he leaped from the wherry without waiting for the bow to touch the beach.

But when he saw only three boys standing on the sands, his eye wandered restlessly about in quest of the fourth; then a deadly pallor overspread his features.

Our story was soon told. A solemn silence fell

upon the crowd of rough boatmen gathered round, interrupted only by a stifled sob from one poor old man, who stood apart from the rest.

The sea was still running too high for any small boat to venture out; so it was arranged that the wherry should take us back to town, leaving the yawl, with a picked crew, to hug the island until daybreak, and then set forth in search of the "Dolphin."

Though it was barely sunrise when we reached town, there were a great many people assembled at the landing eager for intelligence from missing boats. Two picnic parties had started down river the day before, just previous to the gale, and nothing had been heard of them. It turned out that the pleasure seekers saw their danger in time, and ran ashore on one of the least exposed islands, where they passed the night. Shortly after our own arrival they appeared off Rivermouth, much to the joy of their friends, in two shattered, dismasted boats.

The excitement over, I was in a forlorn state, physically and mentally. Captain Nutter put me to bed between hot blankets, and sent Kitty Collins for the doctor. I was wandering in my mind, and fancied myself still on Sandpeep Island; now we were building our brick stove to cook the chowder, and, in my delirium, I laughed aloud and shouted to my comrades; now the sky darkened, and the squall struck the island: now I gave orders to Wallace how to manage the boat, and now I cried because the rain was pouring in on me through the holes in the tent. Toward evening a high fever set in, and it was many days before my grandfather deemed it prudent to tell me that the "Dolphin" had been found, floating keel upwards, four miles southeast of Mackerel Reef.

Poor little Binny Wallace! How strange it seemed, when I went to school again, to see that empty seat in the fifth row! How gloomy the playground was, lacking the sunshine of his gentle, sensitive face! One day a folded sheet slipped from my algebra; it was the last note he ever wrote me. I couldn't read it for the tears.

What a pang shot across my heart the afternoon it was whispered through the town that a body had been washed ashore at Grave Point—the place where we bathed. We bathed there no more! How well I remember the funeral, and what a piteous sight it was afterwards to see his familiar name on a small headstone in the Old South Burying Ground!

Poor little Binny Wallace! Always the same to me. The rest of us have grown up into hard, worldly men, fighting the fight of life; but you are forever young, and gentle, and pure; a part of my own childhood that time cannot wither; always a little boy, always poor little Binny Wallace!

Chapter XV

AN OLD ACQUAINTANCE TURNS UP

A YEAR had stolen by since the death of Binny Wallace—a year of which I have nothing important to record.

The loss of our little playmate threw a shadow over our young lives for many and many a month. The "Dolphin" rose and fell with the tide at the foot of the slippery steps, unused, the rest of the summer. At the close of November we hauled her sadly into the boat house for the winter; but when spring came round we launched the "Dolphin" again, and often went down to the wharf and looked at her lying in the tangled eel-grass, without much inclination to take a row. The associations connected with the boat were too painful as yet; but time, which wears the sharp edge from everything, softened this feeling, and one afternoon we brought out the cobwebbed oars.

The ice once broken, brief trips along the wharves —we seldom cared to go out into the river now—became one of our chief amusements. Meanwhile Gypsy was not forgotten. Every clear morning I was in the saddle before breakfast, and there are few roads or lanes within ten miles of Rivermouth that have not borne the print of her vagrant hoof.

I studied like a good fellow this quarter, carrying off a couple of first prizes. The Captain expressed his gratification by presenting me with a new silver dollar. If a dollar in his eyes was smaller than a cart wheel, it wasn't so very much smaller. I redeemed my pencil case from the treasurer of the Centipedes, and felt that I was getting on in the world.

It was at this time I was greatly cast down by a letter from my father saying that he should be unable to visit Rivermouth until the following year. With that letter came another to Captain Nutter, which he did not read aloud to the family, as usual. It was on business, he said, folding it up in his wallet. He received several of these business letters from time to time, and I noticed that they always made him silent and moody.

The fact is, my father's banking house was not thriving. The unlooked-for failure of a firm largely indebted to him had crippled "the house." When the Captain imparted this information to me I didn't trouble myself over the matter. I supposed— if I supposed anything—that all grown-up people had more or less money, when they wanted it. Whether they inherited it, or whether the government supplied them, was not clear to me. A loose idea that my father had a private gold mine somewhere or other relieved me of all uneasiness.

I was not far from right. Every man has within himself a gold mine whose riches are limited only by his own industry. It is true, it sometimes happens that industry does not avail, if a man lacks that something which, for want of a better name, we call luck. My father was a person of untiring energy and ability; but he had no luck. To use a Rivermouth saying, he was always catching sculpins when everyone else with the same bait was catching mackerel.

It was more than two years since I had seen my parents. I felt that I could not bear a longer separation. Every letter from New Orleans—we got two or three a month—gave me a fit of homesickness; and when it was definitely settled that my father and mother were to remain in the South another twelve months, I resolved to go to them.

Since Binny Wallace's death, Pepper Whitcomb had been my *fidus Achates;* we occupied desks near each other at school, and were always together in play hours. We rigged a twine telegraph from his garret window to the scuttle of the Nutter House, and sent messages to each other in a match box. We shared our pocket money and our secrets—those amazing secrets which boys have. We met in lonely places by stealth, and parted like conspirators; we couldn't buy a jackknife or build a kite without throwing an air of mystery and guilt over the transaction.

I naturally hastened to lay my New Orleans project before Pepper Whitcomb, having dragged him for that purpose to a secluded spot in the dark pine woods outside the town. Pepper listened to me with a gravity which he will not be able to surpass when he becomes Chief Justice, and strongly advised me to go.

"The summer vacation," said Pepper, "lasts six weeks; that will give you a fortnight to spend in New Orleans, allowing two weeks each way for the journey."

I wrung his hand and begged him to accompany me, offering to defray all the expenses. I wasn't anything if I wasn't princely in those days. After considerable urging, he consented to go on terms so liberal. The whole thing was arranged; there was nothing to do now but to advise Captain Nutter of my plan, which I did next day.

The possibility that he might oppose the tour never entered my head. I was therefore totally unprepared for the vigorous negative which met my proposal. I was deeply mortified, moreover, for there was Pepper Whitcomb on the wharf, at the foot of the street, waiting for me to come to let him know what day we were to start.

"Go to New Orleans? Go to Jericho!" exclaimed Captain Nutter. "You'd look pretty, you two, philandering off, like the babes in the wood, twenty-five hundred miles, 'with all the world before you where to choose'!"

And the Captain's features, which had worn an indignant air as he began the sentence, relaxed into a broad smile. Whether it was at the felicity of his own quotation, or at the mental picture he drew of Pepper and myself on our travels I couldn't tell, and

I didn't care. I was heartbroken. How could I face my chum after all the dazzling inducements I had held out to him?

My grandfather, seeing that I took the matter seriously, pointed out the difficulties of such a journey and the great expense involved. He entered into the details of my father's money troubles, and succeeded in making it plain to me that my wishes, under the circumstances, were somewhat unreasonable. It was in no cheerful mood that I joined Pepper at the end of the wharf.

I found that young gentleman leaning against the bulkhead, gazing intently toward the islands in the harbor. He had formed a telescope of his hands, and was so occupied with his observations as to be oblivious of my approach.

"Hullo!" cried Pepper, dropping his hands. "Look there! isn't that a bark coming up the Narrows?"

"Where?"

"Just at the left of Fishcrate Island. Don't you see the foremast peeping above the old derrick?"

Sure enough it was a vessel of considerable size, slowly beating up to town. In a few moments more the other two masts were visible above the green hillocks.

"Fore topmasts blown away," said Pepper. "Putting in for repairs, I guess."

As the bark lazily crept from behind the last of

the islands, she let go her anchors and swung round with the tide. Then the gleeful chant of the sailors at the capstan came to us pleasantly across the water. The vessel lay within three-quarters of a mile of us, and we could plainly see the men at the davits lowering the starboard longboat. It no sooner touched the stream than a dozen of the crew scrambled like mice over the side of the merchantman.

In a neglected seaport like Rivermouth the arrival of a large ship is an event of moment. The prospect of having twenty or thirty jolly tars let loose on the peaceful town excites divers emotions among the inhabitants. The small shopkeepers along the wharves anticipate a thriving trade; the proprietors of the two rival boarding houses—the "Wee Drop" and the "Mariner's Home"—hasten down to the landing to secure lodgers; and the female population of Anchor Lane turn out to a woman, for a ship fresh from sea is always full of possible husbands and long-lost prodigal sons.

But aside from this there is scant welcome given to a ship's crew in Rivermouth. The toil-worn mariner is a sad fellow ashore, judging him by a severe moral standard.

Once, I remember, a United States frigate came into port for repairs after a storm. She lay in the river a fortnight or more, and every day sent us a gang of sixty or seventy of our country's gallant defenders, who spread themselves over the town, doing all sorts of mad things. They were good-natured enough, but full of old Sancho. The "Wee Drop" proved a drop too much for many of them. They went singing through the streets at midnight, wringing off door knockers, shinning up waterspouts, and frightening the Oldest Inhabitant nearly to death by popping their heads into his second-story window, and shouting "Fire!" One morning a bluejacket was discovered in a perilous plight, halfway up the steeple of the South Church, clinging to the lightning rod. How he got there nobody could tell, not even the bluejacket himself. All he knew was, that the leg of his trousers had caught on a nail, and there he stuck, unable to move either way. It cost the town twenty dollars to get him down again. He directed the workmen how to splice the ladders brought to his assistance, and called his rescuers "butter-fingered landlubbers" with delicious coolness.

But those were man-of-war's men. The sedate-looking craft now lying off Fishcrate Island wasn't likely to carry any such cargo. Nevertheless, we watched the coming in of the longboat with considerable interest.

As it drew near, the figure of the man pulling the bow oar seemed oddly familiar to me. Where could I have seen him before? When and where? His back was toward me, but there was something about that closely cropped head that I recognized instantly.

"Way enough!" cried the steersman, and all the oars stood upright in the air. The man in the bow seized the boat hook, and, turning round quickly, showed me the honest face of Sailor Ben of the "Typhoon."

"It's Sailor Ben!" I cried, nearly pushing Pepper Whitcomb overboard in my excitement.

Sailor Ben, with the wonderful pink lady on his arm, and the ships and stars and anchors tattooed all over him, was a well-known hero among my playmates. And there he was, like something in a dream come true!

I didn't wait for my old acquaintance to get firmly on the wharf, before I grasped his hand in both of mine.

"Sailor Ben, don't you remember me?"

He evidently did not. He shifted his quid from one cheek to the other, and looked at me meditatively.

"Lord love ye, lad, I don't know you. I was never here afore in my life."

"What!" I cried, enjoying his perplexity, "have you forgotten the voyage from New Orleans in the 'Typhoon,' two years ago, you lovely old picture book?"

Ah! then he knew me, and in token of the recollection gave my hand such a squeeze that I am sure an unpleasant change came over my countenance.

"Bless my eyes, but you have growed so. I

shouldn't have knowed you if I had met you in Singapore!"

Without stopping to inquire, as I was tempted to do, why he was more likely to recognize me in Singapore than anywhere else, I invited him to come at once up to the Nutter House, where I insured him a warm welcome from the Captain.

"Hold steady, Master Tom," said Sailor Ben, slipping the painter through the ringbolt and tying the loveliest knot you ever saw, "hold steady till I see if the mate can let me off. If you please, sir," he continued, addressing the steersman, a very red-faced, bowlegged person, "this here is a little ship-mate o'mine as wants to talk over back times along of me, if so it's convenient."

"All right, Ben," returned the mate, "shan't want you for an hour."

Leaving one man in charge of the boat, the mate and the rest of the crew went off together. In the meanwhile Pepper Whitcomb had got out his cunner line, and was quietly fishing at the end of the wharf, as if to give me the idea that he wasn't so very much impressed by my intimacy with so renowned a character as Sailor Ben. Perhaps Pepper was a little jealous. At any rate, he refused to go with us to the house.

Captain Nutter was at home reading the River-mouth Barnacle. He was a reader to do an editor's heart good; he never skipped over an advertisement, even if he had read it fifty times before. Then the paper went the rounds of the neighborhood, among the poor people, like the single portable eye which the three blind crones passed to each other in the legend of King Acrisius. The Captain, I repeat, was wandering in the labyrinths of the Rivermouth Barnacle when I led Sailor Ben into the sitting room.

My grandfather, whose inborn courtesy knew no distinctions, received my nautical friend as if he had been an admiral instead of a common forecastle hand. Sailor Ben pulled an imaginary tuft of hair on his forehead, and bowed clumsily. Sailors have a way of using their forelock as a sort of handle to bow with.

The old tar had probably never been in so handsome an apartment in all his days, and nothing could induce him to take the inviting mahogany chair which the Captain wheeled out from the corner.

The abashed mariner stood up against the wall, twirling his tarpaulin in his two hands and looking extremely silly. He made a poor show in a gentleman's drawing room, but what a fellow he had been in his day, when the gale blew great guns and the topsails wanted reefing! I thought of him with the Mexican squadron off Vera Cruz, where

"The rushing battle-bolt sung from the three-decker out of the foam,"

and he didn't seem awkward or ignoble to me, for all his shyness.

As Sailor Ben declined to sit down, the Captain did not resume his seat; so we three stood in a constrained manner until my grandfather went to the door and called to Kitty to bring in a decanter of Madeira and two glasses.

"My grandson, here, has talked so much about you," said the Captain, pleasantly, "that you seem quite like an old acquaintance to me."

"Thankee, sir, thankee," returned Sailor Ben, looking as guilty as if he had been detected in picking a pocket.

"And I'm very glad to see you, Mr. — Mr. —"

"Sailor Ben," suggested that worthy.

"Mr. Sailor Ben," added the Captain, smiling. "Tom, open the door, there's Kitty with the glasses."

I opened the door, and Kitty entered the room bringing the things on a waiter, which she was about to set on the table, when suddenly she uttered a loud shriek; the decanter and glasses fell with a crash to the floor, and Kitty, as white as a sheet, was seen flying through the hall.

"It's his wraith! It's his wraith!"* we heard Kitty shrieking, in the kitchen.

My grandfather and I turned with amazement to Sailor Ben. His eyes were standing out of his head like a lobster's.

"It's my own little Irish lass!" shouted the sailor, and he darted into the hall after her.

* Ghost, spirit.

Miss Abigail came ambling downstairs with a bottle of the infallible hot drops in her hand

Even then we scarcely caught the meaning of his words, but when we saw Sailor Ben and Kitty sobbing on each other's shoulder in the kitchen we understood it all.

"I begs your honor's parden, sir," said Sailor Ben, lifting his tear-stained face above Kitty's tumbled hair, "I begs your honor's parden for kicking up a rumpus in the house, but it's my own little Irish lass as I lost so long ago!"

"Heaven preserve us!" cried the Captain, blowing his nose violently—a transparent ruse to hide his emotion.

Miss Abigail was in an upper chamber, sweeping; but on hearing the unusual racket below, she scented an accident and came ambling downstairs with a bottle of the infallible hot drops in her hand. Nothing but the firmness of my grandfather prevented her from giving Sailor Ben a tablespoonful on the spot. But when she learned what had come about—that this was Kitty's husband, that Kitty Collins wasn't Kitty Collins now, but Mrs. Benjamin Watson of Nantucket—the good soul sat down on the meal chest and sobbed as if—to quote from Captain Nutter—as if a husband of her own had turned up!

A happier set of people than we were never met together in a dingy kitchen or anywhere else. The Captain ordered a fresh decanter of Madeira, and made all hands, excepting myself, drink a cup to the return of the "the prodigal sea son," as he persisted in calling Sailor Ben.

After the first flush of joy and surprise was over Kitty grew silent and constrained. Now and then she fixed her eyes thoughtfully on her husband. Why had he deserted her all these long years? What right had he to look for a welcome from one he had treated so cruelly? She had been true to him, but had he been true to her? Sailor Ben must have guessed what was passing in her mind, for presently he took her hand and said:

"Well, lass, it's a long yarn, but you shall have it all in good time. It was my hard luck as made us part company, an' no will of mine, for I loved you dear."

Kitty brightened up immediately, needing no other assurance of Sailor Ben's faithfulness.

When his hour had expired, we walked with him down to the wharf, where the Captain held a consultation with the mate, which resulted in an extension of Mr. Watson's leave of absence, and afterwards in his discharge from his ship. We then went to the "Mariner's Home" to engage a room for him, as he wouldn't hear of accepting the hospitalities of the Nutter House.

"You see, I'm an uneddicated man," he remarked to my grandfather, by way of explanation.

CHAPTER XVI

IN WHICH SAILOR BEN SPINS A YARN

OF course we were all very curious to learn what had befallen Sailor Ben that morning long ago, when he bade his little bride good-by and disappeared so mysteriously.

After tea, that same evening, we assembled around the table in the kitchen—the only place where Sailor Ben felt at home—to hear what he had to say for himself.

The candles were snuffed, and a pitcher of foaming nut-brown ale was set at the elbow of the speaker, who was evidently embarrassed by the respectability of his audience, consisting of Captain Nutter, Miss Abigail, myself, and Kitty, whose face shone with happiness like one of the polished tin platters on the dresser.

"Well, my hearties," commenced Sailor Ben— then he stopped short and turned very red, as it struck him maybe this was not quite the proper way to address a dignitary like the Captain and a severe elderly lady like Miss Abigail Nutter, who sat bolt upright staring at him as she would have stared at the Tycoon of Japan himself.

"I ain't much of a hand at spinnin' a yarn," remarked Sailor Ben, apologetically, "'specially when the yarn is all about a man as has made a fool of hisself, an' 'specially when that man's name is Benjamin Watson."

"Bravo!" cried Captain Nutter, rapping on the table encouragingly.

"Thankee, sir, thankee. I go back to the time when Kitty an' me was livin' in lodgin's by the dock in New York. We was as happy, sir, as two porpusses, which they toil not neither do they spin. But when I seed the money gittin' low in the locker— Kitty's starboard stockin', savin' your presence, marm—I got downhearted like, seen' as I should be obleeged to ship again, for it didn't seem as I could do much ashore. An' then the sea was my nat'ral spear of action. I wasn't exactly born on it, look you, but I fell into it the fust time I was let out arter my birth. My mother slipped her cable for a heavenly port afore I was old enough to hail her; so I larnt to look on the ocean for a sort of stepmother—an' a precious hard one she has been to me.

"The idee of leavin' Kitty so soon arter our marriage went agin my grain considerable. I cruised along the docks for somethin' to do in the way of stevedore: an' though I picked up a stray job here and there, I didn't arn enough to buy ship bisket for a rat, let alone feedin' two human mouths. There wasn't nothin' honest I wouldn't have turned a hand to; but the longshoremen gobbled up all the work, an' a outsider like me didn't stand a show.

"Things got from bad to worse; the month's rent took all our cash except a dollar or so, an' the sky looked kind o' squally fore an' aft. Well, I set out one mornin'—that identical unlucky mornin'—determined to come back an' toss some pay into Kitty's lap, if I had to sell my jacket for it. I spied a brig unloadin' coal at pier No. 47—how well I remembers it! I hailed the mate, an' offered myself for a coal heaver. But I wasn't wanted, as he told me civilly enough, which was better treatment than usual. As I turned off rather glum I was signaled by one of them sleek, smooth-spoken rascals with a white hat an' a weed on it, as is always goin' about the piers a-seekin' who they may devower.

"We sailors know 'em for rascals from stem to starm, but somehow every fresh one fleeces us jest as his mate did afore him. We don't larn nothin' by exper'ence; we're jest no better than a lot of babbys with no brains.

" 'Good mornin', my man,' sez the chap, as iley as you please.

" 'Mornin', sir,' sez I.

" 'Lookin' for a job?' sez he.

" 'Through the big end of a telescope,' sez I—meanin' that the chances for a job looked very small from my pint of view.

" 'You're the man for my money,' sez the sharper, smilin' as innocent as a cherubim, 'jest step in here till we talk it over.'

'So I goes with him like a nat'ral-born idiot, into a little grocery shop near-by, where we sets down at a table with a bottle between us. Then it comes out as there is a New Bedford whaler about to start for the fishin' grounds, an' jest one able-bodied sailor like me is wanted to make up the crew. Would I go? Yes, I wouldn't on no terms.

" 'I'll bet you fifty dollars,' sez he, 'that you'll come back fust mate.'

" 'I'll bet you a hundred,' sez I, 'that I don't, for I've signed papers as keeps me ashore, an' the parson has witnessed the deed.'

"So we sat there, he urgin' me to ship, an' I chaffin' him cheerful over the bottle.

"Arter a while I begun to feel a little queer; things got foggy in my upper works, an' I remembers, faintlike, of signin' a paper; then I remembers bein' in a small boat; an' then I remembers nothin' until I heard the mate's whistle pipin' all hands on deck. I tumbled up with the rest, an' there I was—on board of a whaler outward bound for a three years' cruise, an' my dear little lass ashore awaitin' for me."

"Miserable wretch!" said Miss Abigail, in a voice that vibrated among the tin platters on the dresser. This was Miss Abigail's way of testifying her sympathy.

"Thankee, marm," returned Sailor Ben, doubtfully.

"No talking to the man at the wheel," cried the

Captain. Upon which we all laughed. "Spin!" added my grandfather.

Sailor Ben resumed:

"I leave you to guess the wretchedness as fell upon me, for I've not got the gift to tell you. There I was down on the ship's books for a three years' viage, an' no help for it. I feel nigh to six hundred years old when I think how long that viage was. There isn't no hourglass as runs slow enough to keep a tally of the slowness of them fust hours. But I done my duty like a man, seein' there wasn't no way of gettin' out of it. I told my shipmates of the trick as had been played on me, an' they tried to cheer me up a bit; but I was sore sorrowful for a long spell. Many a night on watch I put my face in my hands and sobbed for thinkin' of the little woman left among the land-sharks, an' no man to have an eye on her, God bless her!"

Here Kitty softly drew her chair nearer to Sailor Ben, and rested one hand on his arm.

"Our adventures among the whales, I take it, doesn't consarn the present company here assembled. So I give that the go by. There's an end to every-thin', even to a whalin' viage. My heart all but choked me the day we put into New Bedford with our cargo of ile. I got my three years' pay in a lump, an' made for New York like a flash of lightnin'. The people hove to and looked at me, as I rushed through the streets like a madman, until I came to the spot

where the lodgin' house stood on West Street. But,
Lord love ye, there wasn't no sech lodgin' house
there, but a great new brick shop.

"I made bold to go in an' ask arter the old place,
but nobody knowed nothin' about it, save as it had
been torn down two years or more. I was adrift now,
for I had reckoned all them days and nights on gittin'
word of Kitty from Dan Shackford, the man as kept
the lodgin'.

"As I stood ther with all the wind knocked out of
my sails, the idee of runnin' alongside the perlice
station popped into my head. The perlice was
likely to know the latitude of a man like Dan Shackford, who wasn't over an' above respecktible. They
did know—he had died in the Tombs jail that day
twelvemonth. A coincydunce, wasn't it? I was ready
to drop when they told me this; howsomever, I
bore up an' give the chief a notion of the fix I was in.
He writ a notice which I put into the newspaper every
day for three months; but nothin' come of it. I
cruised over the city week in and week out; I went
to every sort of place where they hired women hands;
I didn't leave a thing undone that a uneddicated
man could do. But nothin' come of it. I don't
believe there was a wretcheder soul in that big city of
wretchedness than me. Sometimes I wanted to lay
down in the streets and die.

"Driftin' disconsolate one day among the ship-
pin', who should I overhaul but the identical smooth-

spoken chap with a white hat an' a weed on it! I
didn't know if there was any sperit left in me, till I
clapped eye on his very onpleasant countenance.
'You villain!' sez I, 'where's my little Irish lass as
you dragged me away from?' an' I lighted on him,
hat and all, like that!"

Here Sailor Ben brought his fist down on the deal
table with the force of a sledge hammer. Miss Abigail gave a start, and the ale leaped up in the pitcher
like a miniature fountain.

"I begs your parden, ladies and gentlemen all;
but the thought of that feller with his ring an' his
watch chain an' his walrus face, is alus too many for
me. I was for pitchin' him into the North River,
when a perliceman prevented me from benefitin' the
human family. I had to pay five dollars for hittin'
the chap (they said it was salt and buttery), an'
that's what I call a neat, genteel luxury. It was
worth double the money jest to see that white hat,
with a weed on it, layin' on the wharf like a busted
accordiun.

"Arter months of useless sarch, I went to sea agin.
I never got into a foren port but I kept a watch out
for Kitty. Once I thought I seed her in Liverpool,
but it was only a gal as looked like her. The numbers
of women in different parts of the world as looked
like her was amazin'. So a good many years crawled
by, an' I wandered from place to place, never givin'
up the sarch. I might have been chief mate scores of

times, maybe master; but I hadn't no ambition. I seed many strange things in them years—outlandish people an' cities, storms, shipwrecks, an' battles. I seed many a true mate go down, an' sometimes I envied them what went to their rest. But these things is neither here nor there.

"About a year ago I shipped on board the 'Belphoebe' yonder, an' of all the strange winds as ever blowed, the strangest an' the best was the wind as blowed me to this here blessed spot. I can't be too thankful. That I'm as thankful as it is possible for an uneddicated man to be, He knows as reads the heart of all."

Here ended Sailor Ben's yarn, which I have written down in his own homely words as nearly as I can recall them. After he had finished, the Captain shook hands with him and served out the ale.

As Kitty was about to drink, she paused, rested the cup on her knee, and asked what day of the month it was.

"The twenty-seventh," said the Captain, wondering what she was driving at.

"Then," cried Kitty, "it's ten years this night sence—"

"Since what?" asked my grandfather.

"Sence the little lass and I got spliced!" roared Sailor Ben. "There's another coincydunce for you!"

On hearing this we all clapped hands, and the Captain, with a degree of ceremony that was almost painful, drank a bumper to the health and happiness of the bride and bridegroom.

It was a pleasant sight to see the two old lovers sitting side by side, in spite of all, drinking from the same little cup—a battered zinc dipper which Sailor Ben had unslung from a strap round his waist. I think I never saw him without this dipper and a sheath knife suspended just back of his hip, ready for any convivial occasion.

We had a merry time of it. The Captain was in great force this evening, and not only related his famous exploit in the war of 1812, but regaled the company with a dashing sea song from Mr. Shakespeare's play of "The Tempest." He had a mellow tenor voice (not Shakespeare, but the Captain), and rolled out the verse with a will—

"The master, the swabber, the boatswain, and I,
    The gunner, and his mate,
Lov'd Mall, Meg, and Marian, and Margery,
    But none of us car'd for Kate."

"A very good song, and very well sung," says Sailor Ben, "but some of us does care for Kate. Is this Mr. Shawkespear a seafarin' man, sir?"

"Not at present," replied the Captain, with a monstrous twinkle in his eye.

The clock was striking ten when the party broke up. The Captain walked to the "Mariner's Home" with his guest, in order to question him regarding his future movements.

"Well, sir," said he, "I ain't as young as I was, an' I don't cal'ulate to go to sea no more. I proposes to drop anchor here, an' hug the land until the old hulk goes to pieces. I've got two or three thousand dollars in the locker, an' expects to get on uncommon comfortable without askin' no odds from the Assylum for Decayed Mariners."

My grandfather indorsed the plan warmly, and Sailor Ben did drop anchor in Rivermouth, where he speedily became one of the institutions of the town.

His first step was to buy a small one-story cottage located at the head of the wharf, within gunshot of the Nutter House. To the great amusement of my grandfather, Sailor Ben painted the cottage a light sky blue, and ran a broad, black stripe around it just under the eaves. In this stripe he painted white portholes, at regular distances, making his residence look as much like a man-of-war as possible. With a short flagstaff projecting over the door like a bowsprit, the effect was quite magical. My description of the exterior of this palatial residence is complete when I add that the proprietor nailed a horseshoe against the front door to keep off the witches—a very necessary precaution in these latitudes.

The inside of Sailor Ben's abode was not less striking than the outside. The cottage contained two rooms; the one opening on the wharf he called his cabin; here he ate and slept. His few tumblers and a frugal collection of crockery were set in a rack nailed round the edge to prevent the dishes from sliding off in case of a heavy sea. Hanging against the walls were three or four highly colored prints of celebrated frigates, and a lithograph picture of a rosy young woman insufficiently clad in the American flag. This was labeled "Kitty," though I'm sure it looked no more like her than I did. A walrus tooth with an Eskimo engraved on it, a shark's jaw, and the blade of a swordfish were among the enviable decorations of this apartment. In one corner stood his bunk, or bed, and in the other his well-worn sea chest, a perfect Pandora's box of mysteries. You would have thought yourself in the cabin of a real ship.

The little room aft, separated from the cabin by a sliding door, was the caboose. It held a cooking stove, pots, pans, and groceries; also a lot of fishing lines and coils of tarred twine, which made the place smell like a forecastle, and a delightful smell it is—to those who fancy it.

Kitty didn't leave our service, but played housekeeper for both establishments, returning at night to Sailor Ben's. He shortly added a wherry to his worldly goods, and in the fishing season made a very handsome income. During the winter he employed himself manufacturing crabnets, for which he found no lack of customers.

His popularity among the boys was immense. A jack knife in his expert hand was a whole chest of tools. He could whittle out anything from a wooden chain to a Chinese pagoda, or a full-rigged seventy-four a foot long. To own a ship of Sailor Ben's building was to be exalted above your fellow creatures. He didn't carve many, and those he refused to sell, choosing to present them to his young friends, of whom Tom Bailey, you may be sure, was one.

How delightful it was of winter nights to sit in his cosy cabin, close to the ship's stove (he wouldn't hear of having a fireplace), and listen to Sailor Ben's yarns! In the early summer twilights, when he sat on the doorstep splicing a rope or mending a net, he always had a bevy of blooming young faces alongside.

The dear old fellow! How tenderly the years touched him after this!—all the more tenderly, it seemed, for having roughed him so cruelly in other days.

Chapter XVII

HOW WE ASTONISHED THE
RIVERMOUTHIANS

SAILOR Ben's arrival partly drove the New Orleans project from my brain. Besides, there was just then a certain movement on foot by the Centipede Club which helped to engross my attention.

Pepper Whitcomb took the Captain's veto philosophically, observing that he thought from the first the governor wouldn't let me go. I don't think Pepper was quite honest in that.

But to the subject in hand.

Among the few changes that have taken place in Rivermouth during the past twenty years there is one which I regret. I lament the removal of all those varnished iron cannon which used to do duty as posts at the corners of streets leading from the river. They were quaintly ornamental, each set upon end with a solid shot soldered into its mouth, and gave to that part of the town a picturesqueness very poorly atoned for by the conventional wooden stakes that have deposed them.

These guns ("old sogers" the boys called them) had their story, like everything else in Rivermouth.

When that everlasting last war—the war of 1812, I
mean—came to an end, all the brigs, schooners, and
barks fitted out at this port as privateers were as
eager to get rid of their useless twelve-pounders and
swivels as they had previously been to obtain them.
Many of the pieces had cost large sums, and now they
were little better than so much crude iron—not so
good, in fact, for they were clumsy things to break up
and melt over. The government didn't want them;
private citizens didn't want them; they were a drug
in the market.

But there was one man, ridiculous beyond his
generation, who got it into his head that a fortune
was to be made out of these same guns. To buy them
all, to hold on to them until war was declared
again (as he had no doubt it would be in a few
months), and then sell out at fabulous prices—this
was the daring idea that addled the pate of Silas
Trefethen, "Dealer in E. & W. I. Goods and Groceries," as the faded sign over his shop door informed
the public.

Silas went shrewdly to work, buying up every old
cannon he could lay hands on. His back yard was
soon crowded with broken-down gun carriages, and
his barn with guns, like an arsenal. When Silas's
purpose got wind it was astonishing how valuable
that thing became which just now was worth nothing
at all.

"Ha, ha!" thought Silas, "somebody else is

13

tryin' tu git control of the market.   But I guess I've got the start of him."

So he went on buying and buying, oftentimes paying double the original price of the article.   People in the neighboring towns collected all the worthless ordnance they could find, and sent it by the cart load to Rivermouth.

When his barn was full, Silas began piling the rubbish in his cellar, then in his parlor.   He mortgaged the stock of his grocery store, mortgaged his house, his barn, his horse, and would have mortgaged himself, if anyone would have taken him as security, in order to carry on the grand speculation.   He was a ruined man, and as happy as a lark.

Surely poor Silas was cracked, like the majority of his own cannon.   More or less crazy he must have been always.   Years before this he purchased an elegant rosewood coffin, and kept it in one of the spare rooms in his residence.   He even had his name engraved on the silver plate, leaving a blank after the word "Died."

The blank was filled up in due time, and well it was for Silas that he secured so stylish a coffin in his opulent days, for when he died his worldly wealth would not have bought him a pine box, to say nothing of rosewood.   He never gave up expecting a war with Great Britain.   Hopeful and radiant to the last, his dying words were, *England—war—few days— great profits!*

It was that sweet old Lady, Dame Jocelyn, who told me the story of Silas Trefethen; for these things happened long before my day.   Silas died in 1817.

At Trefethen's death his unique collection came under the auctioneer's hammer.   Some of the larger guns were sold to the town, and planted at the corners of divers streets; others went off to the iron foundry; the balance, numbering twelve, were dumped down on a deserted wharf at the foot of Anchor Lane, where, summer after summer, they rested at their ease in the grass and fungi, pelted in autumn by the rain and annually buried by the winter snow.   It is with these twelve guns that our story has to deal.

The wharf where they reposed was shut off from the street by a high fence—a silent, dreamy old wharf, covered with strange weeds and mosses.   On account of its seclusion and the good fishing it afforded, it was much frequented by us boys.

There we met many an afternoon to throw out our lines, or play leapfrog among the rusty cannon. They were famous fellows in our eyes.   What a racket they had made in the heyday of their unchastened youth!   What stories they might tell now, if their puffy, metallic lips could only speak!   Once they were lively talkers enough; but there the grim sea dogs lay, silent and forlorn in spite of all their former growlings.

They always seemed to me like a lot of venerable, disabled tars, stretched out on a lawn in front of a

hospital, gazing seaward, and mutely lamenting their
lost youth.

But once more they were destined to lift up their
dolorous voices—once more ere they keeled over and
lay speechless for all time. And this is how it
befell.

Jack Harris, Charley Marden, Harry Blake, and
myself were fishing off the wharf one afternoon, when
a thought flashed upon me like an inspiration.

"I say, boys!" I cried, hauling in my line hand
over hand, "I've got something!"

"What does it pull like, youngster?" asked Harris,
looking down at the taut line and expecting to see a
big perch at least.

"Oh, nothing in the fish way," I returned, laughing, "it's about the old guns."

"What about them?"

"I was thinking what jolly fun it would be to set
one of the old sogers on his legs and serve him out a
ration of gunpowder."

Up came the three lines in a jiffy. An enterprise
better suited to the disposition of my companions
could not have been proposed.

In a short time we had one of the smaller cannon
over on its back and were busy scraping the green
rust from the touchhole. The mold had spiked
the gun so effectually, that for a while we fancied we
should have to give up our attempt to resuscitate the
old soger.

"A long gimlet would clear it out," said Charley Marden, "if we only had one."

I looked to see if Sailor Ben's flag was flying at the cabin door, for he always took in the colors when he went off fishing.

"When you want to know if the Admiral's aboard, jest cast an eye to the buntin', my hearties," says Sailor Ben.

Sometimes in a jocose mood he called himself the Admiral, and I am sure he deserved to be one. The Admiral's flag was flying and I soon procured a gimlet from his carefully kept tool chest.

Before long we had the gun in working order. A newspaper lashed to the end of a lath served as a swab to dust out the bore. Jack Harris blew through the touchhole and pronounced all clear.

Seeing our task accomplished so easily, we turned our attention to the other guns, which lay in all sorts of postures in the rank grass. Borrowing a rope from Sailor Ben, we managed with immense labor to drag the heavy pieces into position and place a brick under each muzzle to give it the proper elevation. When we beheld them all in a row, like a regular battery, we simultaneously conceived an idea, the magnitude of which struck us dumb for a moment.

Our first intention was to load and fire a single gun. How feeble and insignificant was such a plan compared to that which now sent the light dancing into our eyes!

"What could we have been thinking of?" cried Jack Harris. "We'll give 'em a broadside, to be sure, if we die for it!"

We turned to with a will, and before nightfall had nearly half the battery overhauled and ready for service. To keep the artillery dry we stuffed wads of loose hemp into the muzzles, and fitted wooden pegs to the touchholes.

At recess the next noon the Centipedes met in a corner of the school yard to take over the proposed lark. The original projectors, though they would have liked to keep the thing secret, were obliged to make a club matter of it, inasmuch as funds were required for ammunition. There had been no recent drain on the treasury, and the society could well afford to spend a few dollars in so notable an undertaking.

It was unanimously agreed that the plan should be carried out in the handsomest manner, and a subscription to that end was taken on the spot. Several of the Centipedes hadn't a cent, excepting the one strung around their necks; others, however, were richer. I chanced to have a dollar, and it went into the cap quicker than lightning. When the club, in view of my munificence, voted to name the guns Bailey's Battery I was prouder than I have ever been since over anything.

The money thus raised, added to that already in the treasury, amounted to nine dollars—a fortune in those days; but not more than we had use for. This sum was divided into twelve parts, for it would not do for one boy to buy all the powder, nor even for us all to make our purchases at the same place. That would excite suspicion at any time, particularly at a period so remote from the Fourth of July.

There were only three stores in town licensed to sell powder; that gave each store four customers. Not to run the slightest risk of remark, one boy bought his powder on Monday, the next boy on Tuesday, and so on until the requisite quantity was in our possession. This we put into a keg and carefully hid in a dry spot on the wharf.

Our next step was to finish cleaning the guns, which occupied two afternoons, for several of the old sogers were in a very congested state indeed. Having completed the task, we came upon a difficulty. To set off the battery by daylight was out of the question; it must be done at night; it must be done with fuses, for no doubt the neighbors would turn out after the first two or three shots, and it would not pay to be caught in the vicinity.

Who knew anything about fuses? Who could arrange it so the guns would go off one after the other, with an interval of a minute or so between?

Theoretically we knew that a minute fuse lasted a minute; double the quantity, two minutes; but practically we were at a standstill. There was but one person who could help us in this extremity—

Sailor Ben. To me was assigned the duty of obtaining what information I could from the ex-gunner, it being left to my discretion whether or not to intrust him with our secrets.

So one evening I dropped into the cabin and artfully turned the conversation to fuses in general, and then to particular fuses, but without getting much out of the old boy, who was busy making a twine hammock. Finally, I was forced to divulge the whole plot.

The Admiral had a sailor's love for a joke, and entered at once and heartily into our scheme. He volunteered to prepare the fuses himself, and I left the labor in his hands, having bound him by several extraordinary oaths—such as "Hope-I-may-die" and "Shiver-my-timbers"—not to betray us, come what would.

This was Monday evening. On Wednesday the fuses were ready. That night we were to unmuzzle Bailey's Battery. Mr. Grimshaw saw that something was wrong somewhere, for we were restless and absent-minded in the classes, and the best of us came to grief before the morning session was over. When Mr. Grimshaw announced "Guy Fawkes" as the subject for our next composition, you might have knocked down the Mystic Twelve with a feather.

The coincidence was certainly curious, but when a man has committed, or is about to commit an offense, a hundred trifles, which would pass unnoticed at another time, seem to point at him with convicting fingers. No doubt Guy Fawkes himself received many a start after he had got his wicked kegs of gunpowder neatly piled up under the House of Lords.

Wednesday, as I have mentioned, was a half holiday, and the Centipedes assembled in my barn to decide on the final arrangements. These were as simple as could be. As the fuses were connected, it needed but one person to fire the train. Hereupon arose a discussion as to who was the proper person. Some argued that I ought to apply the match, the battery being christened after me, and the main idea, moreover, being mine. Others advocated the claim of Phil Adams as the oldest boy. At last we drew lots for the post of honor.

Twelve slips of folded paper, upon one of which was written "Thou art the man," were placed in a quart measure, and thoroughly shaken; then each member stepped up and lifted out his destiny. At a given signal we opened our billets. "Thou art the man," said the slip of paper trembling in my fingers. The sweets and anxieties of a leader were mine the rest of the afternoon.

Directly after twilight set in Phil Adams stole down to the wharf and fixed the fuses to the guns, laying a train of powder from the principal fuse to the fence, through a chink of which I was to drop the match at midnight.

At ten o'clock Rivermouth goes to bed. At

eleven o'clock Rivermouth is as quiet as a country churchyard. At twelve o'clock there is nothing left with which to compare the stillness that broods over the little seaport.

In the midst of this stillness I arose and glided out of the house like a phantom bent on an evil errand; like a phantom I flitted through the silent street, hardly drawing breath until I knelt down beside the fence at the appointed place.

Pausing a moment for my heart to stop thumping, I lighted the match and shielded it with both hands until it was well under way, and then dropped the blazing splinter on the slender thread of gunpowder.

A noiseless flash instantly followed, and all was dark again. I peeped through the crevice in the fence, and saw the main fuse spitting out sparks like a conjurer. Assured that the train had not failed, I took to my heels, fearful lest the fuse might burn more rapidly than we calculated, and cause an explosion before I could get home. This, luckily, did not happen. There's a special Providence that watches over idiots, drunken men, and boys.

I dodged the ceremony of undressing by plunging into bed, jacket, boots, and all. I am not sure I took off my cap; but I know that I had hardly pulled the coverlid over me, when "BOOM!" sounded the first gun of Bailey's Battery.

I lay as still as a mouse. In less than two minutes

I lighted a match and then dropped the blazing splinter on the slender
thread of gunpowder

there was another burst of thunder, and then another. The third gun was a tremendous fellow and fairly shook the house.

The town was waking up. Windows were thrown open here and there, and people called to each other across the streets asking what that firing was for.

"BOOM!" went gun number four.

I sprung out of bed and tore off my jacket, for I heard the Captain feeling his way along the wall to my chamber. I was half undressed by the time he found the knob of the door.

"I say, sir," I cried, "do you hear those guns?"

"Not being deaf, I do," said the Captain, a little tartly—any reflection on his hearing always nettled him, "but what on earth they are for I can't conceive. You had better get up and dress yourself."

"I'm nearly dressed, sir."

"BOOM! BOOM!"—two of the guns had gone off together.

The door of Miss Abigail's bedroom opened hastily, and that pink of maidenly propriety stepped out into the hall in her nightgown—the only indecorous thing I ever knew her to do. She held a lighted candle in her hand and looked like a very aged Lady Macbeth.

"O Dan'el, this is dreadful! What do you suppose it means?"

"I really can't suppose," said the Captain, rubbing his ear, "but I guess it's over now."

"BOOM!" said Bailey's Battery.

Rivermouth was wide awake now, and half the male population were in the streets, running different ways, for the firing seemed to proceed from opposite points of the town. Everybody waylaid everybody else with questions; but as no one knew what was the occasion of the tumult, people who were not usually nervous began to be oppressed by the mystery.

Some thought the town was being bombarded; some thought the world was coming to an end, as the pious and ingenious Mr. Miller had predicted it would; but those who couldn't form any theory whatever were the most perplexed.

In the meanwhile Bailey's Battery bellowed away at regular intervals. The greatest confusion reigned everywhere by this time. People with lanterns rushed hither and thither. The town watch had turned out to a man, and marched off, in admirable order, in the wrong direction. Discovering their mistake, they retraced their steps, and got down to the wharf just as the last cannon belched forth its lightning.

A dense cloud of sulphurous smoke floated over Anchor Lane, obscuring the starlight. Two or three hundred people, in various stages of excitement, crowded about the upper end of the wharf, not liking to advance farther until they were satisfied that the explosions were over. A board was here and there blown from the fence, and through the openings thus afforded a few of the more daring spirits at length ventured to crawl.

The cause of the racket soon transpired. A suspicion that they had been sold gradually dawned on the Rivermouthians. Many were exceedingly indignant, and declared that no penalty was severe enough for those concerned in such a prank; others—and these were the very people who had been terrified nearly out of their wits—had the assurance to laugh, saying that they knew all along it was only a trick.

The town watch boldly took possession of the ground, and the crowd began to disperse. Knots of gossips lingered here and there near the place, indulging in vain surmises as to who the invisible gunners could be.

There was no more noise that night, but many a timid person lay awake expecting a renewal of the mysterious cannonading. The Oldest Inhabitant refused to go to bed on any terms, but persisted in sitting up in a rocking-chair, with his hat and mittens on, until daybreak.

I thought I should never get to sleep. The moment I drifted off in a doze I fell to laughing and woke myself up. But toward morning slumber overtook me, and I had a series of disagreeable dreams, in one of which I was waited upon by the ghost of Silas Trefethen with an exorbitant bill for the use of his guns. In another, I was dragged before a

court-martial and sentenced by Sailor Ben, in a
frizzled wig and three-cornered cocked hat, to be
shot to death by Bailey's Battery—a sentence which
Sailor Ben was about to execute with his own hand,
when I suddenly opened my eyes and found the sunshine lying pleasantly across my face. I tell you I
was glad!

That unaccountable fascination which leads the
guilty to hover about the spot where his crime was
committed drew me down to the wharf as soon as I
was dressed. Phil Adams, Jack Harris, and others
of the conspirators were already there, examining with
a mingled feeling of curiosity and apprehension the
havoc accomplished by the battery.

The fence was badly shattered and the ground
plowed up for several yards round the place where
the guns formerly lay—formerly lay, for now they
were scattered every which way. There was scarcely
a gun that hadn't burst. Here was one ripped open
from muzzle to breech, and there was another with
its mouth blown into the shape of a trumpet. Three
of the guns had disappeared bodily, but on looking
over the edge of the wharf we saw them standing on
end in the tide mud. They had popped overboard
in their excitement.

"I tell you what, fellows," whispered Phil Adams,
"it is lucky we didn't try to touch 'em off with punk.
They'd have blown us all to flinders."

The destruction of Bailey's Battery was not, unfortunately, the only catastrophe. A fragment of one of the cannon had carried away the chimney of Sailor Ben's cabin. He was very mad at first, but having prepared the fuse himself he didn't dare complain openly.

"I'd have taken a reef in the blessed stovepipe," said the Admiral, gazing ruefully at the smashed chimney, "if I had known as how the Flagship was agoin' to be under fire."

The next day he rigged out an iron funnel, which, being in sections, could be detached and taken in at a moment's notice. On the whole, I think he was resigned to the demolition of his brick chimney. The stovepipe was a great deal more shipshape.

The town was not so easily appeased. The selectman determined to make an example of the guilty parties, and offered a reward for their arrest, holding out a promise of pardon to any one of the offenders who would furnish information against the rest. But there were no faint hearts among the Centipedes. Suspicion rested for a while on several persons—on the soldiers at the fort; on a crazy fellow, known about town as "Bottle-Nose"; and at last on Sailor Ben.

"Shiver my timbers!" cries that deeply injured individual. "Do you suppose, sir, as I have lived to sixty year, an' ain't got no more sense than to go for to blaze away at my own upper riggin? It doesn't stand to reason."

It certainly did not seem probable that Mr.

Watson would maliciously knock over his own chimney, and Lawyer Hackett, who had the case in hand, bowed himself out of the Admiral's cabin convinced that the right man had not been discovered.

People living by the sea are always more or less superstitious. Stories of specter ships and mysterious beacons, that lure vessels out of their course and wreck them on unknown reefs, were among the stock legends of Rivermouth, and not a few people in the town were ready to attribute the firing of those guns to some supernatural agency. The Oldest Inhabitant remembered that when he was a boy a dim-looking sort of schooner hove to in the offing one foggy afternoon, fired off a single gun that didn't make any report, and then crumbled to nothing, spar, mast, and hulk, like a piece of burned paper.

The authorities, however, were of the opinion that human hands had something to do with the explosions, and they resorted to deep-laid stratagems to get hold of the said hands. One of their traps came very near catching us. They artfully caused an old brass fieldpiece to be left on a wharf near the scene of our late operations. Nothing in the world but the lack of money to buy powder saved us from falling into the clutches of the two watchmen who lay secreted for a week in a neighboring sail loft.

It was many a day before the midnight bombardment ceased to be the town talk. The trick was so audacious and on so grand a scale that nobody thought for an instant of connecting us lads with it. Suspicion at length grew weary of lighting on the wrong person, and as conjecture—like the physicians in the epitah—was in vain, the Rivermouthians gave up the idea of finding out who had astonished them.

They never did find out, and never will, unless they read this veracious history. If the selectmen are still disposed to punish the malefactors, I can supply Lawyer Hackett with evidence enough to convict Pepper Whitcomb, Phil Adams, Charley Marden, and the other honorable members of the Centipede Club. But really I don't think it would pay now.

CHAPTER XVIII

A FROG HE WOULD A-WOOING GO

IF the reader supposes that I lived all this while in Rivermouth without falling a victim to one or more of the young ladies attending Miss Dorothy Gibbs's Female Institute, why, then, all I have to say is the reader exhibits his ignorance of human nature.

Miss Gibbs's seminary was located within a few minutes' walk of the Temple Grammar School, and numbered about thirty-five pupils, the majority of whom boarded at the Hall—Primrose Hall, as Miss Dorothy prettily called it. The Primroses, as we called them, ranged from seven years of age to sweet seventeen, and a prettier group of sirens never got together even in Rivermouth; for Rivermouth, you should know, is famous for its pretty girls.

There were tall girls and short girls, rosy girls and pale girls, and girls as brown as berries; girls like Amazons, slender girls, weird and winning like Undine, girls with black tresses, girls with auburn ringlets, girls with every tinge of golden hair. To behold Miss Dorothy's young ladies of a Sunday morning walking to church two by two, the smallest toddling at the end of the procession, like the bobs at the tail of a kite, was a spectacle to fill with tender emotion the least susceptible heart. To see Miss Dorothy marching grimly at the head of her light infantry, was to feel the hopelessness of making an attack on any part of the column.

She was a perfect dragon of watchfulness. The most unguarded lifting of an eyelash in the fluttering battalion was sufficient to put her on the lookout. She had had experiences with the male sex, this Miss Dorothy so prim and grim. It was whispered that her heart was a tattered album scrawled over with love lines, but that she had shut up the volume long ago.

There was a tradition that she had been crossed in love; but it was the faintest of traditions. A gay young lieutenant of marines had flirted with her at a country ball (A. D. 1811), and then marched carelessly away at the head of his company to the shrill music of the fife, without so much as a sigh for the girl he left behind him. The years rolled on, the gallant gay Lothario—which wasn't his name— married, became a father, and then a grandfather; and at the period of which I am speaking his grandchild was actually one of Miss Dorothy's young ladies. So, at least, ran the story.

The lieutenant himself was dead these many years; but Miss Dorothy never got over his duplicity. She was convinced that the sole aim of mankind was to win the unguarded affection of maidens, and then march off treacherously with flying colors to the heartless music of the drum and fife. To shield the inmates of Primrose Hall from the bitter influences that had blighted her own early affections was Miss Dorothy's mission in life.

"No wolves prowling about my lambs, if you please," said Miss Dorothy. "I will not allow it."

She was as good as her word. I don't think the boy lives who ever set foot within the limits of Primrose Hall while the seminary was under her charge. Perhaps if Miss Dorothy had given her young ladies a little more liberty, they would not have thought it "such fun" to make eyes over the white lattice fence at the young gentlemen of the Temple Grammar School. I say perhaps; for it is one thing to manage thirty-five young ladies and quite another thing to talk about it.

But all Miss Dorothy's vigilance could not prevent the young folks from meeting in the town now and then, nor could her utmost ingenuity interrupt postal arrangements. There was no end of notes passing between the students and the Primroses. Notes tied to the heads of arrows were shot into dormitory windows; notes were tucked under fences, and hidden in the trunks of decayed trees. Every thick place in the boxwood hedge that surrounded the seminary was a possible post office.

It was a terrible shock to Miss Dorothy the day she unearthed a nest of letters in one of the huge wooden urns surmounting the gateway that led to

All Miss Dorothy's vigilance could not prevent the young folks from
hiding notes in the trunks of decayed trees

her dovecot. It was a bitter moment to Miss Phœbe and Miss Candace and Miss Hesba, when they had their locks of hair grimly handed back to them by Miss Gibbs in the presence of the whole school. Girls whose locks of hair had run the blockade in safety were particularly severe on the offenders. But it didn't stop other notes and other tresses, and I would like to know what can stop them while the earth holds together.

Now when I first came to Rivermouth I looked upon girls as rather tame company; I hadn't a spark of sentiment concerning them; but seeing my comrades sending and receiving mysterious epistles, wearing bits of ribbon in their buttonholes and leaving packages of confectionery (generally lemon drops) in the hollow trunks of trees—why, I felt that this was the proper thing to do. I resolved, as a matter of duty, to fall in love with somebody, and I didn't care in the least who it was. In much the same mood that Don Quixote selected the Dulcinea del Toboso for his ladylove, I singled out one of Miss Dorothy's incomparable ladies for mine.

I debated a long while whether I should not select two, but at last settled down on one—a pale little girl with blue eyes, named Alice. I shall not make a long story of this, for Alice made short work of me. She was secretly in love with Pepper Whitcomb. This occasioned a temporary coolness between Pepper and myself.

Not disheartened, however, I placed Laura Rice
—I believe it was Laura Rice—in the vacant niche.
The new idol was more cruel than the old. The
former frankly sent me to the right about, but the
latter was a deceitful lot. She wore my nosegay
in her dress at the evening service (the Primroses
were marched to church three times every Sunday),
she penned me the daintiest of notes, she sent me the
glossiest of ringlets (cut, as I afterwards found out,
from the stupid head of Miss Gibbs's chamber-
maid), and at the same time was holding me and my
pony up to ridicule in a series of letters written to
Jack Harris. It was Harris himself who kindly
opened my eyes.

"I tell you what, Bailey," said that young gentleman, "Laura is an old veteran, and carries too many
guns for a youngster. She can't resist a flirtation;
I believe she'd flirt with an infant in arms. There's
hardly a fellow in the school that hasn't worn her
colors and some of her hair. She doesn't give out
any more of her own hair now. It's been pretty well
used up. The demand was greater than the supply,
you see. It's all very well to correspond with Laura,
but as to looking for anything serious from her, the
knowing ones don't. Hope I haven't hurt your
feelings, old boy" (that was a soothing stroke of
flattery to call me "old boy"), "but 'twas my duty
as a friend and a Centipede to let you know who you
were dealing with."

Such was the advice given me by that time-stricken, careworn, and embittered man of the world, who was sixteen years old if he was a day.

I dropped Laura. In the course of the next twelve months I had perhaps three or four similar experiences, and the conclusion was forced upon me that I was not a boy likely to distinguish myself in this branch of business.

I fought shy of Primrose Hall from that moment. Smiles were smiled over the boxwood hedge, and little hands were occasionally kissed to me; but I only winked my eye patronizingly, and passed on. I never renewed tender relations with Miss Gibbs's young ladies. All this occurred during my first year and a half at Rivermouth.

Between my studies at school, my outdoor recreations, and the hurts my vanity received, I managed to escape for the time being my very serious attack of that love fever which, like the measles, is almost certain to seize upon a boy sooner or later. I was not to be an exception. I was merely biding my time. The incidents I have now to relate took place shortly after the events described in the last chapter.

In a life so tranquil and circumscribed as ours in the Nutter House, a visitor was a novelty of no little importance. The whole household awoke from its quietude one morning when the Captain announced that a young niece of his from New York was to spend a few weeks with us.

The blue-chintz room, into which a ray of sun was never allowed to penetrate, was thrown open and dusted, and its moldy air made sweet with a bouquet of pot roses placed on the old-fashioned bureau. Kitty was busy all the forenoon washing off the sidewalk and sandpapering the great brass knocker on our front door; and Miss Abigail was up to her elbows in a pigeon pie.

I felt sure it was for no ordinary person that all these preparations were in progress; and I was right. Miss Nelly Glentworth was no ordinary person. I shall never believe she was. There may have been lovelier women, though I have never seen them; there may have been more brilliant women; though it has not been my fortune to meet them; but that there was ever a more charming one than Nelly Glentworth is a proposition against which I contend.

I don't love her now. I don't think of her once in five years; and yet it would give me a turn if in the course of my daily walk I should suddenly come upon her eldest boy. I may say that her eldest boy was not playing a prominent part in this life when I first made her acquaintance.

It was a drizzling, cheerless afternoon toward the end of summer that a hack drew up at the door of the Nutter House. The Captain and Miss Abigail hastened into the hall on hearing the carriage stop. In a moment more Miss Nelly Glentworth was seated in our sitting room undergoing a critical examination at the hands of a small boy who lounged uncomfortably on a settee between the windows.

The small boy considered himself a judge of girls, and he rapidly came to the following conclusions: That Miss Nelly was about nineteen; that she had not given away much of her black hair, which hung in two massive chestnut braids over her shoulders; that she was a shade too pale and a trifle too tall; that her hands were nicely shaped and her feet much too diminutive for daily use. He furthermore observed that her voice was musical, and that her face lighted up with an indescribable brightness when she smiled.

On the whole, the small boy liked her well enough and, satisfied that she was not a person to be afraid of, but, on the contrary, one who might be made quite agreeable, he departed to keep an appointment with his friend Sir Pepper Whitcomb.

But the next morning when Miss Glentworth came down to breakfast in a purple dress, her face as fresh as one of the moss roses on the bureau up stairs, and her laugh as contagious as the merriment of a robin, the small boy experienced a strange sensation, and mentally compared her with the loveliest of Miss Gibbs's young ladies, and found those young ladies wanting in the balance.

A night's rest had wrought a wonderful change in Miss Nelly. The pallor and weariness of the journey had passed away. I looked at her through the toast rack and thought I had never seen anything more winning than her smile.

After breakfast she went out with me to the stable to see Gypsy, and the three of us became friends then and there. Nelly was the only girl that Gypsy ever took the slightest notice of.

It chanced to be a half holiday, and a baseball match of unusual interest was to come off on the school ground that afternoon; but, somehow, I didn't go. I hung about the house abstractedly. The Captain went up town, and Miss Abigail was busy in the kitchen making immortal gingerbread. I drifted into the sitting room, and had our guest all to myself for I don't know how many hours. It was twilight, I recollect, when the Captain returned with letters for Miss Nelly.

Many a time after that I sat with her through the dreamy September afternoons. If I had played baseball it would have been much better for me.

Those first days of Miss Nelly's visit are very misty in my remembrance. I try in vain to remember just when I began to fall in love with her. Whether the spell worked upon me gradually or fell upon me all at once, I don't know. I only know that it seemed to me as if I had always loved her. Things that took place before she came were dim to me, like events that had occurred in the Middle Ages.

Nelly was at least five years my senior. But what

of that? Adam is the only man I ever heard of who didn't in early youth fall in love with a woman older than himself, and I am convinced that he would have done so if he had had the opportunity.

I wonder if girls from fifteen to twenty are aware of the glamour they cast over the straggling, awkward boys whom they regard and treat as mere children? I wonder, now. Young women are so keen in such matters. I wonder if Miss Nelly Glentworth never suspected until the very last night of her visit at Rivermouth that I was over ears in love with her pretty self, and was suffering pangs as poignant as if I had been ten feet high and as old as Methuselah? For, indeed, I was miserable throughout all those five weeks. I went down in the Latin class at the rate of three boys a day. Her fresh young eyes came between me and my books, and there was an end of Vergil.

> "O love, love, love!
>   Love is like a dizziness,
>   It winna let a body
>   Gang aboot his business."

I was wretched away from her, and only less wretched in her presence. The especial cause of my woe was this: I was simply a little boy to Miss Glentworth. I knew it. I bewailed it. I ground my teeth and wept in secret over the fact. If I had been aught else in her eyes would she have smoothed my hair so carelessly, sending an electric shock through my whole system? Would she have walked with me, hand in hand, for hours in the old garden? And once when I lay on the sofa, my head aching with love and mortification, would she have stooped down and kissed me if I hadn't been a little boy? How I despised little boys! How I hated one particular little boy—too little to be loved!

I smile over this very grimly even now. My sorrow was genuine and bitter. It is a great mistake on the part of elderly ladies, male and female, to tell a child that he is seeing his happiest days. Don't you be-believe a word of it, my friend. The burdens of child-hood are as hard to bear as the crosses that weigh us down later in life, while the happinesses of child-hood are tame compared with those of our maturer years. And even if this were not so, it is rank cruelty to throw shadows over the young heart by croaking, "Be merry, for tomorrow you die!"

As the last days of Nelly's visit drew near, I fell into a very unhealthy state of mind. To have her so frank and unconsciously coquettish with me was a daily torment; to be looked upon and treated as a child was bitter almonds; but the thought of losing her altogether was distraction.

The summer was at an end. The days were per-ceptibly shorter, and now and then came an evening when it was chilly enough to have a wood fire in our sitting room. The leaves were beginning to take hectic tints, and the wind was practicing the minor pathetic notes of its autumnal dirge. Nature and myself appeared to be approaching our dissolution simultaneously.

One evening, the evening previous to the day set for Nelly's departure—how well I remember it!—I found her sitting alone by the wide chimney piece looking musingly at the crackling backlog. There were no candles in the room. On her face and hands, and on the small golden cross at her throat, fell the flickering firelight—that ruddy, mellow firelight in which one's grandmother would look poetical.

I drew a low stool from the corner and placed it by the side of her chair. She reached out her hand to me, as was her pretty fashion, and so we sat for several moments silently in the changing glow of the burning logs. At length I moved back the stool so that I could see her face in profile without being seen by her. I lost her hand by this movement, but I couldn't have spoken with the listless touch of her fingers on mine. After two or three attempts I said "Nelly" a good deal louder than I intended.

Perhaps the effort it cost me was evident in my voice. She raised herself quickly in the chair and half turned toward me.

"Well, Tom?"

"I—I am very sorry you are going away."

"So am I. I have enjoyed every hour of my visit."

"Do you think you will ever come back here?"

"Perhaps," said Nelly, and her eyes wandered off into the fitful firelight.

"I suppose you will forget us all very quickly."

"Indeed I shall not. I shall always have the pleasantest memories of Rivermouth."

Here the conversation died a natural death. Nelly sank into a sort of dream, and I meditated. Fearing every moment to be interrupted by some member of the family, I nerved myself to make a bold dash.

"Nelly."

"Well."

"Do you—" I hesitated.

"Do I what?"

"Love anyone very much?"

"Why, of course I do," said Nelly, scattering her revery with a merry laugh. "I love Uncle Nutter, and Aunt Nutter, and you—and Towser."

Towser, our new dog! I couldn't stand that. I pushed back the stool impatiently and stood in front of her.

"That's not what I mean," I said angrily.

"Well, what do you mean?"

"Do you love anyone to marry him?"

"The idea of it," cried Nelly, laughing.

"But you must tell me."

"Must, Tom?"

"Indeed you must, Nelly."

She had risen from the chair with an amused, perplexed look in her eyes. I held her an instant by the dress.

"Please tell me."

"Oh, you silly boy!" cried Nelly. Then she rumpled my hair all over my forehead and ran laughing out of the room.

Suppose Cinderella had rumpled the prince's hair all over his forehead, how would he have liked it? Suppose the Sleeping Beauty, when the King's son with a kiss set her and all the old clocks agoing in the spell-bound castle—suppose the young minx had looked up and coolly laughed in his eye, I guess the king's son wouldn't have been greatly pleased.

I hesitated a second or two and then rushed after Nelly just in time to run against Miss Abigail, who entered the room with a couple of lighted candles.

"Goodness gracious, Tom!" exclaimed Miss Abigail, "are you possessed?"

I left her scraping the warm spermaceti from one of her thumbs.

Nelly was in the kitchen talking quite unconcernedly with Kitty Collins. There she remained until supper time. Supper over, we all adjourned to the sitting room. I planned and plotted, but could manage in no way to get Nelly alone. She and the Captain played cribbage all the evening.

The next morning my lady did not make her appearance until we were seated at the breakfast table. I had got up at daylight myself. Immediately after

breakfast the carriage arrived to take her to the railway station. A gentleman stepped from this carriage,
and greatly to my surprise was welcomed by the
Captain and Miss Abigail, and by Miss Nelly herself, who seemed unnecessarily glad to see him. From
the hasty conversation that followed I learned that
the gentleman had come somewhat unexpectedly to
conduct Miss Nelly to Boston. But how did he
know that she was to leave that morning? Nelly
bade farewell to the Captain and Miss Abigail, made
a little rush and kissed me on the nose, and was
gone.

As the wheels of the hack rolled up the street and
over my finer feelings, I turned to the Captain.

"Who was that gentleman, sir?"

"That was Mr. Waldron."

"A relation of yours, sir?" I asked craftily.

"No relation of mine—a relation of Nelly's,"
said the Captain, smiling.

"A cousin," I suggested, feeling a strange hatred
spring up in my bosom for the unknown.

"Well, I suppose you might call him a cousin for
the present. He's going to marry little Nelly next
summer."

In one of Peter Parley's valuable historical works
is a description of an earthquake at Lisbon. "At the
first shock the inhabitants rushed into the streets;
the earth yawned at their feet, and the houses tottered
and fell on every side." I staggered past the Captain

15

into the street; a giddiness came over me; the earth yawned at my feet, and the houses threatened to fall in on every side of me. How distinctly I remember that momentary sense of confusion when everything in the world seemed toppling over into ruins.

As I have remarked, my love for Nelly is a thing of the past. I had not thought of her for years until I sat down to write this chapter, and yet, now that all is said and done, I shouldn't care particularly to come across Mrs. Waldron's eldest boy in my afternoon's walk. He must be fourteen or fifteen years old by this time—the young villain!

CHAPTER XIX

I BECOME A BLIGHTED BEING

WHEN a young boy gets to be an old boy, when the hair is growing rather thin on the top of the old boy's head, and he has been tamed sufficiently to take a sort of chastened pleasure in allowing the baby to play with his watch seals— when, I say, an old boy has reached this stage in the journey of life, he is sometimes apt to indulge in sportive remarks concerning his first love.

Now, though I bless my stars that it wasn't in my power to marry Miss Nelly, I am not going to deny my boyish regard for her nor laugh at it. As long as it lasted it was a very sincere and unselfish love, and rendered me proportionately wretched. I say as long as it lasted, for one's first love doesn't last forever.

I am ready, however, to laugh at the amusing figure I cut after I had really ceased to have any deep feeling in the matter. It was then I took it into my head to be a Blighted Being. This was about two weeks after the spectral appearance of Mr. Waldron.

For a boy of a naturally vivacious disposition the part of a blighted being presented difficulties. I had an excellent appetite, I liked society, I liked out-of-door sports, I was fond of handsome clothes. Now

219

all these things were incompatible with the doleful character I was to assume, and I proceeded to cast them from me. I neglected my hair. I avoided my playmates. I frowned abstractedly. I didn't eat as much as was good for me. I took lonely walks. I brooded in solitude. I not only committed to memory the more turgid poems of the late Lord Byron— "Fare thee well, and if forever," etc.—but I became a despondent poet on my own account, and composed a string of "Stanzas to One who will understand them." I think I was a trifle too hopeful on that point; for I came across the verses several years afterwards, and was quite unable to understand them myself.

It was a great comfort to be so perfectly miserable and yet not suffer any. I used to look in the glass and gloat over the amount and variety of mournful expressions I could throw into my features. If I caught myself smiling at anything, I cut the smile short with a sigh. The oddest thing about all this is, I never once suspected, that I was not unhappy. No one, not even Pepper Whitcomb, was more deceived than I.

Among the minor pleasures of being blighted were the interest and perplexity I excited in the simple souls that were thrown in daily contact with me, Pepper especially. I nearly drove him into a corresponding state of mind.

I had from time to time given Pepper slight but impressive hints of my admiration for Someone (this was in the early part of Miss Glentworth's visit); I had also led him to infer that my admiration was not altogether in vain. He was therefore unable to explain the cause of my strange behavior, for I had carefully refrained from mentioning to Pepper the fact that Someone had turned out to be Another's.

I treated Pepper shabbily. I couldn't resist playing on his tenderer feelings. He was a boy bubbling over with sympathy for anyone in any kind of trouble. Our intimacy since Binny Wallace's death had been uninterrupted; but now I moved in a sphere apart, not to be profaned by the step of an outsider.

I no longer joined the boys on the playground at recess. I stayed at my desk reading some lugubrious volume—usually The Mysteries of Udolpho, by the amiable Mrs. Radcliffe. A translation of The Sorrows of Werter fell into my hands at this period, and if I could have committed suicide without killing myself, I should certainly have done so.

On half holidays, instead of fraternizing with Pepper and the rest of our clique, I would wander off alone to Grave Point.

Grave Point—the place where Binny Wallace's body came ashore—was a narrow strip of land running out into the river. A line of Lombardy poplars, stiff and severe, like a row of grenadiers, mounted guard on the waterside. On the extreme end of the peninsula was an old disused graveyard, tenanted principally by the early settlers who had been scalped by the

Indians. In a remote corner of the cemetery, set apart from the other mounds, was the grave of a woman who had been hanged in the old colonial times for the murder of her infant. Goodwife Polly Haines had denied the crime to the last, and after her death there had arisen strong doubts as to her actual guilt. It was a belief current among the lads of the town, that if you went to this grave at nightfall on the 10th of November—the anniversary of her execution—and asked, "For what did the magistrates hang you?" a voice would reply, "Nothing."

Many a Rivermouth boy has tremblingly put this question in the dark, and, sure enough, Polly Haines invariably answered nothing!

A low red-brick wall, broken down in many places and frosted over with silvery moss, surrounded this burial ground of our Pilgrim Fathers and their immediate descendants. The latest date on any of the headstones was 1780. A crop of very funny epitaphs sprung up here and there among the overgrown thistles and burdocks, and almost every tablet had a death's-head with crossbones engraved upon it, or else a puffy, round face with a pair of wings stretching out from the ears, like this:

These mortuary emblems furnished me with congenial food for reflection. I used to lie in the long grass, and speculate on the advantages and disadvantages of being a cherub.

I forget what I thought the advantages were, but I remember distinctly of getting into an inextricable tangle on two points: How could a cherub, being all head and wings, manage to sit down when he was tired? To have to sit down on the back of his head struck me as an awkward alternative. Again, where did a cherub carry those indispensable articles (such as jackknives, marbles, and pieces of twine) which boys in an earthly state of existence usually stow away in their trousers pockets?

These were knotty questions, and I was never able to dispose of them satisfactorily.

Meanwhile Pepper Whitcomb would scour the whole town in search of me. He finally discovered my retreat, and dropped in on me abruptly one afternoon, while I was deep in the cherub problem.

"Look here, Tom Bailey!" said Pepper, shying a piece of clam shell indignantly at the *Hic jacet* on a neighboring gravestone, "you are just going to the dogs! Can't you tell a fellow what in thunder ails you, instead of prowling round among the tombs like a jolly old vampire?"

"Pepper," I replied, solemnly, "don't ask me. All is not well here"—touching my breast mysteriously. If I had touched my head instead, I should have been nearer the mark. Pepper stared at me.

"Earthly happiness," I continued, "is a delusion

and a snare. You will never be happy, Pepper, until you are a cherub."

Pepper, by the by, would have made an excellent cherub, he was so chubby. Having delivered myself of these gloomy remarks, I arose languidly from the grass and moved away, leaving Pepper staring after me in mute astonishment. I was Hamlet and Werter and the late Lord Byron all in one.

You will ask what my purpose was in cultivating this factitious despondency. None whatever, Blighted beings never have any purpose in life excepting to be as blighted as possible.

Of course my present line of business could not long escape the eye of Captain Nutter. I don't know if the Captain suspected my attachment for Miss Glentworth. He never alluded to it; but he watched me. Miss Abigail watched me, Kitty Collins watched me, and Sailor Ben watched me.

"I can't make out his signals," I overheard the Admiral remark to my grandfather one day. "I hope he ain't got no kind of sickness aboard."

There was something singularly agreeable in being an object of so great interest. Sometimes I had all I could do to preserve my dejected aspect, it was so pleasant to be miserable. I incline to the opinion that people who are melancholy without any particular reason, such as poets, artists, and young musicians with long hair, have rather an enviable time of it. In a quiet way I never enjoyed myself better in my life than when I was a Blighted Being.

Chapter XX

IN WHICH I PROVE MYSELF TO BE THE GRANDSON OF MY GRANDFATHER

IT was not possible for a boy of my temperament to be a blighted being longer than three consecutive weeks.

I was gradually emerging from my self-imposed cloud when events took place that greatly assisted in restoring me to a more natural frame of mind. I awoke from an imaginary trouble to face a real one.

I suppose you don't know what a financial crisis is? I will give you an illustration.

You are deeply in debt—say to the amount of a quarter of a dollar—to the little knicknack shop round the corner, where they sell picture papers, spruce gum, needles, and Malaga raisins. A boy owes you a quarter of a dollar, which he promises to pay at a certain time. You are depending on this quarter to settle accounts with the small shopkeeper. The time arrives—and the quarter doesn't. That's a financial crisis, in one sense—in twenty-five senses, if I may say so.

When this same thing happens, on a grander scale, in the mercantile world, it produces what is called a panic. One man's inability to pay his debts

225

ruins another man, who, in turn, ruins someone else, and so on, until failure after failure makes even the richest capitalists tremble. Public confidence is suspended, and the smaller fry of merchants are knocked over like tenpins.

These commercial panics occur periodically, after the fashion of comets and earthquakes and other disagreeable things. Such a panic took place in New Orleans in the year 18—, and my father's banking house went to pieces in the crash.

Of a comparatively large fortune nothing remained after paying his debts excepting a few thousand dollars, with which he proposed to return North and embark in some less hazardous enterprise. In the meantime it was necessary for him to stay in New Orleans to wind up the business.

My grandfather was in some way involved in this failure, and lost, I fancy, a considerable sum of money; but he never talked much on the subject. He was an unflinching believer in the spilt-milk proverb.

"It can't be gathered up," he would say, "and it's no use crying over it. Pitch into the cow and get some more milk, is my motto."

The suspension of the banking house was bad enough, but there was an attending circumstance that gave us, at Rivermouth, a great deal more anxiety. The cholera, which someone predicted would visit the country that year, and which, indeed, had made its appearance in a mild form at several points along the Mississippi River, had broken out with much violence at New Orleans.

The report that first reached us through the newspapers was meager and contradictory; many people discredited it; but a letter from my mother left us no room for doubt. The sickness was in the city. The hospitals were filling up, and hundreds of the citizens were flying from the stricken place by every steamboat. The unsettled state of my father's affairs made it imperative for him to remain at his post; his desertion at that moment would have been at the sacrifice of all he had saved from the general wreck.

As he would be detained in New Orleans at least three months, my mother declined to come North without him.

After this we awaited with feverish impatience the weekly news that came to us from the South. The next letter advised us that my parents were well, and that the sickness, so far, had not penetrated to the faubourg, or district, where they lived. The following week brought less cheering tidings. My father's business, in consequence of the flight of the other partners, would keep him in the city beyond the period he had mentioned. The family had moved to Pass Christian, a favorite watering place on Lake Pontchartrain, near New Orleans, where he was able to spend part of each week. So the return North was postponed indefinitely.

It was now that the old longing to see my parents came back to me with irresistible force. I knew my grandfather would not listen to the idea of my going to New Orleans at such a dangerous time, since he had opposed the journey so strongly when the same objection did not exist. But I determined to go, nevertheless.

I think I have mentioned the fact that all the male members of our family, on my father's side—as far back as the Middle Ages—have exhibited in early youth a decided talent for running away. It was a hereditary talent. It ran in the blood to run away. I do not pretend to explain the peculiarity. I simply admit it.

It was not my fate to change the prescribed order of things. I, too, was to run away, thereby proving, if any proof were needed, that I was the grandson of my grandfather. I do not hold myself responsible for the step any more than I do for the shape of my nose, which is said to be a facsimile of Captain Nutter's.

I have frequently noticed how circumstances conspire to help a man, or a boy, when he has thoroughly resolved on doing a thing. That very week the Rivermouth Barnacle printed an advertisement that seemed to have been written on purpose for me. It read as follows:

WANTED.—A Few Able-Bodied Seamen and a Cabin Boy, for the ship "Rawlings," now loading for New Orleans at Johnson's Wharf, Boston. Apply in person, within four days, at the office of Messrs. —— —— & Co., or on board the Ship.

How I was to get to New Orleans with only $4.62 was a question that had been bothering me. This advertisement made it as clear as day. I would go as cabin boy.

I had taken Pepper into my confidence again; I had told him the story of my love for Miss Glentworth, with all its harrowing details; and now conceived it judicious to confide in him the change about to take place in my life, so that, if the "Rawlings" went down in a gale, my friends might have the limited satisfaction of knowing what had become of me.

Pepper shook his head discouragingly, and sought in every way to dissuade me from the step. He drew a disenchanting picture of the existence of a cabin boy, whose constant duty (according to Pepper) was to have dishes broken over his head whenever the captain or the mate chanced to be out of humor, which was mostly all the time. But nothing Pepper said could turn me a hair's breadth from my purpose.

I had little time to spare, for the advertisement stated explicity that applications were to be made in person within four days. I trembled to think of the bare possibility of some other boy snapping up that desirable situation.

It was on Monday I stumbled upon the advertisement. On Tuesday my preparations were completed. My baggage—consisting of four shirts, half a dozen collars, a piece of shoemaker's wax (Heaven knows what for!) and seven stockings, wrapped in a silk handkerchief—lay hidden under a loose plank of the stable floor. This was my point of departure.

My plan was to take the last train for Boston, in order to prevent the possibility of immediate pursuit, if any should be attempted. The train left at 4 P. M.

I ate no breakfast and little dinner that day. I avoided the Captain's eye, and wouldn't have looked Miss Abigail or Kitty in the face for the wealth of the Indies.

When it was time to start for the station I retired quietly to the stable and uncovered my bundle. I lingered a moment to kiss the white star on Gypsy's forehead, and was nearly unmanned when the little animal returned the caress by lapping my cheek. Twice I went back and patted her.

On reaching the station I purchased my ticket with a bravado air that ought to have aroused the suspicion of the ticket master, and hurried to the car, where I sat fidgeting until the train shot out into the broad daylight.

Then I drew a long breath and looked about me. The first object that saluted my sight was Sailor Ben, four or five seats behind me, reading the Rivermouth Barnacle!

Reading was not an easy art to Sailor Ben; he

I was nearly unmanned when Gypsy returned the caress by lapping
my cheek

grappled with the sense of a paragraph as if it were a
polar bear, and generally got the worst of it. On the
present occasion he was having a hard struggle,
judging by the way he worked his mouth and rolled
his eyes. He had evidently not seen me. But what
was he doing on the Boston train?

Without lingering to solve the question, I stole
gently from my seat and passed into the forward car.
This was very awkward, having the Admiral on
board. I couldn't understand it at all. Could it be
possible that the old boy got tired of land and was
running away to sea himself? That was too absurd.
I glanced nervously toward the car door now and
then, half expecting to see him come after me.

We had passed one or two way stations, and I had
quieted down a good deal, when I began to feel as if
somebody was looking steadily at the back of my
head. I turned round involuntarily, and there was
Sailor Ben again, at the farther end of the car, wrest-
ling with the Rivermouth Barnacle as before.

I began to grow very uncomfortable indeed. Was
it by design or chance that he thus dogged my steps?
If he was aware of my presence, why didn't he speak
to me at once? Why did he steal round, making no
sign, like a particularly unpleasant phantom? Maybe it wasn't Sailor Ben. I peeped at him slyly. There
was no mistaking that tanned, genial phiz of his.
Very odd he didn't see me!

Literature, even in the mild form of a country

newspaper, always had the effect of poppies on the Admiral. When I stole another glance in his direction his hat was tilted over his right eye in the most dissolute style, and the Rivermouth Barnacle lay in a confused heap beside him. He had succumbed. He was fast asleep. If he would only keep asleep until we reached our destination!

By and by I discovered that the rear car had been detached from the train at the last stopping place. This accounted satisfactorily for Sailor Ben's singular movements, and considerably calmed my fears. Nevertheless I did not like the aspect of things.

The Admiral continued to snooze like a good fellow and was snoring melodiously as we glided at a slackened pace over a bridge and into Boston.

I grasped my pilgrim's bundle, and, hurrying out of the car, dashed up the first street that presented itself.

It was a narrow, noisy, zigzag street, crowded with trucks and obstructed with bales and boxes of merchandise. I didn't pause to breathe until I had placed a respectable distance between me and the railway station. By this time it was nearly twilight.

I had got into the region of dwelling houses, and was about to seat myself on a doorstep to rest, when, lo! there was the Admiral trundling along on the opposite sidewalk, under a full spread of canvas, as he would have expressed it.

I was off again in an instant at a rapid pace; but

16

in spite of all I could do he held his own without any perceptible exertion. He had a very ugly gait to get away from, the Admiral. I didn't dare to run, for fear of being mistaken for a thief, a suspicion which my bundle would naturally lend color to.

I pushed ahead, however, at a brisk trot, and must have got over one or two miles—my pursuer neither gaining nor losing ground—when I concluded to surrender at discretion. I saw that Sailor Ben was determined to have me, and, knowing my man, I knew that escape was highly improbable.

So I turned round and waited for him to catch up with me, which he did in a few seconds, looking rather sheepish at first.

"Sailor Ben," said I, severely, "do I understand that you are dogging my steps?"

"Well, little messmate," replied the Admiral, rubbing his nose, which he always did when he was disconcerted, "I am kind o' followin' in your wake."

"Under orders?"

"Under orders."

"Under the Captain's orders?"

"Sure-ly."

"In other words, my grandfather has sent you to fetch me back to Rivermouth?"

"That's about it," said the Admiral, with a burst of frankness.

"And I must go with you whether I want to or not?"

"The Capen's very identical words!"

There was nothing to be done. I bit my lips with suppressed anger, and signified that I was at his disposal, since I couldn't help it. The impression was very strong in my mind that the Admiral wouldn't hesitate to put me in irons if I showed signs of mutiny.

It was too late to return to Rivermouth that night—a fact which I communicated to the old boy sullenly, inquiring at the same time what he proposed to do about it.

He said we would cruise about for some rations, and then make a night of it. I didn't condescend to reply, though I hailed the suggestion of something to eat with inward enthusiasm, for I had not taken enough food that day to keep life in a canary.

We wandered back to the railway station, in the waiting room of which was a kind of restaurant presided over by a severe-looking young lady. Here we had a cup of coffee apiece, several tough doughnuts, and some blocks of venerable sponge cake. The young lady who attended on us, whatever her age was then, must have been a mere child when that sponge cake was made.

The Admiral's acquaintance with Boston hotels was slight; but he knew of a quiet lodging house nearby, much patronized by sea captains, and kept by a former friend of his.

In this house, which had seen its best days, we

were accommodated with a moldy chamber containing two cot beds, two chairs, and a cracked pitcher on a washstand. The mantel shelf was ornamented with three big pink conch shells, resembling pieces of petrified liver; and over these hung a cheap lurid print, in which a United States sloop of war was giving a British frigate particular fits. It is very strange how our own ships never seem to suffer any in these terrible engagements. It shows what a nation we are.

An oil-lamp on a deal table cast a dismal glare over the apartment, which was cheerless in the extreme. I thought of our sitting room at home, with its flowery wall paper and gay curtains and soft lounges; I saw Major Elkanah Nutter (my grandfather's father) in powdered wig and Federal uniform, looking down benevolently from his gilt frame between the bookcases; I pictured the Captain and Miss Abigail sitting at the cosy round table in the moonlike glow of the astral lamp; and then I fell to wondering how they would receive me when I came back. I wondered if the Prodigal Son had any idea that his father was going to kill the fatted calf for him, and how he felt about it, on the whole.

Though I was very low in spirits, I put on a bold front to Sailor Ben, you will understand. To be caught and caged in this manner was a frightful shock to my vanity. He tried to draw me into conversation, but I answered in icy monosyllables. He again suggested we should make a night of it, and hinted broadly that he was game for any amount of riotous dissipation, even to the extent of going to see a play if I wanted to. I declined haughtily. I was dying to go.

He threw out a feeler on the subject of dominos and checkers, and observed in a general way that "seven up" was a capital game; but I repulsed him at every point.

I saw that the Admiral was beginning to feel hurt by my systematic coldness. We had always been such hearty friends until now. It was too bad of me to fret that tender, honest old heart even for an hour. I really did love the ancient boy, and when, in a disconsolate way, he ordered up a pitcher of beer, I unbent so far as to partake of some in a teacup. He recovered his spirits instantly, and took out his cuddy clay pipe for a smoke.

Between the beer and the soothing fragrance of the navy plug, I fell into a pleasanter mood myself, and, it being too late now to go to the theater, I condescended to say—addressing the northwest corner of the ceiling—that "seven up" was a capital game. Upon this hint the Admiral disappeared, and returned shortly with a very dirty pack of cards.

As we played, with varying fortunes, by the flickering flame of the lamp, he sipped his beer and became communicative. He seemed immensely tickled by the fact that I had come to Boston. It leaked out presently that he and the Captain had had a wager on the subject.

The discovery of my plans and who had discovered them were points on which the Admiral refused to throw any light. They had been discovered, however, and the Captain had laughed at the idea of my running away. Sailor Ben, on the contrary, had stoutly contended that I meant to slip cable and be off. Whereupon the Captain offered to bet him a dollar that I wouldn't go. And it was partly on account of this wager that Sailor Ben refrained from capturing me when he might have done so at the start.

Now, as the fare to and from Boston, with the lodging expenses, would cost him at least five dollars, I didn't see what he gained by winning the wager. The Admiral rubbed his nose violently when this view of the case presented itself.

I asked him why he didn't take me from the train at the first stopping place and return to Rivermouth by the down train at 4.30. He explained: having purchased a ticket for Boston, he considered himself bound to the owners (the stockholders of the road) to fulfil his part of the contract! To use his own words, he had "shipped for the viage."

This struck me as being so deliciously funny, that after I was in bed and the light was out, I couldn't help laughing aloud once or twice. I suppose the Admiral must have thought I was meditating another escape, for he made periodical visits to my bed throughout the night, satisfying himself by kneading me all over that I hadn't evaporated.

I was all there the next morning, when Sailor Ben half awakened me by shouting merrily, "All hands on deck!" The words rang in my ears like a part of my own dream, for I was at that instant climbing up the side of the "Rawlings" to offer myself as cabin boy.

The Admiral was obliged to shake me roughly two or three times before he could detach me from the dream. I opened my eyes with effort, and stared stupidly round the room. Bit by bit my real situation dawned on me. What a sickening sensation that is, when one is in trouble, to wake up feeling free for a moment, and then to find yesterday's sorrow all ready to go on again!

"Well, little messmate, how fares it?"

I was too much depressed to reply. The thought of returning to Rivermouth chilled me. How could I face Captain Nutter, to say nothing of Miss Abigail and Kitty? How the Temple Grammar School boys would look at me! How Conway and Seth Rodgers would exult over my mortification! And what if the Rev. Wibird Hawkins should allude to me in his next Sunday's sermon?

Sailor Ben was wise in keeping an eye on me, for after these thoughts took possession of my mind, I wanted only the opportunity to give him the slip.

The keeper of the lodgings did not supply meals

to his guests; so we breakfasted at a small chop-house in a crooked street on our way to the cars. The city was not astir yet, and looked glum and careworn in the damp morning atmosphere.

Here and there as we passed along was a sharp-faced shopboy taking down shutters; and now and then we met a seedy man who had evidently spent the night in a doorway. Such early birds and a few laborers with their tin kettles were the only signs of life to be seen until we came to the station, where I insisted on paying for my own ticket. I didn't relish being conveyed from place to place, like a felon changing prisons, at somebody else's expense.

On entering the car I sunk into a seat next the window, and Sailor Ben deposited himself beside me, cutting off all chance of escape.

The car filled up soon after this, and I wondered if there was anything in my mien that would lead the other passengers to suspect I was a boy who had run away and was being brought back.

A man in front of us—he was nearsighted, as I discovered later by his reading a guidebook with his nose—brought the blood to my cheeks by turning round and peering at me steadily. I rubbed a clear spot on the cloudy window glass at my elbow, and looked out to avoid him.

There, in the travelers' room, was the severe-looking young lady piling up her blocks of sponge cake in alluring pyramids and industriously in-

trenching herself behind a breastwork of squash pie.
I saw with cynical pleasure numerous victims walk
up to the counter and recklessly sow the seeds of
death in their constitutions by eating her doughnuts.
I had got quite interested in her, when the whistle
sounded and the train began to move.

The Admiral and I did not talk much on the
journey. I stared out of the window most of the
time, speculating as to the probable nature of the
reception in store for me at the terminus of the road.

What would the Captain say? and Mr. Grimshaw, what would he do about it? Then I thought
of Pepper Whitcomb. Dire was the vengeance I
meant to wreak on Pepper, for who but he had be-
trayed me? Pepper alone had been the repository
of my secret—perfidious Pepper!

As we left station after station behind us, I felt
less and less like encountering the members of our
family. Sailor Ben fathomed what was passing in
my mind, for he leaned over and said:

"I don't think as the Capen will bear down very
hard on you."

But it wasn't that. It wasn't the fear of any
physical punishment that might be inflicted; it was
a sense of my own folly that was creeping over me;
for during the long, silent ride I had examined my
conduct from every standpoint, and there was no
view I could take of myself in which I did not look
like a very foolish person indeed.

As we came within sight of the spires of River-mouth, I wouldn't have cared if the up train, which met us outside the town, had run into us and ended me.

Contrary to my expectation and dread, the Captain was not visible when we stepped from the cars. Sailor Ben glanced among the crowd of faces, apparently looking for him, too. Conway was there—he was always hanging about the station—and if he had intimated in any way that he knew of my disgrace and enjoyed it, I should have walked into him, I am certain.

But this defiant feeling entirely deserted me by the time we reached the Nutter House. The Captain himself opened the door.

"Come on board, sir," said Sailor Ben, scraping his left foot and touching his hat sea fashion.

My grandfather nodded to Sailor Ben, somewhat coldly I thought, and much to my astonishment kindly took me by the hand.

I was unprepared for this, and the tears, which no amount of severity would have wrung from me, welled up to my eyes.

The expression of my grandfather's face, as I glanced at it hastily, was grave and gentle; there was nothing in it of anger or reproof. I followed him into the sitting room, and, obeying a motion of his hand, seated myself on the sofa. He remained standing by the round table for a moment, lost in thought, then leaned over and picked up a letter.

It was a letter with a great black seal.

Chapter XXI

IN WHICH I LEAVE RIVERMOUTH

A LETTER with a great black seal!
I knew then what had happened as well as
I know it now. But which was it, father or
mother? I do not like to look back to the agony
and suspense of that moment.

My father had died at New Orleans during one
of his weekly visits to the city. The letter bearing
these tidings had reached Rivermouth the evening
of my flight—had passed me on the road by the down
train.

I must turn back for a moment to that eventful
evening. When I failed to make my appearance at
supper, the Captain began to suspect that I had
really started on my wild tour southward—a conjecture which Sailor Ben's absence helped to confirm.
I had evidently got off by the train and Sailor Ben
had followed me.

There was no telegraphic communication between Boston and Rivermouth in those days; so my
grandfather could do nothing but await the result.
Even if there had been another mail to Boston, he
could not have availed himself of it, not knowing
how to address a message to the fugitives. The

post office was naturally the last place either I or the Admiral would think of visiting.

My grandfather, however, was too full of trouble to allow this to add to his distress. He knew that the faithful old sailor would not let me come to any harm, and even if I had managed for the time being to elude him, was sure to bring me back sooner or later.

Our return, therefore, by the first train on the following day did not surprise him.

I was greatly puzzled, as I have said, by the gentle manner of his reception; but when we were alone together in the sitting room, and he began slowly to unfold the letter, I understood it all. I caught a sight of my mother's handwriting in the superscription, and there was nothing left to tell me.

My grandfather held the letter a few seconds irresolutely, and then commenced reading it aloud; but he could get no further than the date.

"I can't read it, Tom," said the old gentleman, breaking down. "I thought I could."

He handed it to me. I took the letter mechanically, and hurried away with it to my little room, where I had passed so many happy hours.

The week that followed the receipt of this letter is nearly a blank in my memory. I remember that the days appeared endless; that at times I could not realize the misfortune that had befallen us, and my heart upbraided me for not feeling a deeper grief; that a full sense of my loss would now and then sweep over me like an inspiration, and I would steal away to my chamber or wander forlornly about the gardens. I remember this, but little more.

As the days went by my first grief subsided, and in its place grew up a want which I have experienced at every step in life from boyhood to manhood. Often, even now, after all these years, when I see a lad of twelve or fourteen walking by his father's side, and glancing merrily up at his face, I turn and look after them, and am conscious that I have missed companionship most sweet and sacred.

I shall not dwell on this portion of my story. There were many tranquil, pleasant hours in store for me at that period, and I prefer to turn to them.

One evening the Captain came smiling into the sitting room with an open letter in his hand. My mother had arrived at New York, and would be with us the next day. For the first time in weeks—years, it seemed to me—something of the old cheerfulness mingled with our conversation round the evening lamp. I was to go to Boston with the Captain to meet her and bring her home. I need not describe that meeting. With my mother's hand in mine once more, all the long years we had been parted appeared like a dream. Very dear to me was the sight of that slender, pale woman passing from room to room, and lending a patient grace and beauty to the saddened life of the old house.

Everything was changed with us now. There

were consultations with lawyers, and signing of papers, and correspondence; for my father's affairs had been left in great confusion. And when these were settled, the evenings were not long enough for us to hear all my mother had to tell of the scenes she had passed through in the ill-fated city.

Then there were old times to talk over, full of reminiscences of Aunt Chloe and little black Sam. Little black Sam, by the by, had been taken by his master from my father's service ten months previously, and put on a sugar plantation near Baton Rouge. Not relishing the change, Sam had run away, and by some mysterious agency got into Canada, from which place he had sent back several indecorous messages to his late owner. Aunt Chloe was still in New Orleans, employed as nurse in one of the cholera hospital wards, and the Desmoulins, near neighbors of ours, had purchased the pretty stone house among the orange trees.

How all these simple details interested me will be readily understood by any boy who has been long absent from home.

I was sorry when it became necessary to discuss questions more nearly affecting myself. I had been removed from school temporarily, but it was decided, after much consideration, that I should not return, the decision being left, in a manner, in my own hands.

The Captain wished to carry out his son's intention and send me to college, for which I was nearly fitted; but our means did not admit of this. The Captain, too, could ill afford to bear the expense, for his losses by the failure of the New Orleans business had been heavy. Yet he insisted on the plan, not seeing clearly what other disposal to make of me.

In the midst of our discussions a letter came from my Uncle Snow, a merchant in New York, generously offering me a place in his counting house. The case resolved itself into this: If I went to college, I should have to depend on Captain Nutter for several years, and at the end of the collegiate course would have no settled profession. If I accepted my uncle's offer, I might hope to work my way to independence without loss of time. It was hard to give up the long-cherished dream of being a Harvard boy, but I gave it up.

The decision once made, it was Uncle Snow's wish that I should enter his counting house immediately. The cause of my good uncle's haste was this—he was afraid that I would turn out to be a poet before he could make a merchant of me. His fears were based upon the fact that I had published in the Rivermouth Barnacle some verses addressed in a familiar manner "To the Moon." Now, the idea of a boy, with his living to get, placing himself in communication with the moon, struck the mercantile mind as monstrous. It was not only a bad investment, it was lunacy.

We adopted Uncle Snow's view so far as to accede

to his proposition forthwith. My mother, I neglected to say, was also to reside in New York.

I shall not draw a picture of Pepper Whitcomb's disgust when the news was imparted to him, nor attempt to paint Sailor Ben's distress at the prospect of losing his little messmate.

In the excitement of preparing for the journey I didn't feel any very deep regret myself. But when the moment came for leaving, and I saw my small trunk lashed up behind the carriage, then the pleasantness of the old life and a vague dread of the new came over me, and a mist filled my eyes, shutting out the group of schoolfellows, including all the members of the Centipede Club, who had come down to the house to see me off.

As the carriage swept round the corner, I leaned out of the window to take a last look at Sailor Ben's cottage, and there was the Admiral's flag flying at half-mast.

So I left Rivermouth, little dreaming that I was not to see the old place again for many and many a year.

Chapter XXII

EXEUNT OMNES

WITH the close of my schooldays at Rivermouth this modest chronicle ends.

The new life upon which I entered, the new friends and foes I encountered on the road, and what I did and what I did not, are matters that do not come within the scope of these pages. But before I write Finis to the record as it stands, before I leave it—feeling as if I were once more going away from my boyhood—I have a word or two to say concerning a few of the personages who have figured in the story, if you will allow me to call Gypsy a personage.

I am sure that the reader who has followed me thus far will be willing to hear what became of her, and Sailor Ben and Miss Abigail and the Captain.

First about Gypsy. A month after my departure from Rivermouth the Captain informed me by letter that he had parted with the little mare, according to agreement. She had been sold to the ring master of a traveling circus (I had stipulated on this disposal of her), and was about to set out on her travels. She did not disappoint my glowing anticipations, but became quite a celebrity in her way—by dancing the

17   249

polka to slow music on a pine-board ballroom constructed for the purpose.

I chanced once, a long while afterwards, to be in a country town where her troupe was giving exhibitions; I even read the gaudily illumined show bill, setting forth the accomplishments of

The Far-famed Italian Trick Pony,
Z U L E I K A ! !
FORMERLY OWNED BY
THE PRINCE SHAZ-ZAMAN OF DAMASCUS,

—but failed to recognize my dear little Mustang girl behind those high-sounding titles, and so, alas! did not attend the performance. I hope all the praises she received and all the spangled trappings she wore did not spoil her; but I am afraid they did, for she was always overmuch given to the vanities of this world!

Miss Abigail regulated the domestic destinies of my grandfather's household until the day of her death, which Dr. Theophilus Tredick solemnly averred was hastened by the inveterate habit she had contracted of swallowing unknown quantities of hot drops whenever she fancied herself out of sorts. Eighty-seven empty phials were found in a bonnet box on a shelf in her bedroom closet.

The old house became very lonely when the family got reduced to Captain Nutter and Kitty; and when Kitty passed away, my grandfather divided his time between Rivermouth and New York.

Sailor Ben did not long survive his little Irish lass, as he always fondly called her. At his demise, which took place about six years since, he left his property in trust to the managers of a "Home for Aged Mariners." In his will, which was a very whimsical document—written by himself, and worded with much shrewdness, too—he warned the Trustees that when he got "aloft" he intended to keep his "weather eye" on them, and should send "a speritual shot across their bows" and bring them to, if they didn't treat the Aged Mariners handsomely.

He also expressed a wish to have his body stitched up in a shotted hammock and dropped into the harbor; but as he did not strenuously insist on this, and as it was not in accordance with my grandfather's preconceived notions of Christian burial, the Admiral was laid to rest beside Kitty, in the Old South Burying Ground, with an anchor that would have delighted him neatly carved on his headstone.

I am sorry the fire has gone out in the old ship's stove in that sky-blue cottage at the head of the wharf; I am sorry they have taken down the flagstaff and painted over the funny portholes; for I loved the old cabin as it was. They might have let it alone!

For several months after leaving Rivermouth I carried on a voluminous correspondence with Pepper Whitcomb; but it gradually dwindled down to a single letter a month, and then to none at all. But while he remained at the Temple Grammar School he kept me advised of the current gossip of the town and the doings of the Centipedes.

As one by one of the boys left the academy—Adams, Harris, Marden, Blake, and Langdon—to seek their fortunes elsewhere, there was less to interest me in the old seaport; and when Pepper himself went to Philadelphia to read law, I had no one to give me an inkling of what was going on.

There wasn't much to go on, to be sure. Great events no longer considered it worth their while to honor so quiet a place. One Fourth of July Temple Grammar School burned down—set on fire, it was supposed, by an eccentric squib that was seen to bolt into an upper window—and Mr. Grimshaw retired from public life, married, "and lived happily ever after," as the story books say.

The Widow Conway, I am able to state, did not succeed in enslaving Mr. Meeks, the apothecary, who united himself clandestinely to one of Miss Dorothy Gibbs's young ladies, and lost the patronage of Primrose Hall in consequence.

Young Conway went into the grocery business with his ancient chum, Rodgers—RODGERS & CONWAY! I read the sign only last summer when I was down in Rivermouth, and had half a mind to pop into the shop and shake hands with him, and ask him if he wanted to fight. I contented myself, however, with flattening my nose against his dingy shop window, and beheld Conway, in red whiskers and blue overalls, weighing out sugar for a customer —giving him short weight, I'll bet anything!

I have reserved my pleasantest word for the last. It is touching the Captain. The Captain is still hale and rosy, and if he doesn't relate his exploit in the war of 1812 as spiritedly as he used to, he makes up by relating it more frequently and telling it differently every time! He passes his winters in New York and his summers in the Nutter House, which threatens to prove a hard nut for the destructive gentleman with the scythe and the hourglass, for the seaward gable has not yielded a clapboard to the east wind these twenty years. The Captain has now become the Oldest Inhabitant in Rivermouth, and so I don't laugh at the Oldest Inhabitant any more, but pray in my heart that he may occupy the post of honor for half a century to come!

So ends the Story of a Bad Boy—but not such a very bad boy, as I told you to begin with.

FINIS

FAMILY GERRHOSAURIDAE

The family Gerrhosauridae is a small group of about two dozen species that are found mainly in South Africa and Madagascar. One of the more familiar species is the yellow-throated plated lizard, *Gerrhosaurus flavigularis*. Like many other members of its family, this species does well in a dry terrarium with rocky hiding places and a fairly high temperature. Some of the gerrhosaurids reach a length of two feet and all are oviparous.

FAMILY SCINCIDAE

Some of the most desirable and long-lived of the lizards belong to the family Scincidae. The life histories of only a few of the family's more than 600 species have been worked out in any detail. Known as skinks, they are mostly secretive reptiles that elude observation in the field. Larger members of the family reach two feet, but most skinks are tiny lizards of a few inches. Every continent has its skinks, but it is Australia that produces some of the most desirable types for captivity. The blue-tongued skinks (*Tiliqua scincoides*, *Tiliqua occipitalis*, *Tiliqua nigrolutea*) are large Australian lizards that are very similar in general appearance and habits. They live entirely on

Plated lizard, *Gerrhosaurus* sp. Photo by G. Marcuse.

False hognose snake, *Lioheterodon modestus*, Madagascar. Photo by H. Hansen, Aquarium Berlin.

Banded krait, *Bungarus fasciatus*. Photo by G. Marcuse.

Tentacled snake, *Herpeton tentacularum*. Photo by J. K. Langhammer.

the ground, move slowly, have broad and flat bodies with attractive crossbands or blotches, and flat, blue tongues. Large blue-tongues may reach two feet, but the average is closer to fifteen inches. They become very tame in captivity and do well on chopped raw beef particles mixed with raw beaten eggs. This may be varied with occasional feedings of insects or even young mice and birds. Under favorable conditions mating sometimes occurs; the babies are born alive after undergoing a primitive placental development within the body of the mother. Most live-bearing lizards simply retain the eggs, allowing them to hatch internally rather than buried in the earth or under a stone. With the blue-tongues and certain other skinks, the babies are nourished by the body of the parent while developing.

The skinks of the genus *Egernia* are a varied group, consisting of smooth-scaled types that burrow, others that have taken to a life in trees, and still others that live in rocky areas and have a coarse

Shingleback skink, *Trachydosaurus rugosus.* Photo by J. Warham.

scalation. Of the latter, the short-tailed spiny skink, *Egernia depressa*, and Cunningham's skink, *Egernia cunninghami*, are well known in zoological collections, where they thrive for many years if kept dry and warm. The oddest-looking Australian skink is the stump-tail or shingleback, *Trachydosaurus rugosus*. This inhabitant of dry areas has protruding scales and a short, thick tail. Coloration is some shade of brown or grayish black with lighter underparts. It is a large, thick-bodied lizard which may approach two feet in length in exceptional instances. Insects, snails, fruits, and flowers form the natural diet of Australian skinks, but all of these reptiles are re-

Red ground skink, *Lygosoma fernandi*, Africa. Photo by R.G. Sprackland, Jr.

markable in the ease with which they adjust to foods they never encounter in the wild state. Individuals have been kept for long periods on table scraps! The stump-tailed skink's babies are born alive and almost always number two. These are quite large and begin to forage for themselves at once.

FAMILY ANGUIDAE

It is interesting that two closely related members of the family Anguidae have established longevity records of a quarter of a century or more in captivity. One of these, the "slow-worm," is a diminutive reptile of about eighteen inches when fully grown. The other, the European glass snake, *Ophisaurus apodus*, is a robust lizard which may reach four feet. Both are limbless lizards, like many others of

Shield snake, *Aspidelaps scutatus*, South Africa. Photo by H. Hansen, Aquarium Berlin.

Egyptian cobra, *Naja hajae,* northern Africa. Photo by G. Marcuse.

Arizona coral snake, *Micruroides euryxanthus,* southwestern U.S. Photo by J. K. Langhammer.

their family. The slow-worm, *Anguis fragilis*, is probably the most satisfactory reptile one can keep in captivity where space is very limited. The species is serpentine of body and without limbs, progress being made in graceful undulations. The coloration of the slow-worm is subdued, yet quite attractive in its various shades of metallic brown. These small lizards become very tame, learning to recognize their keeper and feed readily from his fingers. They seem to display an intelligence that is out of keeping with their appearance. Breeding in captivity takes place frequently; the three-inch-long babies are born alive and raised easily on a diet of finely chopped beef and raw eggs, well-mixed and proffered in a shallow dish. Insects, earthworms, and slugs are taken with equal relish. A dish of water should be available always, and means of burrowing and hiding provided. A temperature range of 70 to 75 degrees is suitable.

The European glass snake is a large lizard and one which does exceedingly well in captivity. A simple cage with a layer of fine gravel and a good-sized container of water provides the essential requirements. Eggs and chopped beef—that standby of lizard keepers—is readily taken by captives, as well as a variety of arthropods and small vertebrate animals.

European glass snake, *Ophisaurus apodus*. Photo by G. Marcuse.

Spiny-tailed monitor, *Varanus acanthurus*, Australia. Photo by Muller-Schmida.

FAMILY VARANIDAE

Monitors (genus *Varanus*) belong to the family Varanidae. Some are small reptiles of less than a foot in total length, while others grow to a very large size. The Komodo dragon, *Varanus komodoensis*, may reach twelve feet and a weight of 300 pounds, making it the world's largest lizard. All of the monitors are tropical reptiles and should be kept at a temperature in the 80 to 90-degree range in captivity. They are active lizards, and freshly caught specimens can be expected to spend much of their time seeking a means of escape from their cage. Like snakes, they often rub their snouts sore in their probing of corners and attempts to push out screening or hardware cloth. Fortunately, most specimens will tame after a while. Some, though, remain hostile over long periods—lashing out with their tails upon the slightest provocation. Even a very small monitor can produce a stinging lash with its tail. If such a blow is inflicted on a hand, it will develop into a raised welt. The claws of monitors are long and very sharp and a carelessly handled wild monitor can do much damage with them as well as with its strong jaws. Monitors are amazingly strong animals, and it is quite difficult to hold one without being bitten. They do not readily relinquish a hold they have secured; any effort to pull a specimen away from a seized

Dark sea snake, *Astrotia stokesii,* Pacific Ocean. Photo by R. Steene.

Rhinoceros viper, *Bitis nasicornis.* Photo by J. K. Langhammer.

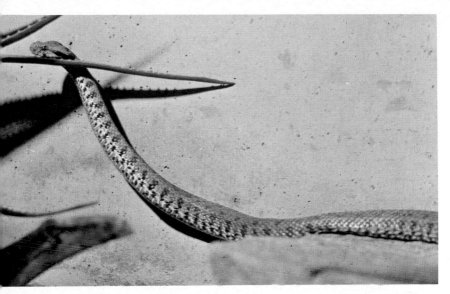

Radde's viper, *Vipera xanthina,* Armenia. Photo by Dr. Otto Kloe.

Gaboon viper, *Bitis gabonica.* Photo by J. K. Langhammer.

Tree monitor, *Varanus prasinus*. Photo by G. Marcuse.

object will only result in a tightening of the hold. A young Nile monitor, *Varanus niloticus*, once seized hold of a forefinger while I was moving it during cage-cleaning. Though only two feet in length, it produced a laceration which served as a practical illustration of what a big specimen could do. It refused to let go until placed under water.

In my opinion, the monitors are among the most interesting of reptiles. Some are extraordinarily beautiful animals, especially when young. None seems to grow very rapidly, though detailed observations are lacking in the literature. A baby water monitor, *Varanus salvator*, in my collection grew from 13 inches to 19 inches in less than a year. It could be expected that its subsequent growth would be at a slower pace.

A few of the monitors which are commonly imported are the lace monitor, *Varanus varius*, the yellow monitor, *Varanus flavescens*, and the sand monitor, *Varanus gouldii*. The tree monitor, *Varanus prasinus*, is an arboreal animal that seldom reaches the United States.

Ocellated monitor, *Varanus timorensis*, Australia. Photo by Dr. Otto Klee.

Palm viper, *Bothrops lateralis,* South America. Photo by G. Marcuse.

Russell's viper, *Vipera russelli.* Photo by H. Hansen, Aquarium Berlin.

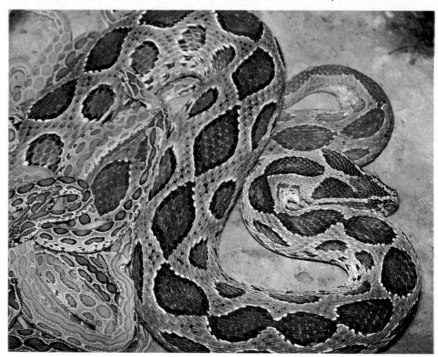

Bushmaster, *Lachesis muta.* Photo by H. Schultz.

Rough-neck monitor, *Varanus rudicollis,* Malaya to Borneo. Photo by Dr. Otto Klee.

Among the different species of monitors there is to be noted a difference in temperament similar to that found among the various species of crocodilians.

Monitors are carnivorous and will devour anything they are capable of dismembering and gulping down. The species which live in or near water will readily eat fish and some, like the water monitor, seem as well adapted to an aquatic existence as the crocodiles. Whole animals should be fed to monitors whenever this is possible, to provide the vitamins and minerals required to prevent the nutritional

Papuan monitor, *Varanus salvadorii,* Papua New Guinea. Photo by Dr. Otto Klee.

Copperhead, *Agkistrodon contortrix*, two subspecies. Photo by G. Marcuse.

Cantil, *Agkistrodon bilineatus*. Photo by J. K. Langhammer.

Eastern pigmy rattlesnake, *Sistrurus miliaris miliaris*. Photo by J. K. Langhammer.

deficiencies that develop among improperly cared-for monitors, especially the juveniles. If meat is fed, it should be fortified with bone meal and a multi-vitamin preparation. Rickets quickly manifests itself among young monitors that are not adequately nourished. A weakening of the rear limbs is the first symptom. Young monitors cannot be bought cheaply from retailers in the United States. Some kinds rarely come on the animal market at all.

Monitors do not require in their enclosures the imitative accessories of soil or rocks that are provided to other kinds of lizards. Ease of cage-cleaning should be the foremost consideration. Generally, this can be best accomplished with a plain floor covered with several thicknesses of paper. A large container of water should be available, and the aquatic species will spend much of their time submerged. It is a fascinating experience to raise a baby of one of the larger types. The Asiatic water monitor is a most attractive little creature during its early years and will quickly develop into a veritable pet. Monitors do not divest themselves of their tails, like some other lizards. Once lost, the tail of a monitor does not grow back. Small specimens should be handled like small crocodiles, a firm grasp being taken just back of the head while the other hand restrains the rear legs and supports that part of the reptile's body. With tame specimens, such precautions are unnecessary.

FAMILY AMPHISBAENIDAE

We will close our discussion of exotic lizards with a few remarks about the worm lizards of the family Amphisbaenidae. If it were not for the fact that they are sometimes offered for sale I would be inclined to bypass them in a general book on reptiles. Persistent burrowers, the worm lizards of the tropics are seldom seen above ground. Most burrowing reptiles do poorly in captivity unless provided with a means of tunneling through soil or sand. But the few accounts we have of the present strange creatures indicate that they will thrive in a container with only a thin layer of wood pulp which is kept moderately damp. The white-bellied worm lizard, *Amphisbaena alba*, is imported occasionally and is one of the larger species, measuring as much as two feet in length. It resembles a giant reddish earthworm. Worm lizards of this and other species may have little place in a small collection of reptiles, but any specimen would surely be a conversation piece among herptile enthusiasts!

Bornean earless monitor,
Lanthanotus borneensis
(above), Borneo. A very rare
family of one species, related to
the monitors. Photo by R. G.
Sprackland, Jr.

Flattened girdle-lizard,
Platysaurus torquatus (right),
southern Africa. The
Cordylidae is a rare family
with few species. Photo by
R. G. Sprackland, Jr.

Cape flattened girdle-lizard, *Platysaurus capensis*, southern Africa.
Photo by G. Marcuse.

Southern pigmy rattlesnake, *Sistrurus miliaris barbouri*. Photo by F. J. Dodd, Jr.

Western pigmy rattlesnake, *Sistrurus miliaris streckeri*. Photo by F. J. Dodd, Jr.

Massasauga, *Sistrurus catenatus*. Photo by J. K. Langhammer.

Eastern diamondback rattlesnake, *Crotalus adamanteus*. Photo by F. J. Dodd, Jr.

Tuatara, *Sphenodon punctatus*. Photo by Malcom Davis.

THE TUATARA

The tuataras of the order Rhynchocephalia, family Sphenodontidae, resemble somewhat the iguanids and the agamids. They are confined to the offshore islands of New Zealand, where they are under the strictest protection. Therefore, they are seldom seen in captivity.

In its habitat, the tuatara is mostly nocturnal, inhabiting during the daytime burrows dug by petrels, seagull-like birds. At night it emerges to feed upon such invertebrates as it may come across. Like many true lizards, it is able to regenerate a lost tail.

Tuataras do not reach sexual maturity until nearly twenty years of age, and the species may, indeed, be one of the longest-lived reptiles. The species—there is only one, *Sphenodon punctatus*—reaches an adult length of about twenty-two inches. Females are smaller and their eggs are deposited in holes. Clutches may number up to two dozen and require fifteen months to hatch.

There is little possibility that the average reader will ever come into contact with a living tuatara. Perhaps no other reptile can thrive in such a low temperature—the captive tuatara seems to thrive best with an ambient Fahrenheit temperature of approximately 55 degrees!

VI

Harmless
North American Snakes

SNAKES IN GENERAL

With the opening of the present chapter I must make a confession: among the multitude of living creatures inhabiting this planet, the snakes have always been my favorites. People who have a frank and open liking for snakes have, in the past, been regarded as a bit peculiar. To some extent, this attitude still prevails. Among enlightened people, however, there is a slowly-growing awareness of the inter-relationship and oneness of all forms of life—nothing vanishes without leaving the whole poorer as a result. As a boy, I was frequently embarrassed when asked why I liked snakes. In the face of the wide-spread prejudice against them, it seemed, somehow, wrong to regard such creatures with friendly interest. The situation is gradu-ally changing as more and more people are getting to know snakes as they really are. This trend will continue and in time an interest in reptiles generally, and snakes in particular, will be regarded as no more unusual or demanding of explanation than a special interest in birds, mammals, or any of the other fascinating forms of life about us.

Snakes are the easiest of backboned animals to keep alive and in good health in captivity. A clean, dry cage with a container for drinking water is all that many species require. Like other reptiles, snakes are cold-blooded, and their activities are circumscribed by the temperature of their surroundings. With those from temperate

Western diamondback rattlesnake, *Crotalus atrox.* Photo by F. J. Dodd, Jr.

Mojave rattlesnake, *Crotalus scutulatus,* southwestern U.S. Photo by F. J. Dodd, Jr.

Prairie rattlesnake, *Crotalus viridis viridis.* Photo by F. J. Dodd, Jr.

Prairie rattlesnake, *Crotalus viridis nuntius.* Photo by F. J. Dodd, Jr.

climates, the temperature range for normal activity may be quite broad and is not likely to present any difficulties to those who keep them in captivity. Species which normally hibernate in the wild state seem able, in captivity, to relinquish this period of winter rest without harmful results. Many snakes feed infrequently, especially when out of the juvenile stage, and this further lightens the burden on their keeper. In a cage snakes do not exercise much, and a liberal feeding once a week will keep most species in good health. If a snake begins to fatten noticeably, the feeding intervals can be stretched to ten days or even two weeks. Usually but one defecation will follow a meal, and this makes it very easy to keep a snake's cage clean.

Snakes live exclusively on animal matter—none is known to accept vegetable substances. It will be noted from reading the chapters on turtles, crocodilians, and lizards that many of the troubles plaguing these reptiles in captivity arise from the lack of an adequate diet. Since snakes will accept only their natural foods or a reasonable approximation of them, they almost never suffer from dietary deficiencies. They either eat what is good for them—or not at all; those in the latter category are individuals which cannot adjust and constitute a very small minority. Such individuals can be forcibly fed, but more will be said about this in a later chapter.

In North America we have a well-varied and very interesting serpent fauna, consisting of well over a hundred species.

BLIND SNAKES AND BOAS

The blind snakes (family Leptotyphlopidae) and the boas (family Boidae) are mostly tropical snakes, but both families have a few representatives in North America. The Texas blind snake, *Leptotyphlops dulcis*, and the western blind snake, *Leptotyphlops humilis*, are diminutive burrowing reptiles that are confined to the south-central and southwestern portions of the continent. They are commonly twelve to fifteen inches long, brownish or even pink in color, with degenerate eyes that have all but lost their function. Ants and their pupae, as well as termites, make up the bulk of the diet of these snakes. In captivity, an aquarium with several inches of loose soil makes the best home for them. Most of their time will be spent beneath the surface in tunnels, but they occasionally make an appearance at night. They reproduce from eggs; their wormlike babies measure around four inches when they hatch. Because of the difficulty of providing captives with their natural diet and the fact that only seldom will they emerge from their burrows, they are probably the least suitable of snakes to keep. None of them will live very long if deprived of a burrowing medium, which should be kept slightly moist. A temperature of 78 to 85 degrees seems to suit them quite well.

The boas of North America appear as pygmies when compared with the large forms of the tropics. Rubber boas, *Charina bottae*, are stout-bodied, blunt-tailed snakes which seldom exceed two feet in length. Though quite secretive, they can climb well and seem at home even in water. Most specimens are captured near streams, in relatively damp situations. Instead of defending themselves by biting, rubber boas are likely to contract their bodies into a ball when handled. They remain timid in captivity and spend most of their time hiding or burrowing. Many do not feed readily, but those which do prefer lizards, small mammals, and birds. Babies number around six, usually, and are produced alive.

Rubber boa, *Charina bottae*. Photo by F. J. Dodd, Jr.

Sidewinder, *Crotalus cerastes,* southwestern deserts. Photo by F. J. Dodd, Jr.

Rock rattlesnake, *Crotalus lepidus,* southwestern Texas to Arizona and Mexico. Photo by J. K. Langhammer.

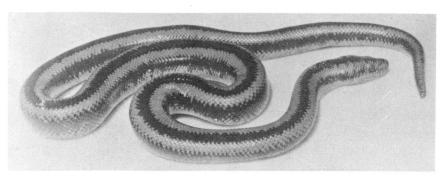

Rosy boa, *Lichanura trivirgata*. From Klauber.

The rosy boa, *Lichanura trivirgata*, is also a western snake and has habits similar to the preceding. It is a variable species in color—grayish, tan, or pinkish—with three fairly distinct dark bands running the length of the body. Like their larger relatives, the rosy and the rubber boas are constrictors, feeding mostly on warm-blooded prey. The males usually have tiny anal spurs.

All of the better-known non-poisonous snakes of North America belong to the family Colubridae. These are the typical snakes that are found nearly everywhere in any habitat that is capable of supporting reptile life. The colubrids vary much in size, form, and habits. It is much beyond the scope of this book to catalogue in detail structural differences among the species, range definitions, and subspecific variations. Rather, the aim is to present a broad picture of our serpent life, with special reference to the adaptability of the various species of snakes to life in captivity.

GARTER SNAKES

The garter snakes (genus *Thamnophis*) are perhaps the best-known snakes of this country. Most are characterized by the presence of stripes running the length of their bodies on a dark background. These stripes may be very vivid, somewhat obscure, or entirely absent, depending on the species, subspecies, or mutation in hand. A single population of the eastern garter snake, *Thamnophis s. sirtalis*, may have striped individuals, others in which the stripes are obscure or replaced by a checkerboard pattern, and others which are coal-black and lack all trace of pattern. Some of the western species, like

Checkered garter snake, *Thamnophis marcianus*. Photo by C. A. Hewitt.

the checkered garter snake, *Thamnophis marcianus*, and certain western varieties of *T. sirtalis*, are extremely pretty snakes.

Most garter snakes show their close affinity to the water snakes in frequenting areas that are plentifully supplied with ponds, streams, and other permanent water bodies. The types which are found in desert country follow the courses of streams and rivers. A few kinds are really aquatic, taking to the water when alarmed and swimming with the ease of the true water snakes. They depend on flight to escape enemies but when caught will put up a good show of defense, biting vigorously and often smearing their captor with a discharge from the anal glands. Captives tame quickly and permit themselves to be handled without the slightest intimation of hostility. A young friend of mine has a varied collection of reptiles and his special favorite is a black-necked garter snake, *Thamnophis cyrtopsis*, from Arizona. It is allowed the freedom of his dresser-top and has certain favorite resting places from which it never wanders far. The most extended foray of the handsome and trusting little reptile is to an adjoining desk, where it reposes beneath the keyboard of a portable typewriter. At first I was somewhat skeptical of an arrangement which allowed a small snake so much freedom, feeling that eventually it would wander away and become lost. But for months now it has been kept uncaged and serves as a practical illustration of the degree to which snakes can be tamed. Garter snakes average two to three feet in length. A few, like Butler's garter snake, *Thamnophis butleri*, may be fully grown when eighteen inches long; the giant garter snake, *Thamnophis couchi gigas*, on the other hand, grows to over four feet!

Garter snakes breed in the spring and the young are born alive in late summer, the broods occasionally numbering several dozens. Baby garter snakes can be reared without difficulty under the most ordinary of cage conditions. The eastern garter snakes feed largely upon earthworms and frogs; the western species and varieties tend to favor small fishes.

Black-necked garter snake, *Thamnophis cyrtopsis*. Photo by G. Marcuse.

Ribbon snake, *Thamnophis sauritus*. Photo courtesy American Museum of Natural History, from Pope's *Reptile World*.

RIBBON SNAKES

Ribbon snakes (*Thamnophis sauritus* and *Thamnophis proximus*) are slender, semi-aquatic members of the garter snake genus. They are frequently to be found basking on bushes which overhang a stream or pond. When alarmed they drop into the water, diving beneath the surface and hiding among aquatic plants. The eastern ribbon snake, *Thamnophis sauritus sauritus*, is a particularly attractive form, its bright yellow stripes standing out vividly on a black or dark brown body. Ribbon snakes are very active reptiles; captives usually remain alert and nervous for some time, though feeding readily enough on frogs, salamanders, and small fishes. Their babies are born alive and in smaller numbers than those of the typical garter snakes. The snakes of this group do not display the bewildering array of color variations seen among the garter snakes. Like the latter, they should be kept in dry cages with only a small container for drinking water.

BROWN SNAKES, RED-BELLIED SNAKES

The brown snakes (genus *Storeria*) are small reptiles, not often measuring more than a foot in length. The most familiar of the two species is the northern brown snake, *Storeria dekayi*, a secretive little

292

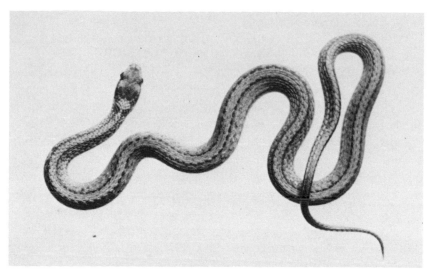
Red-bellied snake, *Storeria occipitomaculata.*

reptile which often lives in large numbers close to human habitations. In fact, in many years of collecting I have seldom found brown snakes in any wilderness area. However incongruous it may seem, any consideration of the habitat of the species immediately brings to mind city dumps and vacant lots. In such places they often abound, sometimes in company with the smooth green snake, *Opheodrys vernalis.* The really small kinds of snakes, like this species, seem much better able to tolerate moderately damp conditions in captivity than their larger relatives. Brown snakes can be successfully maintained under terrarium conditions, with a floor covering of earth and moss. They will also thrive in a plain wooden cage with bare floor, but means of hiding are a necessity for such a secretive reptile. Even when first caught the little brown snake will not bite. Its food consists largely of earthworms and slugs. The red-bellied snake, *Storeria occipitomaculata,* is closely related to the brown snake but differs in color, having a grayish or black dorsal surface and a bright red venter. Unlike the brown snake, the red-belly sticks to forest areas. Often many will be found around farm land that is skirted by areas of open woods. Their usual hiding places are under boards and flat rocks.

WATER SNAKES

Water snakes (genus *Natrix*) are common reptiles over much of the country. In the southeast they abound in numbers of species and in individuals. Most water snakes have brown, dark green, or black upper surfaces, more or less obscurely banded. They have keeled scales and stout bodies with conspicuously distinct heads. Frequenting the environs of water, they take to that element when alarmed and quickly dive out of sight. Aquatic animals of all kinds are eaten; most captives take readily to a diet of fresh fishes. In size, our water snakes range from small forms to species which exceed five feet in length. Large water snakes are formidable-looking and are often confused with the water moccasin, *Agkistrodon piscivorus*. The latter has a pit located between the eye and nostril, and this feature will immediately separate it from the harmless water snakes. Some water snakes fight viciously when cornered or noosed, and large specimens can produce lacerations which bleed freely but are not, of course, dangerous.

Green water snake, *Natrix cyclopion*, southern United States. Photo by F. J. Dodd, Jr.

The northern water snake, *Natrix sipedon sipedon*, lives well in captivity and becomes very tame, readily feeding from the hand. Perhaps no snake is more easily taken care of than a water snake. Their easily-procured diet of fresh or canned fish is at once an asset and a drawback—for fish tend to leave a lingering odor about the quarters of water snakes. This can be minimized by feeding the reptiles—at least the tamer ones—out of their cages. Correlated with their feeding habits is the production of watery feces which are odoriferous and often smeared over the cage bottom. These, then, are the drawbacks of keeping water snakes. A single water snake will require more attention to the cleanliness of its cage than six or more mouse-eating snakes of the same size.

The red-bellied water snake, *Natrix erythrogaster*, of our southeastern waterways is a truly beautiful reptile in the contrast between its rich brown dorsum and bright red belly. It tames readily and makes a most attractive exhibit. The green water snake, *Natrix cyclopion*, and the brown water snake, *Natrix taxispilota*, grow to a huge size and are somewhat less adaptable to cage-life. Baby water snakes of all species are handsomely blotched little creatures, and most are easily raised.

Red-bellied water snake, *Natrix erythrogaster*. From Ditmars, *Reptiles of North America*.

Juvenile racer, *Coluber constrictor*. From Ditmars, *Reptiles of North America*.

RACERS AND WHIPSNAKES

The sleek, fast-moving racers, *Coluber constrictor*, are particularly interesting snakes. In one variety or another they are found from coast to coast. Those of the West are plain olive or brownish snakes with light bellies, while the eastern variety is a plain black snake with an area of white confined to the chin. The young, which are hatched from eggs, differ very much from the adults, being grayish or white with reddish-brown blotches. These begin to fade in the second summer and some racers only slightly over two feet in length have already turned completely black. As adults, the racers average between four and five feet. Among the many specimens I have caught, I have failed to find any that were a full six feet, though this measurement is often cited as the uppermost limit of their growth potential.

Racers are snakes with personality—one never knows what to expect from a specimen encountered in the field. Nearly all books on reptiles say that these snakes glide away like a streak when encountered. This may be true of racers that are met while prowling for food, but I have found that like many other snakes, racers often make no attempt to escape when discovered. This may be particularly true in the more remote areas where their contact with humans has been minimal. On a warm day only a few months ago, while hunting for rattlers, I came upon a cloister of four racers on a rocky hillside. They had recently emerged from their hibernating quarters and all about them were holes and crevices that would have provided a secure retreat. Each of the snakes was awake and alert and fully aware of the presence of my hunting companion and me, as evidenced by their head movements and the flicking of their tongues. Not one of these snakes made any attempt to escape until I had actually clamped my hands down over the mass of them. Two managed to squirm out of my grasp and two were made captive. On countless other occasions I have noted a tendency on the part of racers to scorn flight unless actually molested. I am speaking of racers in rather wild country, where they have been little persecuted. Possibly those which have had frequent contact with people have come to learn the advantage of the flight pattern.

Angry racers will fight viciously, but even the largest specimens can produce little more than superficial scratches with their teeth. Here again, we find racers that do not even attempt to bite when first caught. Many reptile hobbyists have given up on racers, considering them delicate and difficult to handle in captivity. Kept in a cage which has no hiding place and constantly harassed by a procession of people, the captive racer is likely to spend most of its time seeking escape or angrily striking at the objects of its annoyance. Such an animal rarely shows any interest in food, and is likely to damage its snout beyond repair. All racers dislike handling or restraint of any kind; this is true even of those which are well adjusted and have been in captivity and feeding well for many months. Sympathetically cared for, with allowance made for its flighty nature, a racer can become the favorite of a collection of snakes. My method of taming racers is the same I use with the other more nervous types of reptiles. First, I attempt to capture the reptile with as little shock to its nervous system as possible. This generally means seizing it by mid-body, then restraining the head while it is being put into a collecting bag. The snake is never allowed to dangle or attempt to shake loose from a neck-grasp. I never put more than one specimen in a collecting bag. This is securely tied and the snake remains in it for three or four days at least, the bag not being opened during this time. Awaiting the snake at the end of this quieting-down period is a clean and dry cage of moderate size—not more than two-thirds the length of the reptile. This has a glass front but the sides and top are of wooden construction. A small cardboard box with a two-inch hole cut in the side is held in place in one corner of the cage with a heavy rock. The bag is placed in the cage, after being untied, and the snake is allowed to make an acquaintance with its new home. After a couple of days the bag is removed and a container of water which cannot be tipped is furnished. By this time, the snake will have come to regard the cardboard box as a place of refuge and for a while will not venture from it very often. Food in the form of a dead mouse is now offered. If this is not eaten within a few daylight hours, it is removed and the snake is allowed a further few days to adjust before the feeding attempt is repeated. Live mice will serve only to further agitate an already nervous reptile, and in my opinion have little advantage over

Adult racer, *Coluber constrictor*, midwestern subspecies. From Ortenburger, courtesy University of Michigan Museum of Zoology.

dead ones in the feeding of snakes. It was once thought necessary to feed snakes live animals only, but experience has repeatedly demonstrated that any snake which will eat a live mouse will eat a dead one just as readily. The converse is not true, for many snakes which will readily eat dead mice show little interest in live ones.

Getting back to our racer—once it has accepted a mouse it is on its way toward becoming a contented and longlived captive. Eventually it will come to show a great deal of recognition toward its keeper and will even feed from the hand. Racers eat practically any small animal they can overcome and this includes smaller snakes of all kinds. Mice are the favorite food of captives. They are diurnal snakes and seldom move about much at night. Non-constrictors, they simply swallow their food alive in the wild state. The young are hatched from eggs and during the first year of their lives feed largely upon insects, small frogs and salamanders.

Whipsnakes (genus *Masticophis*) are closely related to the racers and have similar habits. Some, like the coachwhip, *Masticophis flagellum*, may attain the enormous length—for a snake of this country—of eight feet. The western forms, of which the striped whipsnake, *Masticophis lateralis*, is one, are often very pretty reptiles. None of the whipsnakes can tolerate even the slightest dampness, though they drink frequently and should be provided with a small dish of water that cannot be tipped. Active snakes all, they require proportionately more food than the slower-moving species.

PATCH-NOSED SNAKES

The patch-nosed snakes (genus *Salvadora*) are delicately formed desert reptiles that much resemble the whipsnakes in their habits. They have a broad dorsal stripe of yellow or tan, bordered by darker lines on the sides. The snout is much flattened and enlarged, im-

Coachwhip, *Masticophis flagellum*. Photo courtesy American Museum of Natural History, from Pope's *Reptile World*.

Western patch-nosed snake, *Salvadora hexalepis*. From Van Denburgh.

parting a short-headed appearance. With their large eyes and quick,
nervous movements, snakes of this genus are reminiscent of small
birds. A western patch-nosed snake, *Salvadora hexalepis*, in my
collection at the time of writing is very active by day but strangely,
for a diurnal snake, will accept its weekly meal of a small dead mouse
only at night! It does not attempt to bite when handled, but has the
peculiar habit of suddenly throwing its body into a gyration about its
own axis. This makes it a very difficult snake to hold when it has its
mind set upon going elsewhere.

INDIGO SNAKE

Among the native snakes, an outstanding species is the indigo
snake, *Drymarchon corais*. Commonly six feet or more in length,
the highly-polished blue-black scales of this handsome reptile shine
with an iridescence under good lighting. The variety found in the
southeast is known as *D. c. couperi*; the Texas subspecies is *D. c.
erebennus* and is not as attractive, having a brownish overcast to its
color. Both varieties live very well in captivity, feeding upon small
mammals, birds, reptiles, amphibians, and fishes. Some individuals
can be conditioned to a diet of raw beef strips. Technically classified

Indigo snake, *Drymarchon corais.* Photo courtesy American Museum of Natural History.

as a near relative of the racers and whipsnakes, the indigo is, in its demeanor, an altogether different snake. It is nowhere very abundant, so the capture of an indigo is generally the highlight of a day's collecting. It is generally found in the more remote, sandy areas where tortoise burrows are numerous. Captives do well only if kept warm and dry; if these conditions are fulfilled they can be expected to outlive nearly all other kinds of snakes. Indigo snakes are the most expensive of our native serpents, and the supply seems never equal to the demand for them. Most private collectors do not own more than a single specimen, but those who have collected indigos in numbers tell us that they fight viciously among themselves when caged together. This is a rare trait among snakes of the same species that are of approximately the same size.

RAT SNAKES

Rat snakes (genus *Elaphe*) are common and familiar reptiles over much of the eastern half of the country. Generally of moderate to large size, some kinds are boldly patterned and among the most beautiful snakes in the world. All are constrictors, and their ceaseless search for mice and rats brings them into close proximity to human

301

Corn snake, *Elaphe guttata*. Photo courtesy Univ. Florida Press, from Carr and Goin's *Guide to Reptiles, Amphibians and Freshwater Fishes of Florida*.

Black rat snake, *Elaphe obsoleta obsoleta*. From Ditmars, *Reptiles of North America*.

dwellings, where such rodents often abound. They are not fast-moving snakes, and those encountered in the field will often stand their ground and vigorously defend themselves, contracting their forequarters and striking with a sharp hiss. Individuals may retain a readiness to bite even after months of captivity, but this is very unusual. The average rat snake makes a quick adjustment to cage life and shows little of the nervousness displayed by some other kinds of serpents.

The corn snake, *Elaphe guttata*, is a beautifully blotched species that feeds largely upon mice. Its gray or orange ground-color is overlaid with large red saddles that are bordered by black. The belly is handsomely checkered in black and white. Though the species may rarely reach six feet, such specimens are uncommon and any over four feet must be considered quite large. Like the other rat snakes, the present species climbs well but most often is found on the ground. It is both diurnal and nocturnal, depending in some measure on weather conditions. Few are found abroad on really hot days—but this is true of nearly all kinds of snakes.

The north-central states are the home of the fox snake, *Elaphe vulpina*, another of the blotched rat snakes with rather subdued tones of yellow and brown. The head has a metallic luster and the species is often confused with the copperhead, *Agkistrodon contortrix*. Fox snakes receive their common name from their habit of emitting an odor like that found around a fox den. They do this only when freshly caught; once placed in a cage they become the personification of good nature, feed readily on rodents and birds, and live a seemingly contented existence. The species does not often exceed four feet in length but has a stout build. It is a favorite of those who have kept it in captivity. Unfortunately, it is one of those snakes of rather limited distribution and is not often available from dealers.

The black rat snake, *Elaphe obsoleta obsoleta*, is the largest species of its genus in North America. Six-foot specimens are not rare, and occasional individuals grow much larger. Typically, it is a snake of wooded hillsides, often found in association with timber rattlesnakes, copperheads, and black racers. Superficially, it resembles the latter, but is a stouter snake, has a more angular and distinct head, is slower-moving, and its scales are keeled; those of the racer are smooth.

A conspicuous snake in the Carolinas, Georgia, and Florida is the yellow rat snake, *Elaphe obsoleta quadrivittata*. This brightly-hued

Yellow rat snake, *Elaphe obsoleta quadrivittata.* Photo courtesy University of Florida Press, from Carr and Goin.

Texas rat snake, *Elaphe obsoleta lindheimeri,* Texas and Louisiana. Photo courtesy American Museum of Natural History, from Pope's *Reptile World.*

snake, banded longitudinally with four blackish stripes, is often seen in trees. A more usual habitat is the environs of sheds and abandoned buildings which have become the congregating places of large numbers of rodents. Like other rat snakes, this species deposits about two dozen eggs in early summer. These hatch about eight weeks later, the babies measuring twelve to fourteen inches. In color and pattern they are very much different from the parent snakes. They are boldly blotched with brown on a gray ground color, this coloration fading as growth progresses until the plain yellow of the adult prevails when the young snake is about half-grown. A few adults retain traces of the juvenile pattern in obscure, barely-discernible blotches between their characteristic stripes. Baby rat snakes of this and the other species differ from the adults in the matter of food requirements. Adult rat snakes live exclusively upon warm-blooded prey and the eggs of birds. The juveniles will accept frogs, insects, and lizards.

An especially beautiful rat snake inhabits southern Florida, particularly the Everglades. The Everglades rat snake, *Elaphe obsoleta rossalleni*, as the subspecies is called, is a bright orange snake, growing to very large size, and often entirely lacking the striping of the more widely-distributed yellow rat snake. I would call this the handsomest of the larger North American snakes. Unfortunately, the species loses some of the intensity of its color when it has been in captivity for a long time. Whether this tendency could be overcome by the addition of vitamins to the diet of captives is not known, but it would be interesting to experiment along these lines.

PINE SNAKE, GOPHER SNAKE, BULLSNAKE

The pine, gopher, and bullsnakes were once divided into several species but all are now regarded simply as varieties of *Pituophis melanoleucus*. All are large and showy serpents with pointed heads and strong, constricting bodies. Economically they are among our most valuable reptiles, frequenting agricultural areas where they feed mostly on rodents that are injurious to crops. A small filament in the mouth permits them to hiss more loudly than any other snakes in this country; this, coupled with the vibration of their tails and lunging strikes at the object of their annoyance, causes wild specimens to appear quite formidable.

Pine snake, *Pituophis melanoleucus melanoleucus*. From Ditmars, *Reptiles of North America*.

The pine snake, *Pituophis melanoleucus melanoleucus*, is a large black and white snake which makes the pine barrens of New Jersey a favorite hunting ground of the reptile enthusiasts of nearby cities. Often five feet or more in length, the species is stoutly built and makes a good display animal. Many become very tame in captivity and will feed readily in or out of their cages; a few remain erratic in disposition and tend to bite if provoked. Mice are the favorite food of captives, and the species seems to have but a moderate requirement for water. This means that a permanent water container may be dispensed with and, instead, water offered at weekly intervals. This may assist in maintaining dry quarters for these snakes, for they can easily tip most dishes with the weight of their bodies.

A western relative of the pine snake is the bullsnake, *Pituophis melanoleucus sayi*, a yellow-brown reptile that is one of our largest snakes, with recorded lengths in excess of eight feet. Despite its large size and diurnal habits, this and the other members of the genus tend to spend much of their time hiding if a box or house is provided. Such means of concealment are in no way necessary for the successful maintenance of captives, for they calm down quickly in captivity and show little nervousness. Bullsnakes are large enough to be allowed to roam about a house occasionally, providing there is no means of exit. The various species of *Pituophis* are very responsive to any contact stimuli and seem most contented when confined alone. Recently I had occasion to cage together a large black racer and a bull-snake of similar size, but of greater body bulk. The racer was an active snake and its meanderings brought it into frequent body contact with the bullsnake. At each such contact, the bullsnake would vigorously arch its body, casting the racer away with some force. The racer would retaliate by frequently biting its cagemate. Both snakes fed readily before they were housed together. Occupying the same cage, each refused to eat and persisted in its fast until they were separated. A five-foot bullsnake requires a mouse each week to maintain a normal weight and state of health in captivity.

KINGSNAKES

The eastern kingsnake, *Lampropeltis getulus getulus*, and some of its relatives are famous for their habit of overcoming and devouring other kinds of snakes, even the poisonous species. The present species is lustrous black, banded over its entire length with regularly spaced markings of white or yellow. These fork and connect with each other along the sides, producing an effect like that of a chain. The average

Eastern kingsnake, *Lampropeltis getulus getulus*. From Ditmars, *Reptiles of North America*.

California kingsnake, *Lampropeltis getulus californiae,* two color varieties. From Van Denburgh.

kingsnake is about four feet long and quite thick-bodied and powerfully muscled. It is a constrictor, and captives will subsist indefinitely on a diet of small rodents. Several kingsnakes will get along very well together, but the introduction of an unrelated species will throw a cage of kingsnakes into a state of turmoil. The newcomer will be seized and quickly dispatched, and two kingsnakes are likely to start swallowing it from opposite ends. This can be catastrophic, for when their heads meet the larger specimen will often engulf the smaller one. For this reason, kingsnakes should be carefully watched while feeding. The bites of our native poisonous snakes seem to have little effect on kingsnakes, aside from the mechanical injuries which their needlelike fangs may produce. Rattlers in particular seem to recognize the kingsnake as an enemy and will hump their bodies in an endeavor to thwart the encircling attack of their adversary. They seem to realize that a stabbing strike, so effective against other animals, would be useless in dealing with a kingsnake. They employ their fangs only when actually seized.

Kingsnakes, in their many forms, are secretive reptiles and productive collecting entails the overturning of logs, stones, and pieces of trash. Often they are numerous in the vicinity of ponds and streams, seeming to prefer an environment that is at least moist. Some individuals will bite when first caught but nearly all quickly lose this trait and become the most docile of captives. The species deposits up to two dozen eggs which hatch in about six weeks. Baby kingsnakes of twelve to fourteen inches do not differ from the adults much in color. They feed mostly on newborn rodents, lizards, and smaller snakes.

MILK SNAKE

The eastern milk snake, *Lampropeltis triangulum*, is one of the kingsnake's smaller relatives. It is a slender gray reptile, saddled with closely set blotches of brown or red. The undersurface presents a checkerboard pattern. In snake-poor New England, this species is one of the more attractive, and is quite common in some areas. Usually it can be found basking only in the early spring. At other times it is a nocturnal reptile that spends its days in hiding. Although small in

Speckled kingsnake, *Lampropeltis getulus holbrooki*. Photo by J. G. Walls.

size—the average milk snake is about thirty inches long and has a body diameter of a half-inch, a milk snake can produce a more painful bite than many larger snakes. It has a habit of biting without warning, then chewing, once it has obtained a good hold. Milk snakes have the reputation of doing poorly in captivity. This may be true of most individuals, but occasionally a specimen will feed well and thrive for a number of years. I would regard it essential to provide a piece of bark or other hiding place for so secretive a reptile. Specimens kept in a bare cage tend to wander about hour after hour, seeking seclusion or a means of escape. Of one thing you can be sure—if there exists the smallest opening in a cage housing a milk snake, the reptile will be sure to find it and effect an escape. I once lost a milk snake in this way in an apartment. Curiously, it turned up one early morning many months later and appeared in better condition than when it escaped. What it ate, if it did, or where it obtained liquid nourishment, are puzzling questions.

Milk snake, *Lampropeltis triangulum.* Photo courtesy American Museum of Natural History, from Pope's *Reptile World.*

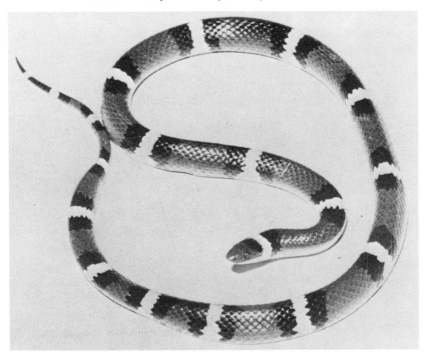

California mountain king snake, *Lampropeltis zonata,* Pacific states. From Van Denburgh.

RAINBOW SNAKE, MUD SNAKE

Although placed in different genera, the rainbow snake, *Abastor erythrogrammus,* and the mud snake, *Farancia abacura,* are closely allied and of similar habits. Both are large, very colorful burrowing species of swampy areas, confined to our southeastern states and the Mississippi valley. The rainbow is handsomely striped with red and black, while the mud is a shiny black species with pink blotches along its sides—extensions of the all-pink belly. Four feet would be an average length for either species. Efforts to keep these attractive snakes in captivity met with little success until it was determined that they fed mostly on the aquatic salamanders of the genera *Amphiuma* and *Siren.* This did not improve the situation much, for these salamanders can seldom be obtained in quantities. Then it was learned that these finicky eaters would accept nearly any aquatic animal that bore the scent of the salamanders. Now collectors can easily keep specimens of these colorful snakes if a frozen salamander

Rainbow snake, *Abastor erythrogrammus*. Photo by F. J. Dodd, Jr.

is rubbed against frogs or fishes before they are offered to the snakes. Either species will live indefinitely in an aquarium with several inches of water and no land area. In the South, newly-hatched babies can often be found crossing causeways in enormous numbers.

HOGNOSE SNAKE

The eastern hognose snake, *Heterodon platyrhinos*, is one of several kinds of curious serpents that are found mostly in dry, sandy areas. Though quite short, their very broad and heavy bodies give them a rather formidable appearance. This is backed by a show of bluff that has few peers among reptiles. The neck is broadly expanded while the diminutive reptile hisses loudly and strikes boldly at its tormentor. If these antics do not succeed in scaring the aggressor, the snake will turn over on its back and violently twist about, as though in agony, then finally lie still with mouth opened and tongue protruded. A specimen in this condition hangs limply if handled, but if placed in a crawling position will quickly flop over on its back and remain so until danger has passed. Tame specimens abandon this behavior and become very desirable inmates of a reptile collection. They will seldom take food other than frogs or toads, however, and this is considered by some a drawback. All-black hognose snakes are not

312

Eastern hognose snake, *Heterodon platyrhinos.* Photo courtesy Illinois Natural History Survey.

rare in elevated regions and, as with other snakes, occasional albinos are found. One such specimen was exhibited for at time at the Trailside Museum near Boston. It presented a beautiful study in pastels—the normally dark blotches faintly discernible in pink.

RINGNECK SNAKES

Ringneck snakes are seldom-seen denizens of our forested areas. Due to differences in size and color, they once were separated into a number of species. Now all are regarded as varieties of *Diadophis punctatus*. Eastern varieties generally do not exceed fifteen inches, while some western types reach a length of over two feet. Characteristic of the ringnecks is a black or slate-colored back and a red or orange stomach surface. The narrow ring just behind the head is a distinguishing feature. Ringnecks are able to tolerate some dampness in their cages and do well in planted terrariums if provided with a flat stone or section of bark for hiding. Earthworms and a variety of other animals are eaten, including snakes which are smaller than the ringnecks themselves.

GREEN SNAKES

The rough green snake, *Opheodrys aestivus,* and the smooth green snake, *Opheodrys vernalis,* are our only native bright green snakes, although this color is common in serpents of the tropics, especially those kinds which spend much of their lives in trees. Our green snakes are small and graceful reptiles; the smooth species has a

Ringneck snake, *Diadophis punctatus.* Photo courtesy American Museum of Natural History, from Pope's *Reptile World.*

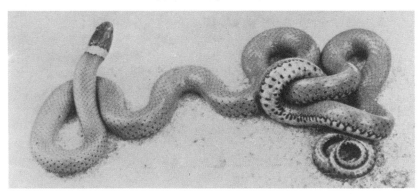

Smooth green snake, *Opheodrys vernalis*. From Ditmars, *Reptiles of North America*.

Rough green snake, *Opheodrys aestivus*. From Ditmars, *Reptiles of North America*.

maximum length of only about twenty inches, while the rough green may reach three feet or more. Either species may be kept in a terrarium, where they will feed on hairless caterpillars, crickets, grasshoppers, and spiders. The rough green snake climbs well and is usually found in bushes near water; the smooth green snake is more at home in damp meadows. The smooth green snake, particularly, tends to form colonies, outside of which specimens are seldom found. As a boy in Boston, I collected green snakes in the vacant lots which dotted the city. These places were nearly barren of vegetation and were, in fact, dumps. Among the rubble and pieces of trash, the beautiful little snakes seemed out of place. I did not realize it at the time, but I was never again to find smooth green snakes in such numbers.

In this chapter we have talked about representatives of our major groups of harmless native snakes. There are many species that are less familiar and about which we do not have much detailed information.

Glossy snake, *Arizona elegans*, western United States. From Klauber.

Longnosed snake, *Rhinocheilus lecontei,* western United States. From Van Denburgh.

Lined snake, *Tropidoclonium lineatum,* northern Mississippi R. valley west to Texas. From Ditmars, *Reptiles of North America.*

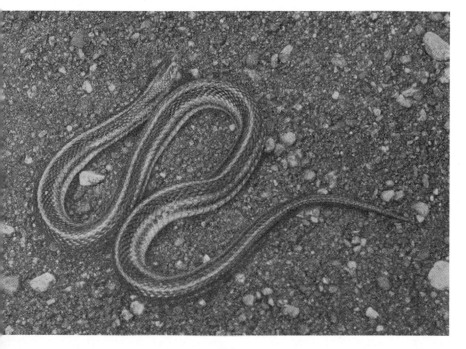

Shovelnosed snake, *Chionactis occipitalis,* southwestern United States. From Van Denburgh.

Most snake fanciers seem to have a preference for the larger species—these are more showy and, in general, easier to care for than the smaller kinds. Most of our larger snakes cannot stand dampness: they quickly develop fungoid conditions. Many of the smaller kinds, on the other hand, will thrive best in surroundings which imitate their natural habitats. It is possible for the herpetologist to elicit much new and interesting information regarding the smaller snakes under the semi-natural conditions of a terrarium.

VII

Non-poisonous Exotic Snakes

FAMILY BOIDAE

The family Boidae includes all of the really huge snakes of the world. Included in this family, however, are numerous smaller forms that have achieved little of the popularity of their larger relatives, but are, nevertheless, very interesting and often beautiful reptiles. Pythons and boas, as the members of this family are called, are very much like each other in many respects. Because of a fundamental difference in the structure of their skulls, they have often been separated and placed in subfamilies of their own. In their manner of reproducing, they differ in that the pythons deposit eggs while the boas give birth to live babies. In their many species and subspecies the Boidae are primitive snakes. Their ancient lineage is evidenced by such features as well-developed, paired lungs and, in most kinds, the trace of hind limbs. These are the "spurs" which may be seen at the base of the tail and are generally larger in a male than in the opposite sex. All pythons and boas kill their prey by constriction. Curiously, wild specimens will strike and hiss like other snakes, but never employ their powerful coils in defense until seized. Among the present snakes are some which tame readily, feed well, and live for a great many years in captivity; other kinds, however, are noted for their quick tempers and general intractability. A large boa or python is capable of producing severe lacerations with its long teeth and should, therefore, be handled with care unless known to be of good temperament. Some of the pythons and boas have exquisitely beautiful color patterns which, combined with large size and good disposition, make them deservedly the most popular of imported snakes. Some reptile hobbyists who once kept varied assortments of herptiles have come to confine their attention to the raising of giant snakes. Even a single specimen, well-cared-for, can provide a fascinating experience when raised from a baby of two feet or less to an adult weighing perhaps 200 pounds. Financially, baby pythons represent the soundest investment. The value of a growing youngster can easily increase tenfold during the first eight to ten years of its life. There is a ready market for large specimens, and those approaching record lengths may be negotiated for in terms of thousands of dollars. The large constrictors are notably inactive snakes and present few problems in the matter of housing. A very large specimen may be confined in a cage which would not do at all for one of the more active colubrids of moderate size. Boas and pythons have successfully been allowed the run of a house where no dogs, cats, or other small mammals are present. Caged, their general demeanor is to accept with indifference the limitation of movement caused by walls and glass. There is little of the probing for an escape route that is noticeable among some freshly caught snakes of other kinds. It may be that the mental processes of pythons and boas are not as highly evolved as those of other serpents, but if this is so we have no proof of it. I prefer to think of them as snakes which do not mind too much a close association with people!

The larger pythons and boas have a life expectancy of twenty to thirty years. This span is not in excess of that achieved by some captive colubrids and crotalids, snakes of only four to six feet in maximum length. This is a little surprising; among reptiles we can generally expect the largest forms to live the longest. Both pythons and boas produce at least one species which attains a length in excess of thirty feet.

RETICULATE PYTHON

Largest of the true pythons is the reticulate python, *Python reticulatus*, of southeastern Asia, the Philippines, and the East Indies. Among the most majestic of living snakes, the present beautiful reptile has a beautifully interwoven pattern of brown, gold, and black. The reddish eyes of an adult can be seen clearly. These, and the narrow line extending from the snout to the back of the head, are features which will distinguish this python from other Asiatic species. Baby pythons of this and other kinds usually feed quite readily and can be raised without difficulty. Larger specimens that have been taken from their native haunts are apt to be too reticent to eat for a long time after capture, so they are much less satisfactory than those which have been captive-reared. Like other large members of the genus *Python*, the reticulate deposits large eggs to the number of a hundred or more, occasionally, and these she broods by coiling about them until hatching time. Hatchlings may measure two feet in length and grow fairly rapidly under good conditions, for the first few years adding twenty inches or more to their length each annum. They prefer mice as food, while the adults can be maintained on a diet of chickens. Eighty degrees is a good cage temperature for pythons and boas of all kinds.

Reticulate python, *Python reticulatus.* Photo by G. Marcuse.

INDIAN PYTHON

The Indian python, *Python molurus*, is equally handsome, especially in its light phase, but is a somewhat smaller reptile than the preceding species. The two are sometimes confused by amateur herpetologists who are not critically familiar with the giant snakes. The colors are somewhat similar but in the present species the head marking has the appearance of an arrowhead, tapering to a point near the snout. It has long been recognized that the lighter variety of the Indian python tames more readily than the darker form and is, in general, a much prettier reptile. The situation is similar to that existing among the boa constrictors, *Boa constrictor*, in which the light phases are not only prettier but adapt much more easily to confinement than the darker forms. India, Ceylon, and the East Indies form the natural range of the Indian python. It spends much of its time in trees, and captives of all the larger pythons appreciate stout limbs in their cages. Like most other pythons, *P. molurus* lays eggs and coils about them during the incubation period. While brooding, the parent has an increase in body temperature.

Indian python, *Python molurus*. Photo by L. E. Perkins.

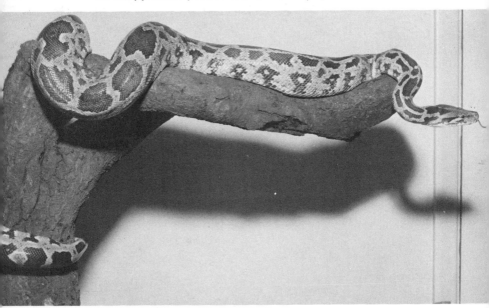

Indian python, *Python molurus*. Photo by G. Marcuse.

ROCK PYTHON

The central and southern portions of the African continent are the home of the rock python, *Python sebae*, another huge constricting snake which may grow to twenty feet or more. This, too, is a very beautiful snake which exhibits some variation in the intensity of its colors. Like the other large constrictors, captives will remain in a tank of water for long periods, especially before shedding or when digesting a meal. Zoos commonly provide these giant snakes with sizeable pools. Food requirements are small mammals in the case of babies; larger specimens take rabbits, chickens, and other warm-blooded prey. Feeding intervals can be spaced at ten days to two weeks with specimens that are well-grown. A twelve-foot python will keep well-nourished with a six-pound chicken every ten days. Larger amounts of food will be devoured if the opportunity presents itself but with snakes, as with humans, obesity shortens life. Overfed pythons may attain an enormous girth and a weight in excess of 250 pounds. Such specimens have difficulty moving about, seldom climb the trees in their cages, and often succumb to heart failure. I recently had the opportunity to examine a python weighing about 260 pounds though but slightly in excess of twenty feet in length. All pythons are relatively heavy-bodied snakes, but this particular example lacked the well-muscled sleekness of those which had a more normal weight and I believe it had been deliberately fattened to establish a weight record. Its demise shortly thereafter occasioned an autopsy which pointed to heart failure as the cause of death.

BLOOD PYTHON, BALL PYTHON

Among the smaller pythons frequently imported are the blood python, *Python curtus*, of Asia and the ball python, *Python regius*, of Africa. These are stout-bodied snakes that adapt quite well to captivity and seldom show any sign of bad temper. The former seems never to exceed ten feet in length, while the latter is fully grown at four or five. The blood python has an exceptionally beautiful coloration—some would call it the handsomest species of its genus. Ball pythons receive their common name from the tendency, noted among other constricting snakes as well, of coiling themselves into a ball when handled. The resultant mass of serpentine coils can be rolled about without relaxation on the part of the reptile.

OTHER PYTHONS

Australia and New Guinea and other Pacific islands have a number of fine pythons that are less frequently imported than the Asiatic and African forms. The carpet python, *Morelia spilotes variegata*, and the diamond python, *Morelia spilotes spilotes*, are, as their scientific names indicate, simply varieties of the same species. Both are handsomely patterned reptiles which average from six to ten feet in length. Unfortunately, captives usually live only a few years. The

Young carpet python, *Morelia spilotes variegata.* Photo by G. Marcuse.

amethystine python, *Liasis amethystinus,* is one of the world's longest snakes, occasionally reaching a length of 25 feet. It is a relatively slender snake with an attractive color pattern of brown and yellow. Particularly interesting is the black-headed python, *Aspidites melano-cephalus,* an eight-foot species that lives largely on the ground and has a black head and neck which contrast strangely with the banded pattern of the remainder of the snake. Pythons are not generally regarded as snake-eating serpents, but the present species is an exception: it attacks without hesitation even the deadliest of the Australian snakes. Its diet is not confined to other snakes, however. Captives become very tame and will eat nearly any warm-blooded creature that they are capable of swallowing. Due to the extreme elasticity of their jaws and skin, all of the pythons and boas are capable of swallowing animals much larger than their heads.

Black-headed python, *Aspidites melanocephalus*. Photo by Dr. Otto Klee.

BOAS

The most familiar of the giant constrictors are those known as boas, *Boa constrictor*. Natives of the tropical Americas, these snakes are a staple in the stocks of pet dealers. The species has a number of races which differ markedly in color and temperament. Those from Mexico and Central America are dark in color with rather obscure crossbars. The babies, with their huge heads, are rather sinister-looking little creatures. These northernmost forms of the boa constrictor are often hard to tame and resent all familiarity from human hands. The variety known as the red-tailed boa is a native of the Amazon jungles and is particularly beautiful—pale tan with ruddy crossbars that are widely separated and become red toward the tail. Boas of this variety make gentle and handsome members of any collection. Fully grown, at perhaps twelve feet, and in the prime of condition, they are among the most beautiful snakes. Babies of the boas are produced alive, generally in May, and a brood may consist of twenty or more infant snakes. These feed readily upon mice

Burrowing python, *Calabaria reinhardtii,* West Africa. Photo by Dr. Otto
Klee.

Boa constrictor, *Boa constrictor*. Photo by L. E. Perkins.

and grow rapidly. Like the pythons, the boas will enter a tank of water and soak for long periods. I do not consider it desirable to permit such baths to extend over a period of more than twenty-four hours, however.

Boa constrictor, showing variation in color pattern. Photos by C. A. Hewitt.

Though not especially adaptable to captivity, the anaconda, *Eunectes murinus*, of South America deserves special mention because it is the largest of New World snakes. A number of forms are recognized and all are very much alike in habits, frequenting jungle watercourses and feeding on mammals, birds, and reptiles. The yellow anaconda, *Eunectes notaeus*, grows to only about fifteen feet and is quite attractively marked as a baby, but these vivid yellow and black colors fade as they grow. The much-larger *E. murinus* is olive-brown with dark spots. Most anacondas tend to retain a morose disposition, in spite of which, however, individuals often live very many years when well cared for. One anaconda, at least, lived twenty-eight years in captivity.

Anaconda, *Eunectes murinus*.

Epicrates is another tropical American genus of boas which includes several well-known species. Because of its docile disposition and the beautiful iridescence of its scales, the rainbow boa, *Epicrates cenchris*, is a favorite in collections. The species ranges over a broad area of Central and South America. Examples from the northernmost portions of the range are brownish-gray and lack the spectacular beauty of those from Brazil, in which a reddish hue predominates. The Cuban boa, *Epicrates angulifer*, is one of the larger species, reaching a length of fourteen feet. It is not a colorful snake, being, for the most part, plain tan or brownish with a series of darker blotches running the length of the body. It is believed to feed mostly upon bats in the wild state; captives will accept other warm-blooded prey, but the species has such a persistently irascible disposition that many individuals cannot be persuaded to eat at all. Several smaller kinds of *Epicrates* occur in the West Indies. The Haitian boa, *Epicrates*

Rainbow boa, *Epicrates cenchris,* young. Photo by G. Marcuse.

angulifer striatus, averages about six feet in length and is rather slender of form. It lives well if kept at a temperature range of 78 to 85 degrees.

Tree boas form a small but interesting group of serpents that are admirably suited to an arboreal existence, having bodies which are much compressed from side to side and strongly prehensile tails. The green tree boa, *Corallus canina,* like its relatives, feeds mostly upon birds and is well able to capture such feathered prey with long and very sharp teeth. It is a beautiful reptile—emerald green above and yellow below, embellished along its back with narrow crossbands of white. As with the other boas, the babies are brought forth fully developed and differ from the adults in being of an orange color. None of the strictly arboreal boas reaches a large size; the present species runs four to six feet in length. It is essential that tree boas have their cage provided with a tree limb, where they will spend most of their time compactly coiled.

Rainbow boa, *Epicrates cenchris,* adult. Photo by G. Marcuse.

Green python, *Chondropython viridis*, New Guinea. Photo by G. Marcuse.

Green tree boa, *Corallus caninus*. Photo by G. Marcuse.

Rough-scaled sand boa, *Eryx conicus*, India. Photo by G. Marcuse

In striking contrast to the tree boas is a group known as sand boas (genus *Eryx*), which are short, stoutly formed snakes with bluntly tipped tails. They spend their lives entirely on the ground or burrowing beneath its surface; they inhabit dry areas of Asia, Europe, and Africa. One of the commonest species is the brown sand boa, *Eryx johni*, of India. Not exceeding a yard in length, this species and its relatives can be kept in a small cage with several inches of fine sand in which they will burrow. Small birds and mice are accepted readily and sand boas do well if kept dry and warm.

FAMILY COLUBRIDAE

The majority of the world's snakes belong to the family Colubridae. There is so much diversification of structure within this family that it has been divided into groups known as subfamilies. No herpetologist, in recent times, has been able to compile anything like a complete account of the snakes of this vast family. Such an endeavor could well occupy a lifetime of research. Changes of names among the many genera and species have been frequent and are still being made, as our studies give us a clearer picture of relation-

Hooded snake, *Xenedon merremi*, Brazil. Photo by H. Schultz.

ships within the groups. The synonymy presented in the literature is enough to discourage any but the most technical worker. Necessarily, therefore, we must glean our knowledge of the various species from fragmentary sources, including regional accounts and papers on individual genera and species. Most of the colubrids, as the snakes of this family are called, are the typical harmless snakes that predominate in every continent except Australia.

Many colubrids possess grooved fangs in the rear of their jaws. These fangs are used to inject venom into the natural prey of the snakes and can seldom be used effectively as a defense against humans. A few exceptions are notable, however, and I would regard it as judicious to handle rear-fanged snakes, especially the large ones, with caution. The boomslang, for instance, can cause the death of a human being.

The rear-fanged snakes' venomous properties have been little investigated. Many of them seldom bite when handled, and of those which do bite many cannot bring the tiny rear teeth into play unless a small, rounded surface is seized or a portion of loose flesh is grasped. The fingers, or the area of skin between two fingers, would be vulnerable. Among human subjects effects similar to those produced by the sting of a bee have been noted. Some of the tinier rear-fanged snakes are unable to break the flesh with their teeth. At our present stage of knowledge or, perhaps more correctly, lack of knowledge, common sense should be exercised in the handling of the rear-fanged serpents. In tropical regions, where the snakes of this type may be numerous, caution should be used in the handling of any snake which is not definitely known to be completely harmless. There is no sure way of identifying a rear-fanged snake in the field, unless one is critically familiar with the snake fauna of the area being collected. Some snakes of this type attain a good size, with a proportionately developed venom apparatus, but only two species, the twig snake and the boomslang, are known to be able to inflict serious bites upon humans. The former species has been recognized as dangerous only for the past decade. As a matter of course, I handle rear-fanged snakes, if they are of any size, with much the same precautions I use in the handling of vipers and others of the so-called deadly species. The characteristic of possessing enlarged and sometimes grooved teeth toward the rear of the mouth crosses several subfamilies of snakes and is found in arboreal, terrestrial, and aquatic forms. It is of little value in establishing relationships among the species. Any listing of all the known rear-fanged serpents would bring together a very artificial grouping of forms, many of whose closest relatives lack any trace of enlarged or grooved teeth.

Contrary to popular supposition, it is not necessary for these snakes to "chew" in order to inject venom. They are quite capable of delivering a serious wound by striking with open mouth, then immediately withdrawing. But in spite of the few known exceptions, we must regard nearly all of the rear-fanged snakes as harmless—at least as far as people are concerned.

WART SNAKE

Snakes show marvelous adaptations to their environments, and in this respect perhaps none exceeds the wart snake, *Acrochordus javanicus*, of Asia and northern Australia. Thoroughly aquatic, if removed from the water this strange snake flounders about and is unable to make much progress. Thick-bodied and blunt-headed, its skin hangs in loose folds and each scale is separated, not overlapping as in other snakes. The species lacks broad ventral plates which enable most snakes to move about on land. Instead, its belly is covered with a granular scalation. Wart snakes, the larger females of which may reach six feet, frequent streams, canals, and rivers and even enter the sea occasionally. They feed principally upon fishes, which they catch by quick snaps of their sharp-toothed jaws. The babies are born alive and may number twenty-five or more. This is one of the snakes which is annually caught by the thousands to supply the leather trade with fine and durable hides, which is perhaps one of the reasons why not many wart snakes are exported alive. They live fairly well under aquarium conditions if the water temperature is kept at a fairly high level...75 to 80 degrees. The valvular nostrils are placed at the tip of the reptile's snout, a peculiarity noted among many reptiles that spend most of their time in water. The species is able to remain submerged for long periods. Specimens are active mainly at night, reposing by day in the quieter shore waters of their native streams.

WATER SNAKES

The snakes of the genus *Natrix*, cosmopolitan in distribution and known commonly as water snakes, seem, in comparison to the highly

European water snake (also called grass snake), *Natrix natrix*. Photo by G. Marcuse.

specialized wart snake, to be but moderately suited for an aquatic existence. While they are excellent swimmers and divers, most spend much of their time on land, sunning near bodies of water into which they plunge and quickly disappear when frightened. Some species lay eggs while others produce their babies alive. While a few species of *Natrix* are prettily colored, most are clad in rather somber hues. The water snake *Natrix natrix* is a very common European species that does well in captivity. Adults are grayish with a yellowish-white collar. A fully grown snake of this species is about three feet long. A species of similar size, but rather more pretty, is the diced water snake, *Natrix tessellata*, of Europe and Asia. It resembles the preceding species in laying eggs, in contradistinction to the water snakes of North America, all of which produce their young alive. An Asiatic species of wide distribution is the checkered water snake, *Natrix piscator*, a reptile which shows much variation in color even among specimens from the same area. Usually a tan or brown snake with squarish black markings over much of the body, the checkered water snake occasionally may be enlivened with splashes of red or yellow. Although vicious when first caught, it soon calms down and makes an agreeable captive. The annulated water snake, *Natrix annularis*, is a pretty Asiatic species which differs from many of the Old World members of the genus in producing its young alive.

COMMON AFRICAN COLUBRIDS

The commoner terrestrial colubrids of Africa are frequently available from dealers in exotic reptiles. Particularly elegant, though not of large size or brilliant coloration, is the mole snake, *Pseudaspis cana*. This fine species is light brown; each scale of its moderately stout body is well defined, imparting a very neat appearance. The file snake, *Mehelya capensis*, has a light vertebral stripe running the length of its otherwise dark body, serving to accentuate the rather triangular body form. However well fed, file snakes have an emaciated appearance because of the prominence of the dorsal ridge. They are rough-scaled and strong constrictors, reaching a length of about five feet and feeding almost entirely upon other snakes. The beauty snake, *Psammophis sibilans*, is one of a group of several active and slender species that frequent relatively dry situations and are commonly known as sand snakes. They are rear-fanged and feed principally upon lizards. From their habit of prowling about human dwellings in search of rodents, snakes of the genus *Boaedon* are called house snakes. The brown house snake, *Boaedon fuliginosus*, is the species most commonly imported.

ORIENTAL RAT SNAKE (PTYAS)

Several very large, long-tailed serpents are prominent among the reptile fauna of Asia. One of these is the Oriental rat snake, *Ptyas mucosus*, an alert, very active snake which occasionally grows to ten feet. The color of this snake is brown or greenish-brown, obscurely crossbanded with rather dark markings. The scales about the mouth are lighter and edged with black; surmounting these are huge, ever-wary eyes. Rat snakes sell their liberty dearly and in captivity retain their wildness over a long period, but if carefully handled some individuals eventually tame down, feed well, and may live over long periods. In general, their actions are similar to those of the familiar coachwhips of the United States. Their diet includes such varied items as frogs, lizards, small mammals, and birds. In parts of their native land they are vigorously protected in recognition of their value as rodent destroyers. Wooded areas near water are favorite prowling grounds, and specimens encountered in the field will race away swiftly if escape is possible. Cornered, they flatten the neck vertically and with a short hiss strike at one's face. Because of this species' large size, a strike from an Oriental rat snake may be received in the would-be captor's face; the reptile's sharp teeth produce generous lacerations. The taming of a large rat snake is an achievement which will tax the patience of its keeper. It is best accomplished in the manner described in the last chapter, relating to the eastern racer of the United States. The cage used should, of course, be larger—in keeping with the much greater length of the present reptile. Oriental rat snakes deposit eggs which may be over two inches in length in the case of a large female.

LESSER INDIAN RAT SNAKE

A smaller species from Asia, sometimes called the lesser Indian rat snake, is known scientifically as *Ptyas korros*. Fully grown at five to six feet, it adapts more readily to captivity than the preceding species. Dark olive or brown is the predominating color, and each scale is margined with black. These Old World rat snakes, all of which are nonpoisonous, bear a resemblance to the cobras which inhabit the same areas. In connection with the use of their common name—rat snakes—it should be pointed out that these snakes are not be be confused with snakes of the genus *Elaphe*, which bear the same title. The latter are snakes of far different temperament.

BLACK AND YELLOW RAT SNAKE

Central and South America have large, partially arboreal snakes which, because of their feeding habits, likewise are called rat snakes. A really spectacular species is the black and yellow rat snake, *Spilotes pullatus*, possibly the largest member of the family, with a maximum length in excess of twelve feet. Like the Asiatic members of its genus, this snake is tamed only with much difficulty and patience. Captives will eat birds and their eggs, and mammals; they should be kept at a temperature no lower than 75 degrees, and care should be taken that freshly caught specimens do not injure themselves by striking against the glass fronts of their cages.

Mussurana, *Clelia clelia*. Photo by G. Marcuse.

MUSSURANA

Particularly handsome among the South American snakes is the species known as the mussurana, *Clelia clelia*. Feeding almost entirely upon other snakes, when fully grown at seven or eight feet the mussurana is able to overcome and devour most of the larger pit vipers that it may chance to encounter. The species is a powerful constrictor and is rear-fanged besides, though it has not been proven to have a bite which is dangerous to humans. The average mussurana is a very mild-tempered snake and will bite only under extreme provocation. It is an egg-laying species; the newly hatched young are very much different from the adults in coloration, having black heads and pinkish bodies with a light-colored band at the neck.

340

ROAD GUARDER

Another snake-eating snake is the tiny road guarder, *Conophis lineatus*, of tropical America. It, too, is one of the rear-fanged snakes and makes use of its venom-conducting teeth to subdue lizards and other smaller snakes.

ORIENTAL KING SNAKES, CHAIN SNAKES

Known variously as Oriental king snakes and chain snakes, the species of the genus *Dinodon* have the habit of rolling themselves into a ball when first captured. Snakes of this genus are confined to Asia, their banded color pattern causing them to be confused often with the dangerous krait of that continent. The head of the krait is but little larger than its neck, while the snakes under consideration have rather broad, flattened heads which are quite distinct. The red-banded chain snake, *Dinodon rufozonatum*, is a four-foot reddish-brown species with dark crossbands. As with the related species, it lays eggs and frequents the borders of streams or other marshy places

Black and yellow rat snake, *Spilotes pullatus.* Photo by Muller-Schmida.

where an abundance of frogs may be found. These, together with smaller snakes and lizards, make up its diet. *Dinodon* species have enlarged teeth, but these lack any trace of a groove. It is a night-roving animal and has eyes which are conspicuous in bulging slightly. The white-banded chain snake, *Dinodon septentrionale*, is a species of similar form and habits, but differs in its colors, having a grayish-brown ground color with more widely separated dark bands.

GOLDEN WATER COBRA

Snakes have picked up a variety of common names which more or less aptly describe their habits. Thus, in the golden water cobra, *Cyclagras gigas*, of South America we have a snake which displays habits like those of the true cobras, though it is not related to them. *C. gigas* has a yellowish belly; in the males this color extends to the back, where it is transversed by black or dark brown markings. The females are rather dull by comparison, being mostly brownish above. The species lays eggs and feeds on frogs and fishes. Imported specimens commonly measure four to five feet.

SPECKLED RACER

The speckled racer, *Drymobius margaritiferus*, is another pretty tropical American snake. It has a wide range in Central America and Mexico and has even been found in the extreme southern portion of Texas. About three feet when fully grown, this snake is black, with a yellowish spot on each scale. It frequents aquatic situations, though it is not a water snake in the sense of spending much of its time actually in that element. Frogs are eaten in captivity, and the snakes of this genus should be kept at a temperature of 75 to 85 degrees, in a dry cage, but with water available for drinking purposes at all times. The speckled racers are swift-moving species which commonly measure about three feet.

GENUS COLUBER

Related to the racers and whipsnakes of North America are a variety of Old World snakes of the genus *Coluber*. Though not constricting snakes, an occasional specimen, in overcoming its prey, will show a trace of what may be an evolutionary trend—toward or away from—the constricting method of overcoming prey. Coils may be used effectively, though loosely, to control and restrict the move-

The small scale wedged between the lower anterior edge of the eye and the upper labials is a hallmark of the genus *Coluber* throughout the world. Photo by L. E. Perkins.

ments of an animal that has been seized. The horse-shoe snake, *Coluber hippocrepis*, of southern Europe and northern Africa is a rather pretty species that is named for the marking on its head. Dark green snakes, *Coluber jugularis*, are part of the European fauna and are also found in Asia. The flowered snake, *Coluber florulentus*, and the Algerian snake, *Coluber algirus*, inhabit northern Africa. None of the snakes of this genus has a reputation for being very hardy in captivity. They range from about three to six feet in length and are very active in the wild state, actively foraging during daylight hours for small mammals, birds, and reptiles. In captivity they should be kept as free from annoyance as possible and, in general, require very warm and dry cages. Though some frequent sandy areas, there is little point in providing sand as a floor covering for their cages, since they are not burrowing serpents. Sand will only make the task of cage-cleaning more difficult, and I consider it especially important to maintain the quarters of these snakes in the strictest state of cleanliness possible.

EUROPEAN CONSTRICTORS

The smooth snake, *Coronella austriaca*, is an inconspicuous reptile of Europe which in many respects resembles the milk snakes of the United States. It is a small snake, two feet in length, and spends much of its time hiding—both in the wild state and in captivity. Its color is brown, with a double row of dark spots along the back. The female produces from four to fifteen babies in the late summer; the babies arrive at sexual maturity in about four years. Captives, when they can be persuaded to eat, show a preference for lizards and baby mice. Other common and harmless constricting snakes of Europe are the leopard snake, *Elaphe situla*; the four-lined snake, *Elaphe quatuorlineata*; and the Aesculapean snake, *Elaphe longissima*. The first-named is a particularly beautiful snake, with black-edged red blotches on a ground color of yellow. Babies will eat lizards or very small mice; the adults feed largely upon grown mice and birds. It is a curious fact that some species of snakes which are considered delicate and short-lived in captivity occasionally produce an individual which thrives for many years. The leopard snake seldom lives a year, yet at least one individual lived in excess of twenty! We can find many parallels to this in the literature relating to the longevity of captive reptiles.

ASIATIC RAT SNAKES (ELAPHE)

Frequently imported from Asia are several species of large rat snakes (genus *Elaphe*) that are handsome in appearance, quiet in demeanor, and in general among the most satisfactory reptiles in captivity. The striped-tail rat snake, *Elaphe taeniurus*, is one of these kinds. Many snakes are striped, or banded, or blotched. In the present yellow, green, and black species we find a combination of all three patterns arranged in the most pleasing fashion. The head is pale, with a dark line extending backward from the eye to the angle of the jaw. The neck remains yellow for several inches, when a series of rather angular and broken dark splotches make their appearance and extend about half the length of the snake. These become smaller, finally disappearing toward the posterior portion of the body, where a broad yellow stripe takes their place, giving way along the sides to narrowly spaced spots. Looking at different sections of the snake's body, one might think that they belonged to at least three different snakes! This species reaches a large size, eight feet at least, and is a strong constrictor, feeding readily in captivity on rodents. Like the other rat snakes of its genus, *E. taeniurus* has a flattened abdomen which is sharply angular to its sides. This assists it greatly in climbing, and wild rat snakes of many species are frequently encountered in bushes and trees.

The keeled rat snake, *Elaphe carinata*, is also a very large species, but it has more sober colors than *E. taeniurus*, being mostly a plain brown reptile with indistinct darker markings on the forward portions of its body. The species is coarsely scaled and has a heavy body; it feeds upon rodents and, to some extent at least, other snakes.

TREE SNAKES

A veritable galaxy of tree snakes occurs throughout the warmer regions of the world. Some are so excessively slender and protectively colored as to be barely discernible when they repose among the vines and bushes which form their habitats. Others are not quite so attenuated in their proportions, and these types occasionally desert their arboreal sanctuaries to prowl on the ground. One of these is the handsome mangrove snake, *Boiga dendrophila*, of the Asiatic mainland and the offshore island groups. Mangrove snakes are commonly six to seven feet long and clad in lustrous black scalation over which are regularly-spaced narrow bands of vivid yellow. Few reptiles are more attractive as exhibits than the present snake as it coils compactly, as is its manner, on a bough in a well-lighted cage. The mangove is a rear-fanged snake and feeds on birds, mammals, reptiles, amphibians, and even fishes! Captives are best housed by themselves, for they will attack and devour other snakes nearly as large as themselves. Fully-grown examples seem to have a preference for birds. Reptile dealers generally offer this snake in four to six-foot-lengths. Juveniles and sub-adults rarely come on the market. Other species of the genus are often to be had, among them Blanding's tree snake, *Boiga blandingi*, and the dog-tooth cat snake, *Boiga cynodon*. Their habits are like those of the mangrove snake.

345

Mangrove snake, *Boiga dendrophila*. Photo by G. Marcuse.

Some of the most daintily-built and beautiful of the tree snakes belong to the genus *Leptophis* (called *Thalerophis* by some writers.) These are the green tree snakes and parrot snakes of the reptile trade. *Leptophis ahaetulla* frequently comes in with shipments from South America; *Leptophis diplotropis* comes from Mexico, as well as other species from other places. As I recall it, the first exotic snake I ever owned was a handsome three-foot *Leptophis*. Like its relatives, it fed readily on lizards. Supplying it with anoles taxed my boyhood financial resources during the months it was with me. This small snake introduced me to the prevalance of mites among tropical snakes. Soon after its arrival the minute red mites could be seen everywhere, in and out of the reptile's cage. Commercial preparations for the control of these pests were not available, so my "treatment" of the snake consisted of allowing it to crawl through a wet cloth which I held closely against its body. This particular tree snake was very adept at escaping from the smallest opening in its cage. I would always find it coiled up someplace nearby. It did not seem inclined to seek exit from the room by descending to the floor. One day, however, it disappeared, and I searched in vain for it for many days. With its escape the mite problem gradually resolved itself, though not to a complete extent for several weeks, at least!

VINE SNAKES

While the foregoing members of the genus *Leptophis* are very slender creatures, they appear robust when compared with the vine snakes (genus *Oxybelis*) of the tropical Americas. The green vine snake, *Oxybelis fulgidus*, reaches a length of five feet or more, while the brown vine snake, *Oxybelis aeneus*, is somewhat inferior in length. Vine snakes are incredibly slender reptiles and are next to impossible to see when coiled loosely in a bush. They feed chiefly upon lizards and possess rear fangs for subduing such quarry. It is absolutely essential to provide these and other true tree snakes with branches in their cages. A temperature of 75 degrees is satisfactory for them.

The long-nosed tree snakes of the genus *Dryophis* (*Ahaetulla*) appear to be closely related to the vine snakes, but are found in the tropics of the Old World. Some, like *Dryophis nasuta*, have a flexible

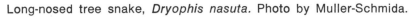

Long-nosed tree snake, *Dryophis nasuta.* Photo by Muller-Schmida.

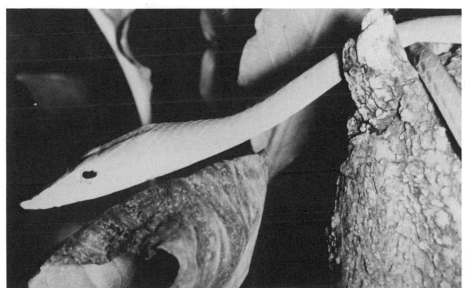

protuberance at the end of their long and slender heads, which feature adds to their grotesque appearance. *Dryophis* species bear living young, thus differing from those of the genera *Leptophis* and *Oxybelis*, both of which are oviparous. They will accept frogs, lizards, small mammals, and birds. Captives can be maintained indefinitely on a diet of American anoles. The bite of these snakes, when they can manage to imbed their tiny rear fangs, will produce, in humans, a swelling and pain like that caused by a wasp's sting. They seldom try to bite, however, depending mostly on bluff with open mouth to frighten enemies.

GOLDEN TREE SNAKE

Stories of flying snakes might be regarded as fanciful travelers' tales if it were not for the fact that the phenomenon has been substantiated in part, at least, by the observations of scientific investigators. The snake figuring in these accounts is the golden tree snake, *Chrysopelia ornata*, and its close relatives. This small but very handsome reptile occurs in Asia and is not a rare snake. It is a tree snake but is somewhat stouter in build than many such serpents and is, perhaps, the prettiest of all in its coloration. There is considerable variation of pattern, but the golden tree snake is essentially a black species that is rather suffusely banded with lighter lines, between which occur delicate shades of red and yellow. The small head of this three-foot species is quite distinct from the neck; the eyes are large, with round pupils. While it cannot actually "fly" in the manner of birds and bats, without question this tree snake—and perhaps other kinds as well—is able to make long glides by compressing its lower surface into a concave form after it has launched itself into the air from a coiled position. Longer glides are in a downward direction but from the impetus of the take-off a position above that of the starting point can be attained if the distance is only a few feet. Motion pictures have recorded the simultaneous volplaning of a number of these snakes in their native jungle habitat. The effect produced is one that is not likely to be soon forgotten. Golden tree snakes make highly interesting and ornamental additions to a reptile collection, but unless confined in a really large cage they cannot be expected to show off their unusual abilities. Attempts to induce a flight artificially generally meet with failure, and I do not believe that the mechanism involved is one which relates particularly to

Golden tree snake, *Chrysopelia ornata*. Photo by Muller-Schmida.

escape from a threat. The species is rear-fanged, and golden tree snakes are quite ready to defend themselves by biting when freshly caught. No ill results from their bites have been recorded among humans, however. A wide variety of food is accepted in captivity, but the preference is for lizards. Captives do well if maintained at 75 to 80 degrees in a cage that has numerous branches for climbing.

BOOMSLANG

Throughout the present chapter there have been references to snakes possessing enlarged and sometimes-grooved rear fangs. None of the species considered so far has been proved capable of producing in a man anything but inconsequential symptoms following a bite, though once again I would urge caution in the handling of specimens, particularly of the larger species like the mangrove snake. Two species of rear-fanged snakes from Africa, however, both tree-dwelling and very slender of build, have caused fatalities among humans. One of these is the boomslang, *Dispholidus typus*, a four-foot snake that occurs over the greater portion of the African continent. It is a very common reptile in some portions of its extensive range, but bites do not occur often, because the boomslang takes rapid flight when disturbed. Fatalities have occurred most often among people who

Boomslang, *Dispholidus typus*. Photo by Muller-Schmida.

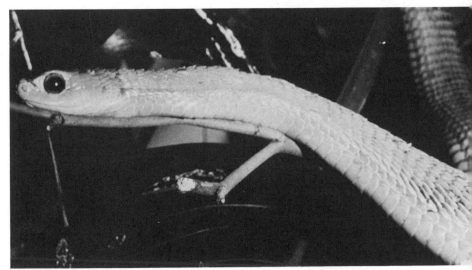

were attempting to capture a snake or were handling one after capture. The species inflates its throat vertically when annoyed; several tree snakes also do this. This is followed by an opened-mouth strike, followed often by a grasping and chewing action on the part of the snake. The boomslang is a plainly colored reptile and feeds mainly upon birds and their eggs, and lizards. This and the other rear-fanged species of snakes are nearly always these days designated as such on the price lists of reptile importers. They so closely resemble some of the harmless snakes, however, that there always exists the possibility of a misidentification. For a very great many years after its discovery the boomslang was not regarded as a dangerously poisonous serpent.

TWIG SNAKE

Another innocuous-appearing rear-fanged snake that is now regarded as dangerous to humans is the twig snake, *Thelotornis kirtlandi*, sometimes called the bird snake or the vine snake. Even more slender than the boomslang, this snake has similar habits, including the inflating of its throat when angry. Its range covers much of Africa, but the twig snake is, of course, missing from desert areas and is absent from the southern tip of the continent.

EGG-EATING SNAKES

A rather inconspicuous little snake of tropical and South Africa is famous for its capacity to swallow whole eggs that are enormous in proportion to the size of the reptile's head. This is the egg-eating snake, *Dasypeltis scaber*, a brown or tan reptile that has a spotted upper-surface and may grow to be a yard long. Egg-eaters are very common snakes and are quite often imported. Since there is a considerable demand for them, they are not among the least expensive snakes. Nearly all of our more familiar snakes have an astonishing ability to swallow large objects, and in the present species this ability has been even further modified to include eggs that appear huge in comparison with the small and slender snake that engulfs them. Egg-eating snakes possess a saw-like arrangement of bony projections in their esophagus. These cut into the shell of a bird's egg as it is being swallowed, and the pressure of the diminutive reptile's neck causes the shell to collapse. The shell fragments are later disgorged. A closely related species, the Indian egg-eating snake, *Elachistodon westermanni*, was once separated from *Dasypeltis* taxonomically because it has rear fangs, while the former does not. Both now occupy the same subfamily status.

SNAIL-EATING SNAKES

In contrast to the egg-eating snakes are the equally-peculiar snail-eating snakes (genera *Amblycephalus* and *Dipsas*), sometimes referred to as chunk-heads. Typically, these are slender tree snakes with string-like necks and tails. Their snouts are blunt and their lower jaws lack the median line which separates the scales of other snakes and makes possible much stretching of the skin when a large object is being swallowed. Snail-eating snakes extract their staple food from their shells with long, sharp teeth. The snail-eating snakes should be given branches among which to climb. They are not difficult to care for if a good supply of slugs or snails is readily obtainable.

Tentacled snake, *Herpeton tentaculatum*. Photo by G. Marcuse.

Cuban racer, *Alsophis angulifer*, Cuba. Photo by G. Marcuse.

OTHER COLUBRIDS

A group of thoroughly aquatic fresh- and brackish-water snakes occupy a section of their own within the broader scope of the family of colubrid serpents. They frequent waters of shallow depth, bring forth their young alive, and are rear-fanged. Some feed largely upon crabs, while others prefer frogs or fishes. The most unusual of the group is the tentacled snake, *Herpeton tentaculatum*, which has been reaching the reptile market in increasing numbers in recent years. These small and rather attractively marked snakes have two scaly appendages protruding from their snouts, the use of which is not known at present. In captivity tentacled snakes should be kept in an aquarium that has no landing place and is securely covered with screening or hardware cloth. A water-soaked branch should be held fixed in position at the bottom of about ten inches of water that is kept within a reasonable range of 78 degrees. The snakes will anchor themselves to the submerged branch with their tails. Small fishes are grasped as they swim near the snakes. Closely related to the tentacled snake, but lacking the nasal adornment of the latter, are the Asian snakes of the genus *Enhydris*. Like the *Herpeton* species they do well in a shoreless aquarium that has several inches of water. They progress in a rather awkward fashion when placed on land; many snap and bite viciously when removed from their element.

FAMILIES TYPHLOPIDAE, ANILIDAE

Distinct families of harmless snakes, members of which have not so far been discussed in this or the preceding chapter, are the Typhlopidae and the Anilidae. Members of the first family are wormlike reptiles ranging in size from a few inches to a couple of feet. Burrowing forms, they are rarely seen even in places where they are most common. Over 150 species are recognized, but they are almost never available commercially. They are related to the snakes of the family Leptotyphlopidae, which were taken up in the last chapter, and their care in captivity is the same. Representing the Anilidae, another family consisting of secretive and little-known snakes, is the beautiful false coral snake, *Anilius scytale*, a South American snake that reaches dealers in some numbers. Ringed brilliantly in scarlet and black, this snake bears some resemblance to the very venomous coral snakes, but is not related to them. It has vestiges of hind limbs, tiny eyes, and is of slender, cylindrical form. Imported specimens are generally around two feet in length and will eat small lizards and snakes. Like many other secretive reptiles, they will do well only if provided with means of burrowing or hiding.

VIII

Poisonous Snakes

Venomous snakes are the star attractions in any collection of reptiles, a fact which may be witnessed in any zoo that is fortunate enough to have a reptile house. Crowds may pass cage after cage, containing huge crocodilians, extremely rare turtles, lizards of bizarre forms and colors, and innocuous snakes, with little more than cursory inspection. But the cobras, mambas, vipers, and rattlesnakes stop such visitors in their tracks to observe with awesome awareness the often beautiful sinuous forms that have achieved notoriety because of their poisonous properties. In the better zoos, the poisonous snakes are treated with the degree of respect that is warranted by their awful capabilities. In the case of the more active and dangerous types, elaborate systems are employed with a view toward minimizing the possibility of bite casualties during such operations as feeding and cage-cleaning. Even so, accidents occur with rather disturbing frequency. Sera covering such medical contingencies are stocked by zoological parks for, in the cases of exotic poisonous snakes, they might otherwise not be available quickly when needed. The sera that are stocked by hospitals, when they have them at all, are usually of types that are antidotal only for the bites of local snakes.

If we were talking about reptiles solely from the standpoint of their suitability as pets, there would be little need to discuss the poisonous kinds. Poisonous snakes can, and often have been, tamed to the point where they permit handling. In this respect they do not differ much from their harmless relatives. Everyone who has kept many snakes knows, however, that even the most docile non-poisonous snake may have an "off-day" when it will bite if handled roughly or if it feels itself threatened. Poisonous snakes may, likewise, have such "moods," and this is one of the things which make them totally unsuitable as pets. One reads, not without a degree of amusement—tempered by concern—the letters which parents write asking herpetologists whether they think rattlers or cobras could be cared for safely by twelve- and fourteen-year-old sons and daughters! While maturity of judgment may be correlated only somewhat intimately with chronological age, I would strongly urge the teenager not to keep poisonous snakes—with or without parental permission. If an older person decides to keep one or more poisonous snakes in a private collection, it should be done with a thorough awareness of the dangers involved. In a few places there are municipal or state laws governing the keeping of poisonous snakes. This aspect should be given some attention before any are acquired. It is to be expected that the future will bring more such statutes, occasioned by the unhappy incidents of bites or escapes by captive specimens. I have been catching poisonous snakes in the field and keeping them under observation in cages for many years. I was bitten once—by a four-foot timber rattler—during an exceptional act of carelessness on my part while providing the creature with water. Severe envenomation accompanied the bite but, fortunately, recovery was uncomplicated, and there were no after-effects. Others have not been so lucky. Snakebite histories make gruesome reading. The subject will be discussed further when we talk about the methods of collecting reptiles in their natural haunts.

FAMILY ELAPIDAE

Some of the world's most infamous snakes belong to the family Elapidae—the group which includes cobras and mambas. Elapid snakes, as they are called, are found on all the continental land masses except Europe. In Australia, they predominate over other kinds, and that continent is the only one which has more venomous species than non-venomous species. Many of the Australian elapids are so small, however, that they are incapable of inflicting dangerous bites. Some are very secretive types which are seldom seen above ground. Australia has rigid codes protecting its fauna, and it is only occasionally that any poisonous Australian species is exported or available from dealers.

TIGER SNAKE

The tiger snake, *Notechis scutatus*, which receives its common name from the series of dark crossbands on a lighter ground color that run from the neck to the tail of the reptile, is a common but very dangerous reptile. This snake is usually three to four feet long, but in exceptional instances it may reach a length of five feet or more. Tiger snakes occur over much of Australia and are believed to be responsible for most of the serious bites in that country. Tested in the laboratory, the venom of this serpent has been found to be one of the most toxic known. The tiger snake produces large broods of living young, often to the number of thirty or more. This usually occurs in February or March, and the babies shift for themselves at once. Adult tiger snakes will eat small rodents and birds; it is likely that juveniles would include lizards in their diet. When angry, the tiger snake will spread its neck like a cobra and strike with great swiftness.

DEATH ADDER

Differing in form from most elapids, the death adder, *Acanthophis antarcticus*, is another Australian reptile that is quite common and widespread. Typically, elapine snakes are rather slender of build;

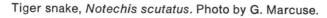

Tiger snake, *Notechis scutatus*. Photo by G. Marcuse.

some may be excessively so. Death adders, however, are thick and chunky, resembling the popular conception of a viper type. They may be gray or brown, with dark crossbands, and seldom exceed two feet in length. A broad, flat head and coarsely-keeled scales add to the picture of a snake which looks, and is, very dangerous. Death adders live fairly well in a dry and warm cage. Mice will be readily accepted by most captives, and a temperature of 75 to 80 degrees is recommended. Progeny are not numerous, a brood of babies numbering less than twelve on the average.

AUSTRALIAN BLACK SNAKE, MULGA SNAKE, SPOTTED BLACK SNAKE

The handsome red-bellied black snake of Australia, *Pseudechis porphyriacus*, is found mostly in swampy places and is an excellent swimmer. Like most other Australian snakes, it is not aggressive but will fight fiercely when cornered. Its venom is of lower toxicity than those of the tiger snake and the death adder. A large black snake may measure seven feet or more and is a very beautiful animal with a shiny black uppersurface and a belly which varies from pink to scarlet red. Angry specimens flatten the neck and strike readily enough, but do not rear from the ground as does a cobra. Babies are born alive. Of the Australian elapids, the black snake is one of the most satisfactory in captivity. It will devour small mammals and birds, as well as frogs and lizards. Closely related to the black snake are the mulga snake, *Pseudechis australis*, a brownish reptile with a pink undersurface, and the spotted black snake, *Pseudechis guttatus*, which differs from *P. porphyriacus* in having a grayish belly.

AUSTRALIAN COPPERHEAD, WESTERN BROWN SNAKE, TAIPAN

The Australian copperhead, *Denisonia superba*, is not related to its namesake of the United States. Southeastern Australia is the natural range of the copperhead; it frequents swampy areas and feeds largely upon frogs. A large example may be five feet long and is dark brown or black. Other Australian elapids which occasionally reach the cages of dealers are the western brown snake, *Demansia nuchalis*, and the taipan, *Oxyuranus scutellatus*, a dreaded reptile which may reach a length of ten feet and is considered the most aggressive and dangerous of that country's snakes.

AFRICAN GARTER SNAKES

A number of small snakes of the genus *Elapsoidea*, some of them prettily marked with bands of red and white, inhabit Africa. Often called garter snakes, they are in no way related to the American reptiles of the same name. Small and secretive, the African garter snakes seldom make any attempt to strike but will bite if much handled. Though only about two feet in length, the pretty members of this genus are true elapids and should be regarded with caution. In captivity, unless given adequate means of burrowing or at least remaining out of sight, they will seldom thrive.

KRAITS

The kraits (genus *Bungarus*) account for many deaths in Asia, where they are among the most common poisonous snakes. Sluggish by nature, they make little effort to get out of one's way and are frequently stepped on at night when they are prowling in search of the other snakes upon which they feed. Though largely terrestrial and secretive, some species ascend trees and have been found even on the roofs of houses. They seldom will make any attempt to bite unless touched, when they will swing their heads around quickly and grasp and chew on the offending object. Even this response cannot usually be elicited, especially during the daylight hours, when a freshly-captured specimen will often roll into a ball which conceals its head and remain in this position while being handled. In Oriental countries kraits are captured and sold as food; it is rather disconcerting to view the indifference with which they are handled in these places. Oriental vendors think nothing of grasping these large snakes with their bare hands, yet bites from them are few. Still, kraits are among the most dangerous of snakes, and one that is stepped on will certainly bite in retaliation. Kraits very often do not live well in captivity, which may be due in part to the fact that they are rarely provided with sufficient means of hiding. Cages for kraits should be quite large; at least a portion of it should be abundantly supplied with hollow logs and a profusion of bark slabs. The snakes can be expected to spend much of their time in seclusion but will issue forth at night in search of food. This is best provided in the form of smaller, harmless snakes, though in the absence of these other small reptiles, frogs, small mammals, and even fishes will be taken by some individuals. Characteristically, the kraits are banded snakes of three to four feet in length. Some of the more commonly imported species are the banded krait, *Bungarus fasciatus*, a quite handsome yellow and black species, and the Chinese krait, *Bungarus multicinctus*, a black and white form. The kraits are subject to much color variation; some may even lack bands, being of a single color over the entire body. As far as is known, all of the krait species lay eggs.

COBRAS

Cobras occupy a rather special niche in the serpents' hall of fame. Popularly, they are visualized as hooded serpents rearing from the basket of Hindu snake charmers and "dancing" to the accompaniment of the discordant tones produced by his fluted instrument. Cobras do not have a sense of hearing, as we understand it, and the specimens used in these performances sway from side to side in an effort to achieve an advantageous striking position at the body of the "charmer," which is also kept constantly in motion, to keep the reptiles off balance. In some cases, these snakes have had their fangs removed, but this is by no means always true. There is little question that the show is a dangerous one, and it is somewhat oversimplified by the foregoing comments. An intimate knowledge of the serpentine material used is a requisite, and this is not acquired without great risk. The spreading of a cobra's hood is accomplished by the serpent's elongated ribs and can be observed only in agitated snakes. Reports that cobras spread their hoods while sunning require confirmation. The development of the hood varies among the different species of cobras; some have little or no ability to expand the neck. Cobras which have become accustomed to cage life lie quietly about and resemble more ordinary types of snakes. Under ordinary conditions they do not make spectacular display animals. Many writers have said that cobras are the most intelligent of snakes. This may or may not be true, but certain it is that they are very alert, sometimes extremely aggressive, and at all times most dangerous reptiles to tamper with.

Several species of cobras have the ability to discharge venom from their fangs directly at the face of an antagonist. The ringhals, *Hemachatus haemachatus*, is especially notable for this, "spitting" accurately over a distance of six to eight feet in the case of an adult cobra which

Cape cobra, *Naja nivea,* southern Africa. Photo by G. Marcuse.

Egyptian cobra, *Naja hajae,* northern Africa. Photo by G. Marcuse.

measures about four feet in length. The ejection of venom is usually accomplished from a raised body stance, with the hood spread. In the case of a standing man, it would be directed upward toward his eyes. Temporary or possible permanent blindness can result if any of the spray enters the eyes, a more than likely occurrence. Immediate remedial measures consist of a thorough rinsing of the eyes and face with water, which should always be carried in spitting-cobra country. Captive ringhals are hardy and thrive over long periods of time if properly cared for. Frogs, rodents, and birds can be fed successfully. The ringhals produces its babies alive.

The typical cobras have an extensive range in Asia and Africa. There is a great deal of variation in colors and markings among the various species and subspecies of the genus *Naja*. The common cobra, *Naja naja*; the black-lipped cobra, *Naja melanoleuca*; and the black-necked cobra, *Naja nigricollis*, are a few of the kinds which are imported. The last-named is an accomplished "spitter"—quite as adept as the ringhals. Adult cobras of the commoner forms are usually five to six feet in length and have a moderately heavy body. All require a considerable amount of warmth and the species from arid situations, in particular, need a very dry atmosphere. They are active reptiles and should have large cages. To someone who has had experience in handling the snakes of the United States, including the poisonous ones, but has not tried to care for a cobra in captivity, I can suggest that a mental picture be drawn of a racer-like snake which has, in addition to its speed, a poisonous bite and the sometime-ability to accurately eject venom into one's eyes. This composite will give the reader some idea of the care which must be exercised in the handling of captive cobras. All retain a high-strung disposition in captivity and are easily provoked. Fights with each other are frequent. The *Naja* species reproduce by means of eggs, and a hatchling will rear its diminutive form, spread its hood, and strike the moment it is completely free of the egg.

A particularly dangerous snake is the king cobra, *Ophiophagus hannah*, of Asia, a species which has been known to reach a length of eighteen feet! An example of this size could rear itself to the height of an average man. Large specimens are often imported and are quite expensive, for the snake is not a really common one. Its color is usually an olive-brown, sometimes with pale bands. Babies are handsomely banded in black and white and may measure about

Monocellate cobra, *Naja naja kaouthiae*. Photo by G. Marcuse.

twenty inches when hatched. The king cobra is one of the species of snakes which guard their eggs, which may number several dozens. Under favorable conditions king cobras have successfully bred and produced fertile eggs in captivity. Unlike the commoner cobras which will take a variety of warm-and-cold blooded animals, the present species prefers other snakes as food. Occasionally, a specimen may be trained to take other foods.

MAMBAS

Mambas (genus *Dendroaspis*) are confined to Africa, where they are justifiably feared by hunters and others who enter their haunts. All are long, very slender snakes; black, brown, or green may be the prevailing color. They look and act like tree snakes and can be confused with some of the innocuous forms of the latter. The black mamba, *Dendroaspis polylepis*, can grow to twelve feet; its relatives, like the green mamba, *Dendroaspis angusticeps*, are somewhat smaller. Mambas can be kept in a large cage which has branches for climbing. Food in the wild state consists of birds, mostly, but captives will take mice and often frogs and lizards. Being extremely active and prone to attack if interfered with, mambas should never be allowed the freedom of a room—as during cage-cleaning. Food and water should be introduced by means of long tongs, a careful watch being kept on the cage's inhabitants during this process. This rule should apply to the feeding and watering of all captive venomous snakes. Complete visibility of the occupant should be had during any work in a cage that does not have a dividing partition. In small cages, particularly, I never keep more than a single individual. Some snakes pay little attention to cage-cleaning, whereas others rush forward to investigate the cause of the disturbance. This may be particularly true of snakes which have been in captivity a long time and have lost their natural timidity. An animal which has lost its fear of humans is more dangerous than a freshly-caught individual, unless the loss of fear is accompanied by a corresponding loss of the inclination to bite when danger threatens. The more nervous types of dangerous snakes can rarely be brought to this degree of tameness, regardless of how kindly treated. Mambas are oviparous snakes and the eggs may

Green mamba, *Dendroaspis angusticeps.* Photo by G. Marcuse.

number about a dozen. Among the really deadly snakes of the world, the mambas must surely occupy a foremost position. I do not think there would be many recoveries from the fully-delivered bite of a large mamba unless the bite were treated rapidly and energetically.

CORAL SNAKES

North, Central, and South America are the homes of a number of small burrowing elapids that are called coral snakes (genus *Micrurus*). Brightly ringed with black, yellow, and red, the small members of this genus are very attractive reptiles and often have a close resemblance to certain harmless snakes which share their habitats. The eastern coral snake, *Micrurus fulvius*, is well known in the United States, where its bite has caused a number of deaths. In habits, the coral snakes are somewhat like the kraits: they remain hidden during the day and emerge at dusk to search for food in the form of other snakes and small lizards; they never bite except when handled or stepped on; they adapt rather poorly to average cage conditions and must be provided with a floor-covering of moss or wood pulp in which to burrow. A temperature range of 75 to 80 degrees is best for them. Most coral snakes do not grow larger than three feet—some are much smaller. The giant coral snake, *Micrurus spixi*, is an exception, attaining dimensions of four to five feet. Despite their gentle demeanor, coral snakes are very venomous reptiles, and no one should attempt to capture one without suitable tools.

FAMILY HYDROPHIIDAE

All of the strictly marine serpents have been placed in one family—the Hydrophiidae. Two sub-classifications have been made, depending on the degree of specialization shown by the various species for an aquatic existence. Most sea snakes give birth to living young in shallow shore waters, but there are several kinds which actually leave the sea and deposit their eggs on land. Marine snakes are widely-ranging and abundant in tropical waters of the Indian and Pacific Oceans. Great numbers of sea snakes are hauled in by commercial fishermen, who pick them up with bare hands and toss them back into the sea. Fatal bites sometimes occur from this carelessness, for all of the known sea snakes are poisonous and very dangerously so, though many species have a mild disposition. Size among the marine snakes runs from a couple of feet to over eight

Eastern coral snake, *Micrurus fulvius*. Photo by C. Hansen.

Banded sea snake, *Laticauda laticaudata*. Photo by G. Budich.

feet. As a group, they show much variation in colors and pattern, and some are quite beautiful. All have flattened tails and seem as thoroughly at home in the water as the eels upon which they feed. Some species have been seen far out to sea in aggregations which numbered in the thousands, if not millions, of individuals. The reason for such concentrations is not known. Sea snakes are seldom available from dealers in reptiles, and we have learned little of their habits in either the wild state or in captivity. It is known that they can be maintained over indefinite periods in ordinary tap water and often accept food under these circumstances. One species, at least, has been cut off from the sea and now resides in fresh water.

Representative of the sea snakes which have not broken away completely from the land are such kinds as the banded sea snakes, *Laticauda laticaudata* and *Laticauda semifasciata*. These species have ventral scales which are broadened, like those of terrestrial serpents, and are able to make awkward progress on land. Some species of *Laticauda* are said to sun themselves on coral atolls; among these species we find the sea snakes that lay their eggs on land. The thoroughly aquatic species are represented by the yellow-bellied sea snake, *Pelamis platurus*, a dark brown or black reptile with a bright yellow belly and a vividly-banded tail. The belly scales of this snake are small and do not differ from the scales of the back. Such species rarely, if ever, voluntarily leave the water; they bear living young. I do not believe that any sea snake has been kept in captivity over a really long period of time, even in salt or brackish water. Most will live out of water for quite a while. The sea snakes are a fascinating group of reptiles and well worthy of the life study of a specialist.

FAMILY VIPERIDAE

Snakes of the family Viperidae, commonly called vipers, are found only in the eastern hemisphere and are absent from Australia. Typically, the snakes of this family are rather stout-bodied terrestrial reptiles, though some have taken to subterranean habits and others live in trees. With proper care, many do exceedingly well in captivity. Vipers and pit vipers do best with an absolute minimum of handling or other disturbances. The best captives are those which have been raised from infancy, and with many of the species this is not a difficult accomplishment if their feeding requirements can be satisfied. Adults which have been handled roughly at time of capture and thereafter often refuse to eat or will feed so sparingly that they starve to death. Force-feeding, a simple and safe operation in the case of a harmless snake, is a dangerous procedure with a poisonous one, and the trauma to the snake which accompanies such forcible handling is likely to outdo any good which may be accomplished. Likewise, the "milking" of a captive poisonous snake is a reprehensible practice and is justified only when there is a clear need for the venom, as in the production of snakebite sera or in experiments to determine the composition or toxicity of the product. In connection with the danger and difficulty of force-feeding venomous snakes, it might be well to bring out that in every aspect of their care in captivity the poisonous snakes present more problems than the harmless kinds. This is true in such everyday occurrences as feeding, cage-cleaning, assistance in the shedding of their skins, and giving treatment for parasites and minor illnesses. These are points to be considered when the time allotted to the care of a collection is limited. On the other hand, there is hardly a more attractive and interesting exhibit than a well-managed collection of poisonous snakes. The colors and patterns of some of the species are positively gorgeous. Most viperine snakes show little interest in escaping from their cages once they have quieted down and started feeding. In this they resemble the more phlegmatic of the boas and pythons.

BURROWING VIPER

The burrowing viper, *Atractaspis bibroni*, and its relatives form an interesting African group. Commonly less than two feet long, their slender and cylindrical forms are ideally suited to the underground life of the reptiles. A curious thing about them is the enormous development of the viper fang mechanism: the fangs are so long that they can be used with little effectiveness when the mouth is open. They often bite with the mouth closed, the viperine teeth exposed and projecting over the sides of the lower jaw. Unlike most other true vipers, the present species deposit eggs. They are nocturnal and feed upon small mammals, lizards, and other snakes. In captivity they should have a means of hiding. Possibly the best arrangement is one which provides a thin layer of soil and flat rocks or slabs of bark.